Kickback

By the same author

DEAD BEAT

Kickback

Val McDermid

St. Martin's Press
New York

ISBN 0-312-09836-7

First published in Great Britain by Victor Gollancz.

First U.S. Edition: September 1993

10 9 8 7 6 5 4 3 2 1

To Lavender Linoleum Lovers Everywhere

Acknowledgements

Writing is a solitary business, but there are always other people who have helped make a book. As far as *Kickback* is concerned, I owe thanks to Diana Cooper, who guided me through the legal minefields as well as providing inspirations of various kinds; Stephen Gaskell, the man from Macclesfield who takes the pain out of conveyancing; Kirstie Blades from the Birkenhead Land Registry who took the time and trouble to make sure I understood what goes on there; Andrew at Information Technology Resource in Horwich; the Longsight cheque squad, who don't even know they helped; my editor, Julia Wisdom; and, as always, the team at Gregory and Radice.

Any mistakes are uniquely mine.

'Property is theft'   Pierre Joseph Proudhon

Kickback

The Case of the Missing Conservatories. Sounds like the Sherlock Holmes story Conan Doyle didn't get round to writing because it was too boring. Let me tell you, I was with Conan Doyle on this one. If it hadn't been for the fact that our secretary's love life was in desperate need of ECT, there's no way I'd have got involved. Which, as it turned out, might have been no bad thing.

I was crouched behind the heavy bulk of the elevator machinery, holding my breath, desperately praying I'd pick the right moment to make my move. I knew I wouldn't get a second chance with a nasty bag of works like Vohaul's hit man. I caught sight of him as he emerged from the stairwell. I leaped to my feet and threw myself at one of the pair of heavy pulley attachments suspended from the ceiling. It shot across the room towards my relentless opponent. At the last minute he turned, spotted it and ducked, letting it whistle over his head. My mouth dried with fear as he caught sight of me and headed menacingly in my direction. I dodged round the elevator machinery, trying to keep it between us so I could make a dash for the stairs. As he rushed after me, I desperately swung the other pulley towards him. It caught him on the side of the head, the momentum plunging him over the lip of the lift shaft into the blackness below. I'd done it! I'd managed to stay alive!

I let my breath out in a slow sigh of relief and leaned back in the chair, hitting the key that offered me the 'Save Game' option. A glance at my watch told me it was time to leave Space Quest III for the day. I'd had the half-hour lunch break that was all I could spare in my partner Bill's absence. Besides, I knew that our secretary Shelley would be returning from her own lunch break any minute now, and I didn't want her wandering in and catching me at it. While the cat's away, the mouse plays Space Quest, and all that, which isn't very businesslike behaviour for a partner in a security consultancy and private investigation agency. Even if I'm only the junior partner.

That particular week, I was the only show in town. Bill had abandoned ship for the fleshpots (or should that be lobster pots?) of the Channel Islands to run a computer security course for a merchant bank. Which meant that Kate Brannigan was the only functioning half of Mortensen and Brannigan, as far as the UK mainland was concerned. Say it fast like that and we sound like major players instead of a two-operative agency that handles a significant chunk of the white-collar crime in the North West of England.

I headed for the cupboard off my office that doubles as the ladies loo and office darkroom. I had a couple of films that needed processing from my weekend surveillance outside a pharmaceutical company's lab. PharmAce Supplies had been having some problems with their stock control. I'd spent a couple of days working on the inside as a temporary lab assistant, long enough to realize that the problem wasn't what went on in working hours. Someone was sneaking in when the lab was locked and helping himself or herself, then breaking into the computer stock records to doctor them. All I needed to discover was the identity of the hacker, which had been revealed after a couple of evenings sat cramped in the back of Mortensen and Brannigan's newest toy, a Little Rascal van that we'd fitted out specifically for stake-out work. Hopefully, the proof that incriminated the senior lab technician was in my hand, captured forever on the fastest film that money could buy.

I was looking forward to half an hour in the darkroom, away from phones that didn't seem to have stopped ringing since Bill left. No such luck. I'd barely closed the blackout curtain when the intercom buzzed at me like that horrible drill dentists use to smooth off a filling. The buzzing stopped and Shelley's distorted voice came at me like Donald Duck on helium. 'Kate, I have a client for you,' I deciphered.

I sighed. The Tooth Fairy's revenge for playing games on the office computer. 'I was playing in my own time,' I muttered, in the vain hope that would appease the old bag. 'Kate? Can you hear me?' Shelley honked.

'There's no appointment in the book,' I tried.

'It's an emergency. Can you come out of the darkroom, please?'

'I suppose so,' I grumbled. I knew there was no point in refusing. Shelley is quite capable of letting a full minute pass, then hammering on the door claiming an urgent case of Montezuma's Revenge from the Mexican taco bar downstairs where she treats herself to lunch once a week. She always varies the days so I can never catch her out in a lie.

Still grumbling, I let myself back into my office. Before I'd taken the three steps back to my chair, Shelley was in the room, closing the door firmly behind her. She looked slightly agitated as she crossed to my desk, an expression about as familiar on her face as genuine compassion is on Baroness Thatcher's. She handed me a new-client form with the name filled in. Ted Barlow. 'Tell me about it,' I said, resigning myself.

'He owns a firm that builds and installs conservatories and his bank are calling in his loans, demanding repayment of his overdraft and refusing him credit. He needs us to find out why and to persuade his bank to change their minds,' Shelley explained, slightly breathlessly. Well out of character. I was beginning to wonder just what had happened to her over lunch.

'Shelley,' I groaned. 'You know that's not our kind of thing. The guy's been up to some fiddle, the bank have cottoned on and he wants someone to pull him out of the shit. Simple as that. There's no money in it, there's no point.'

'Kate, just talk to him, please?' Shelley as supplicant was a new role on me. She never pleads for anything. Even her demands for raises are detailed in precise, well-documented memos. 'The guy's desperate, he really needs some help. He's not on the fiddle, I'd put money on it.'

'If he's not on the fiddle, he's the only builder that hasn't been since Solomon built the temple,' I said.

Shelley tossed her head, the beads woven into her plaits

jangling like wind chimes. 'What's the matter with you, Kate?' she challenged me. 'You getting too high and mighty for the little people? You only deal with rock stars and company chairmen these days? You're always busy telling me how proud you are of your dad, working his way up to foreman from the production line at Cowley. If it was your dad out there with his little problem, would you be telling him to go away? This guy's not some big shot, he's just a working bloke who's got there the hard way, and now some faceless bank manager wants to take it all away from him. Come on, Kate, where's your heart?' Shelley stopped abruptly, looking shocked.

So she should have done. She was bang out of order. But she'd caught my attention, though not for the reason she'd thought. I decided I wanted to see Ted Barlow, not because I'd been guilt tripped. But I was fascinated to see the man who had catapulted Shelley into the role of a lioness protecting her cubs. Since her divorce, I hadn't seen any man raise her enviable cool by so much as a degree.

'Send him in, Shelley,' I replied abruptly. 'Let's hear what the man has to say for himself.'

Shelley stalked over to the door and pulled it open. 'Mr Barlow? Miss Brannigan will see you now.' She simpered. I swear to God, this tough little woman who rules her two teenagers like Attila the Hun *simpered*.

The man who appeared in the doorway made Shelley look as fragile as a Giacometti sculpture. He topped six foot easily, and he looked as if a suit were as foreign to him as a Peruvian nose-flute. Not that he was bulky. His broad shoulders tapered through a deep chest to a narrow waist without a single strain in the seams of his off-the-peg suit. But you could see that he was solid muscle. As if that wasn't enough, his legs were long and slim. It was a body to die for.

Nice legs, shame about the face, though. Ted Barlow was no hunk from the neck up. His nose was too big, his ears stuck out, his eyebrows met in the middle. But his eyes looked kind, with laughter lines radiating out from them. I put him in his mid-thirties, and he didn't seem to have spent too many of those years in an office, if his body language was anything to go by. He stood awkwardly in the doorway, shifting his weight from one foot to the other, a nervous smile not making it as far as the gentle blue eyes.

'Come in, sit down,' I said, standing up and gesturing towards the two exquisitely comfortable leather and wood chairs I'd bought for the clients in a moment of uncharacteristic kindness. He moved uncertainly into the office and stared at the chairs as if not entirely certain he would fit in to them. 'Thank you, Shelley,' I said pointedly as she continued to hang around by the door. She left, reluctantly for once.

Ted lowered himself into the chair and, surprised by the comfort, relaxed slightly. They always work, those chairs. Look like hell, feel like heaven. I pulled a new-client form towards me and said, 'I need to take a few details, Mr Barlow, so we can see if we can give you the help you need.' Shelley might be besotted, but I wasn't giving an inch without good cause. I got the phone numbers and the address – an industrial estate in Stockport – then asked how he'd come to hear of us. I prayed he'd picked us out of Yellow Pages so I could dump him without offending anyone except Shelley, but clearly, wiping out Vohaul's hit man was to be my sole success of the day.

'Mark Buckland at SecureSure said you'd sort me out,' he said.

'You know Mark well, do you?' Foolishly, I was still hanging on to hope. Maybe he only knew Mark because SecureSure had fitted his burglar alarm. If so, I could still give him the kiss-off without upsetting the substantial discount that Mark gives us on all the hardware we order from him.

This time, Ted's smile lit up his face, revealing the same brand of boyish charm I get quite enough of at home, thank you. 'We've been mates for years. We were at school together. We still play cricket together. Opening batsmen for Stockport Viaduct, would you believe?'

I swallowed the sigh and got down to it. 'What exactly is the problem?'

'Well, it's the bank. I got this from them this morning,' he said, tentatively holding out a folded sheet of paper.

I put him out of his misery and took it from him. He looked

as if I'd taken the weight of the world off his broad shoulders. I opened it up and ploughed through the mangled verbiage. The bottom line was he had £74,587.34 outstanding on a £100,000 loan and an overdraft of £6,325.67. The Royal Pennine Bank wanted their money back pronto, or they'd seize his home and his business. And their associate finance company would be writing to him separately, basically to tell him his punters wouldn't be stiffing them for any more loans either. And I thought my bank manager wrote stroppy letters. I could see why Ted was looking gutted. 'I see,' I said. 'And do you have any idea why they wrote this letter?'

He looked confused. 'Well, I rang them up as soon as I got it, like you would. And they said they couldn't discuss it on the phone, would I come in to see them. So I said I'd go in this morning. It wasn't my local branch, you see; all the little branches come under the big branch in Stockport now, so I didn't know the bloke who'd signed the letter or anything.' He paused, waiting for something.

I nodded and smiled encouragingly. That seemed to do the trick.

'Well, I went in, like I said, and I saw the chap that signed the letter. And I asked him what it was all about, and he said that if I checked my paperwork, I would see that he wasn't obliged to give me a reason. Right stuffed shirt, he was. Then he said he wasn't at liberty to discuss the bank's confidential reasons for their decision. Well, I wasn't happy with that, no way, because I've not missed a single payment on that loan, not in the four months I've had it, and I've reduced the overdraft by four grand over the last six months. I told him, I said, you're not being fair to me. And he just shrugged and said he was sorry.' Ted's voice rose in outrage. I could see why.

'So what happened then?' I prompted.

'Well, I'm afraid I lost my rag a bit, you know? I told him he wasn't bloody sorry at all, and that I wasn't going to leave matters there. Then I walked out.'

I struggled to keep a straight face. If that was Ted's idea of losing his rag a bit, I could see that someone like Shelley was just what he needed. 'You must have some idea of what's behind this, Mr Barlow,' I prodded.

He looked genuinely baffled as he shook his head. 'I haven't a clue. I've always given the bank what they were due when it were due. This loan, I took it out so I could expand the business. We've just moved into a new industrial unit at Cheadle Heath, but I knew business was going well enough to pay back the loan on time.'

'Are you sure your orders haven't dropped back because of the recession and the bank's not just taking safety precautions?' I hazarded.

He shook his head, his hand nervously heading for his jacket pocket. He stopped, guiltily. 'Is it all right if I smoke?' he asked.

'Go right ahead,' I responded. I got up to fetch him an ashtray. 'You were saying? About the effects of the recession?'

He dabbed his cigarette nervously at his lips. 'Well, to be honest, we've not seen it. I think what's happening is that people who've been trying to sell their houses have kind of given up on the idea and decided to go for some improvements to the places they're in already. You know, loft conversions for extra bedrooms, that kind of thing? Well, a lot of them go for conservatories, to give them an extra reception room, especially if they've got teenage kids. I mean, if a conservatory's double glazed and you stick a radiator in, it's as warm as a room in the house in the winter. Our business is actually up on this time last year.'

I dragged out of him that he specialized in attaching conservatories to newish properties on the kind of estates where double-glazing salesmen used to graze like cattle. That way, he only ever had to produce a handful of designs in a few standard sizes, thus cutting his overheads to a minimum. He also concentrated on a relatively compact area: the south-west side of Manchester and over to Warrington new town, the little boxes capital of the North West. The two salesmen he employed brought in more than enough orders to keep the factory busy, Ted insisted.

'And you're absolutely positive that the bank gave you no idea why they are foreclosing?' I demanded again, reluctant to believe they had been quite so bloody-minded.

He nodded, uncertainly, then said, 'Well, he said something I didn't understand.'

'Can you remember exactly what that was?' I asked in the tone of voice one uses with a particularly slow child.

He frowned as he struggled to remember. It was like watching an elephant crochet. 'Well, he did say there was an unusual and unacceptably high default rate on the remortgages, but he wouldn't say any more than that.'

'The remortgages?'

'People who can't sell their houses often remortgage to get their hands on their capital. They use the conservatory as the excuse for the remortgage. But I don't understand what that's got to do with me,' he said plaintively.

I wasn't altogether sure that I did. But I knew a man who would. I wasn't excited by Ted Barlow's story, but I'd wrapped up the pharmaceuticals case in less time than I'd anticipated, so the week was looking slack. I thought it wouldn't kill me to play around with his problem for a day or two. I was about to ask Ted to let Shelley have a list of his clients over the last few months when he finally grabbed my attention.

'Well, I was that angry when I left the bank that I decided to go and see some of the people who had done a remortgage. I went back to the office and picked up the names and addresses and went over to Warrington. I went to four of the houses. Two of them were completely empty. And the other two had complete strangers living in them. But – and this is the really weird bit, Miss Brannigan – there were no conservatories there. They'd vanished. The conservatories had just disappeared.'

2

I took a deep breath. I have noticed that there are some people in this world who are congenitally incapable of telling a story that runs in a straight line from the beginning through the middle to the end, incorporating all the relevant points. Some of them win the Booker Prize, and that's fine by me. I just wish they didn't end up in my office. 'Disappeared?' I finally echoed, when it became clear Ted had shot his bolt.

He nodded. 'That's right. They're just not there any more. And the people that are living in two of the houses swear blind there's never been a conservatory there, not since they moved in a few months ago. The whole thing's a complete mystery to me. That's why I thought you might be able to help.' If Shelley had been in the room, she'd have rolled over on her back at the look of trusting supplication on Ted Barlow's face.

As it was, I was hooked. It's not often I get a client with a genuine mystery to solve. And this gave me the added bonus of getting my own back on Ms Supercool. Watching Shelley jumping through hoops for Ted Barlow was going to be the best cabaret in town.

I leaned back in my chair. 'OK, Ted. We'll take a look at it. On one condition. I'm afraid that, since the bank's stopped your line of credit, I'm going to have to ask you for a cash retainer.'

He'd been one step ahead of me. 'Will a grand do?' he asked, pulling a thick envelope from his inside pocket.

It was my turn to nod helplessly. 'I thought you'd want cash,' he went on. 'Us builders can always lay hands on a few bob in readies when we have to. Rainy day money. That way, you always make sure the important people get paid.' He handed the envelope over. 'Go ahead, count it, I won't be offended,' he added.

I did as he said. It was all there, in used twenties. I pressed the intercom. 'Shelley? Can you give Mr Barlow a receipt for one thousand pounds cash on his way out? Thanks.' I got to my feet. 'I've got one or two things to sort out here, Ted, but I'd like to meet you later this afternoon at your office. Four o'clock OK?'

'That's great. Shall I leave the directions with your secretary?' He sounded almost eager. This could get to be a lot of fun, I thought to myself as I showed Ted out. He headed for Shelley's desk like a homing pigeon.

Much as I'd taken to Ted, I learned very early on in this game that liking someone is no guarantee of their honesty. So I picked up the phone and rang Mark Buckland at SecureSure. His secretary didn't mess me about with tales of fictitious meetings since Mark's always pleased to hear from Mortensen and Brannigan. It usually means a nice little earner for him. SecureSure supply a lot of the hardware we recommend in our role as security consultants, and even with the substantial discount he offers us, Mark still makes a tidy profit.

'Hi Kate!' he greeted me, his voice charged with its normal overdose of enthusiasm. 'Now, don't tell me, let me guess. Ted Barlow, am I right?'

'You're right.'

'I'm glad he took my advice, Kate. The guy is in deep shit, and he doesn't deserve it.' Mark sounded sincere. But then, he always does. That's the main reason he can afford to drive around in seventy grand's worth of Mercedes coupé.

'That's what I was ringing you about. No disrespect, but I need to check out that the guy's kosher. I don't want to find myself three days down the road with this and some bank clerk giving me the hard word because our Mr Barlow's got a track record with more twists and turns than a sheep track,' I said.

'He's kosher all right, Kate. The guy is completely straight. He's the kind that gets into trouble because he's too honest, if you know what I mean.'

'Oh, come on, Mark. It's me you're talking to. The guy's a builder, for Christ's sake. He can lay his hands on a grand in cash, just like that. That's not straight, not in the normal definition of the word,' I protested.

'OK, so maybe the taxman doesn't know about every shilling he makes. But that doesn't make you a bad person, now does it, Kate?'

'So give me the truth, not the advertising copy.'

Mark sighed. 'You're a hard woman, Brannigan.' Tell me about it, I thought cynically. 'Right. Ted Barlow is probably my oldest friend. He was my best man, first time round. I was an usher at his wedding. Unfortunately, he married a prize bitch. Fiona Barlow was a slut and the last guy to find out was Ted. He divorced her five years ago and since then he's become a workaholic. He started off as a one-man-band, doing a bit of replacement windows stuff. Then a couple of friends asked him if he could do them a conservatory. They lived in real punter property, you know, Wimpey, Barratt, something like that. They got Ted to create this Victorian-style conservatory, all stained glass and UPVC. Of course, monkey see, monkey want. Half the estate wanted one, and Ted was launched in the conservatory business. Now, he's got a really solid little firm, a substantial turnover, and he's done it the straight way. Which, as you know, is pretty bloody unusual in the home improvement game.'

In spite of my natural scepticism, I was impressed. Whatever was going on with Ted Barlow's conservatories, it looked like it wasn't the man himself who was up to something. 'What about his competitors? Would they be looking to put the shaft in?' I asked.

'Hmm,' Mark mused. 'I wouldn't have thought so. He's not serious enough to be a worry to any of the really big-time boys. He's strictly small, reputable and local. Whatever's going down here needs someone like you to sort it out. And if you do clear it up, because he's such a good friend, I'll even waive my ten per cent commission for sending him to you!'

'If I wasn't a lady, I'd tell you to go fuck yourself, Buckland. Ten per cent!' I snorted. 'Just for that, I'm putting the lunch

invitation on hold. Thanks for the backgrounder, anyway. I'll
do my best for Ted.'

'Thanks, Kate. You won't be sorry. You sort him out, he'll be
your friend for life. Pity you've already got a conservatory, eh?'
He was gone before I could get on my high horse. Just as well,
really. It took me a good thirty seconds to realize he'd been at
the wind-up and I'd fallen for it.

I wandered through to the outer office to give Shelley the
new-client form and the cash, for banking. To my surprise, Ted
Barlow was still there, standing awkwardly in front of Shelley's
desk like a kid who's hung behind after class to talk to the
teacher he has a crush on. As I entered, Shelley looked flustered
and quickly said, 'I'm sure Kate will have no trouble following
these directions, Mr Barlow.'

'Right, well, I'll be off then. I'll be seeing you later, Miss
Brannigan.'

'Kate,' I corrected automatically. Miss Brannigan makes me
feel like my spinster great aunt. She's not one of those indomi-
table old biddies with razor sharp minds that we all want to be
when we're old. She's a selfish, hypochondriacal, demanding
old manipulator and I have this superstitious fear that if I let
enough people call me Miss Brannigan, it might rub off on me.

'Kate,' he acknowledged nervously. 'Thank you very much,
both of you.' He backed through the door. Shelley was head
down, fingers flying over the keyboard before the door was
even halfway closed.

'Amazing how long it takes to give a set of directions,' I said
sweetly, dropping the form in her in-tray.

'I was just sympathizing with the man,' Shelley replied
mildly. It's not always easy to tell with her coffee-coloured skin,
but I'd swear she was blushing.

'Very commendable, too. There's a grand in this envelope.
Can you pop down to the bank with it? I'd rather not leave it
in the safe.'

'You do right. You'd only spend it,' Shelley retorted, getting
her own back. I poked my tongue out at her and returned to
my own office. I picked up the phone again. This time, I rang
Josh Gilbert. Josh is a partner in a financial services company.

They specialize in providing advice and information to the kind of people who are so paranoid about ending up as impoverished senior citizens that they cheerfully do without while they're young enough to enjoy it, just so they can sit back in comfort in their old age, muttering, 'If I had my youth again, I could be waterskiing now ...' Josh persuades them to settle their shekels in the bosoms of insurance companies and unit trusts, then sits back planning for his own retirement on the fat commissions he's just earned. Only difference is, Josh expects his retirement to begin at forty. He's thirty-six now, and tells me he's well on target. I hate him.

Of course, he was with a client. But I'd deliberately made my call at ten minutes to the hour. I figured that way he'd be able to call me back between appointments. Three minutes later, I was talking to him. I briefly outlined Ted Barlow's problem. Josh said 'Mmm,' a lot. Eventually, he said, 'I'll check your guy out. And I'll do some asking around, no names, no pack drill. OK?'

'Great. When can we get together on this?'

Over the phone, I could hear the sound of Josh turning the pages in his diary. 'You hit me on a bad week,' he said. 'I suppose you need this stuff yesterday?'

'Afraid so. Sorry.'

He sucked his breath in over his teeth, the way plumbers are trained to do when they look at your central-heating system. 'Today's Tuesday. I'm snowed under today, but I can get to it tomorrow,' he muttered, half to himself. 'But my time's backed up solid Thursday, Friday I'm in London ... Listen, can you do breakfast Thursday? I meant it when I said it was a bad week.'

I took a deep breath. I'm never at my best first thing, but business is business. 'Thursday breakfast is fine,' I lied. 'Where would you like?'

'You choose, it's your money,' Josh replied.

We settled on the Portland at seven-thirty. They have this team of obliging hall porters who park your car for you, which in my opinion is a major advantage at that time of the morning. I checked my watch again. I didn't have time enough to develop and print my surveillance films. Instead, I settled for opening a file on Ted Barlow in my database.

Colonial Conservatories occupied the last unit before the industrial estate gave way to a sewage farm. What really caught the eye was the conservatory he'd built on the front of the unit. It was about ten foot deep and ran the whole thirty foot width of the building. It had a brick foundation, and was separated into four distinct sections by thin brick pillars. The first section was classic Victorian Crystal Palace style, complete with plastic replica finials on the roof. Next was the Country Diary of an Edwardian Lady school of conservatory, a riot of stained panels whose inaccuracies would give any botanist the screaming habdabs. Third in line was the Spartan conservatory. A bit like mine, in fact. Finally, there was the Last Days of the Raj look – windows forming arches in a plastic veneer that gave the appearance, from a considerable distance, of being mahogany. Just the place to sit on your rattan furniture and summon the punkah wallah to cool you down. You get a lot of that in South Manchester.

Inside the conservatory, I could see Colonial Conservatories' offices. I sat in the car for a moment, taking in the set-up. Just inside the door was a C-shaped reception desk. Behind it, a woman was on the phone. She had a curly perm that looked like Charles I's spare wig. Occasionally, she tapped a key on her word processor and gave the screen a bored stare before returning to her conversation. Over to one side, there were two small desks, each equipped with a phone and a pile of clutter. No one was at either desk. On the back wall, a door led into the main building. Over in the far corner, a small office had been divided off with glass partitions. Ted Barlow was standing in shirtsleeves in this office, his tie hanging loose and the top button of his shirt open, slowly working his way through the contents of a filing cabinet drawer. The rest of the reception was taken up with display panels.

I walked into the conservatory. The receptionist said brightly into the phone, 'Hold the line, please.' She flicked a switch then turned her radiance on me. 'How may I help you?' she asked in a little girl's voice.

'I have an appointment with Mr Barlow. My name's Brannigan. Kate Brannigan.'

'One moment, please.' She ran a finger down the page of her open desk diary. Her nail extensions mesmerized me. Just how could she type with those claws? She looked up and caught my stare, then smiled knowingly. 'Yes,' she said. 'I'll just see if he's ready for you.' She picked up a phone and buzzed through. Ted looked round him in a distracted way, saw me, ignored the phone and rushed across the reception area.

'Kate,' he exclaimed. 'Thanks for coming.' The receptionist cast her eyes heavenwards. Clearly, in her view, the man had no idea how bosses are supposed to behave. 'Now, what do you need to know?'

I steered him towards his office. I had no reason to suspect the receptionist of anything other than unrealistic aspirations, but it was too early in the investigation to trust anyone. 'I need a list of addresses of all the conservatories you've fitted in the last six months where the customers have taken out remortgages to finance them. Do you keep track of that information?'

He nodded, then stopped abruptly just outside his office. He pointed to a display board that showed several houses with conservatories attached. The houses were roughly similar – medium-sized, mostly detached, modern, all obviously surrounded on every side by more of the same. Ted's face looked genuinely mournful. 'That one, that one and that one,' he said. 'I had photographs taken of them after we built them because we were just about to do a new brochure. And when I went back today, they just weren't there any more.'

I felt a frisson of relief. The one nagging doubt I had had about Ted's honesty was resolved. Nasty, suspicious person that I am, I'd been wondering if the conservatories had ever been there in the first place. Now I had some concrete evidence that they had been spirited away. 'Can you give me the name of the photographer?' I asked, caution winning over my desire to believe in Ted.

'Yes, no problem. Listen, while I sort this stuff out for you, would you like me to get one of the lads to show you round the factory? See how we actually do the business?'

I declined politely. The construction of double-glazed conservatories wasn't a gap in my knowledge I felt the need to plug. I settled for the entertaining spectacle of watching Ted wrestle with his filing system. I sat down in his chair and picked up a leaflet about the joys of conservatories. I had the feeling this might be a long job.

The deathless prose of Ted's PR consultant stood no chance against the smartly dressed man who strode into the showroom, dumped a briefcase on one of the two small desks and walked into Ted's office, grinning at me like we were old friends.

'Hi,' he said. 'Jack McCafferty,' he added, thrusting his hand out towards me. His handshake was firm and cool, just like the rest of the image he projected. His brown curly hair was cut close at the sides and longer on top, so he looked like a respectable version of Mick Hucknall. His eyes were blue and had the dull sheen of polished sodalite against the lightly tanned skin of his face. He wore an olive green double-breasted suit, a cream shirt and a burgundy silk tie. The ensemble looked about five hundred pounds' worth to me. I felt quite underdressed in my terracotta linen suit and mustard cowl-necked sweater.

'Kate, Jack's one of my salesmen,' Ted said.

'Sales *team*,' Jack put him right. From his air of amused patience, I gathered it was a regular correction. 'And you are?'

'Kate Brannigan,' I said. 'I'm an accountant. I'm putting together a package with Ted. Pleased to meet you, Jack.'

Ted looked astonished. Lying didn't seem to be his strong suit. Luckily, he was standing behind Jack. He cleared his throat and handed me a bulky blue folder. 'Here are the details you wanted, Kate,' he said. 'If there's anything that's not clear, just give me a call.'

'OK, Ted.' I nodded. I had one or two questions I wanted to ask him, but not ones that fitted my exciting new persona of accountant. 'Nice to meet you, Jack.'

'Nice. That's a word. Not the one I would have used for meeting you, Kate,' he replied, a suggestive lift to one eyebrow.

As I walked back across the reception area and out to my car, I could feel his eyes on me. I felt pretty sure I wouldn't like what he was thinking.

3

I pulled up half a mile down the road and had a quick look through the file. Most of the properties seemed to be over in Warrington, so I decided to leave them till morning. The light was already starting to fade, and by the time I'd driven over there, there would be nothing to see. However, there were half a dozen properties nearby where Ted had fitted conservatories. He'd already visited one of them and discovered that the conservatory had gone. On my way home, I decided I might as well take a quick look at the others. I pulled my *A–Z* out of the glove box and mapped out the most efficient route that included them all.

The first was at the head of a cul-de-sac in a nasty sixties estate, one of a pair of almost-detached houses, linked only by their garages in a bizarre Siamese twinning. I rang the bell, but there was no response, so I walked down the narrow path between the house and the fence to the back garden. Surprise, surprise. There was no conservatory. I studied the plan so I could work out exactly where it had been. Then I crouched down and scrutinized the brickwork on the back wall. I didn't really expect to find anything, since I wasn't at all sure what I should even be looking for. However, even my untrained eye noticed a line of faint markings on the wall. It looked like someone had given it a going over with a wire brush – enough to shift the surface grime and weathering, that was all.

Intrigued, I stood up and headed for the next destination. 6 Wiltshire Copse and 19 Amundsen Avenue were almost identical. And they were both minus conservatories. However, the next two remortgages I visited still had their conservatories firmly anchored to the houses. I trekked back to my car for the fifth time, deeply depressed after too much exposure to the kind of horrid little houses that give modern a bad name. I thought of my own home, a bungalow built only three years before, but constructed by a builder who didn't feel the need to see how small a bedroom you could build before the human mind screams 'No!' My lounge is generous, I don't have to climb over anything to get in and out of bed and my second bedroom is big enough for me to use as an office, complete with sofa bed for unavoidable visitors. But most of these overgrown sheds looked as if they'd have been pressed to provide one decent-sized bedroom, never mind three.

The irony was that they were probably worth more than mine because they were situated on bijou developments in the suburbs. Whereas my little oasis, one of thirty 'professional person's dwellings', was five minutes from every city centre amenity. The downside was that it was surrounded by the kind of inner-city housing they make earnest Channel 4 documentaries about. The locale had brought the price down far enough for me also to afford the necessary state-of-the-art alarm system.

I decided home was where I should head for. Darkness was falling, so I wouldn't be able to continue my fascinating study of late-twentieth-century bricklaying. Besides, people were getting home from work and I was beginning to feel a little conspicuous. It was only a matter of time before some over-zealous Neighbourhood Watch vigilante called the cops, an embarrassment I could well do without. I drove out of the opposite end of the estate to the one I'd come in by, and suddenly realized I was only a couple of streets away from Alexis's house.

Alexis Lee is probably my best friend. She's the crime reporter on the *Manchester Evening Chronicle*. I guess the fact that we're both women who've broken into what is traditionally a male preserve helped build the bond between us. But apart from our common interest in things criminal, she's also saved me more money than anyone else I know. I can think of at least a dozen times when she's prevented me from making very costly mistakes in expensive dress shops. And, at the risk of making her sound like a stereotype, she's got that wonderful, rich Liverpudlian sense of humour that can find the funny side in the blackest tragedy. I couldn't think of anything that would cheer me up faster than a half-hour pit stop.

The earlier rain had turned the fallen leaves into a slick mush. As I braked gently to pull up outside Alexis's, I swear my Vauxhall Nova went sideways. Cursing the Highways Department, I slithered round the car and on to the safer ground of the driveway. I grabbed at a post to steady myself, then realized with a shock that this particular post wasn't a permanent fixture. It was supporting a For Sale sign. I was outraged. How dare they put the house on the market without consulting me? Time I found out what was going on here. I walked round to the back door, knocked and entered the kitchen.

Alexis's girlfriend Chris is a partner in a firm of community architects, which is why their kitchen looks like a Gothic cathedral, complete with flagged floor and vaulted ceiling with beams like whales' ribs. The plasterwork is stencilled with flower and fruit motifs, and there are plaster bas-relief bosses at regular intervals along the roof truss. It's an amazing sight.

Instead of the Quasimodo I always half-expect, Alexis was sitting at the pitch-pine table, a mug of tea at her elbow, some kind of catalogue open in front of her. As I came in, she looked up and grinned. 'Kate! Hey, good to see you, kid! Grab yourself a cuppa, the pot's fresh,' she said, waving at the multi-coloured knitted tea cosy by the kettle. I poured myself a mug of strong tea as Alexis asked, 'What brings you round here? You been doing a job? Anything in it for me?'

'Never mind that,' I said firmly, dropping into a chair. 'You trying to avoid me? What's with the For Sale sign? You put the house on the market and you don't tell me?'

'Why? Were you thinking of buying it? Don't! Don't even let it cross your mind! There's barely enough room for me and Chris, and we agree on what's an acceptable degree of mess. You and Richard would kill within a week here,' Alexis parried.

'Don't try to divert me,' I said. 'Richard and I are fine as we are. Next door neighbours is as close as I'm ever going to let it get.'

'And how is your insignificant other?' Alexis interrupted.

'He sends you his love too.' Alexis and the man I love have a relationship that seems to me to consist entirely of verbal abuse. In spite of appearances, however, I suspect they love each other dearly; once I actually came upon the two of them having a friendly drink together in a corner of the *Chronicle*'s local. They'd both looked extremely sheepish about it. 'Now, about this For Sale board?'

'It's only been up a couple of days. It's all been a bit of a rush. You remember Chris and I talking about how we wanted to buy a piece of land and build our own dream home?'

I nodded. I could more easily have forgotten my own name. 'You're planning on doing it as part of a self-build scheme; Chris is going to design the houses in exchange for other people giving you their labour, yes?' They'd been talking about it for as long as I'd known them. With a lot of people, I'd have written it off as dreaming. But Alexis and Chris were serious. They'd spent hundreds of hours poring over books, plans and their own drawings till they'd come up with their ideal home. All they'd been waiting for was the right plot of land at the right price in the right location. 'The land?' I asked.

Alexis reached along the side of the table and pulled a drawer open. She tossed a packet of photographs at me. 'Look at that, Kate. Isn't it stunning? Isn't it just brilliant?' She pushed her unruly black hair out of her eyes and gazed expectantly at me.

I studied the pictures. The first half-dozen showed a selection of views of an area of rough moorland grass that had sheep grazing all over it. 'That's the land,' Alexis enthused, unable to stay silent. I continued. The rest of the pictures were views of distant hills, woods and valleys. Not a Chinese takeaway in sight. 'And those are the views. Amazing, isn't it? That's why I'm going through this.' She waved the catalogue at me. I could see now it was a building supplies price list. Personally, I'd have preferred a night in with the phone book.

'Where on earth is it?' I asked. 'It looks so . . . rural.' That was the first word I could come up with that was truthful as well as sounding like I approved.

'It's really wild, isn't it? It's only three minutes away from the M66. It's just above Ramsbottom. I can be in the office in twenty minutes outside rush hour, but it's completely isolated from the hassle of city life.'

If that had been me, I'd have ended the sentence six words sooner. If you're more than ten minutes away from a Marks & Spencer Food Hall (fifteen including legal parking), as far as I'm concerned, you're outside the civilized world. 'Right,' I said. 'That's just what you wanted, isn't it?'

'Yeah, it's the business. As soon as we saw it advertised, we called a meeting of the other people we'll be building with, and we all went off to see it. We've agreed a price with the builder, but he wants a quick completion because someone else is interested. Or so he says, but if you ask me, he's just on the make. Anyway, we've put down a deposit of five thousand pounds on each plot, and it's looking good. So it's time to sell this place and get our hands on the readies we'll need to build the new house.'

'But where are you going to live while you're building?' I asked.

'Well, Kate, it's funny you should mention that. We were wondering ...' I nearly panicked. Then I saw the smile twitching at the corner of her mouth. 'We're going to buy a caravan now, at the end of the season when it's cheap, live in it over the winter and sell it in the spring. The house should be just about habitable by then,' Alexis told me cheerfully. I couldn't control the shiver that ran through me.

'Well, any time you need a bath, you're more than welcome,' I said.

'Thanks. I might just take you up on that, you being so handy for the office,' she said.

I drained my mug and got to my feet. 'I've got to run.'

'Don't tell me, you're off on some Deep Throat surveillance,' Alexis teased.

'Wrong again. I can see why you just write about crime rather than detecting it. No, Richard and I are going tenpin bowling.' I said it quickly, but it didn't get past her.

'Tenpin bowling?' Alexis spluttered. 'Tenpin bowling? Shit, Brannigan, it'll be snogging in the back row of the pictures next.'

I left her giggling to herself. All through history, the pioneers have been mocked by lesser minds. All you can do is rise above it.

There are probably worse ways to spend a wet Wednesday in Warrington than wandering round modern housing developments talking to the local inhabitants. If so, I haven't discovered them. I got to the first address soon after nine, which wasn't bad considering it had taken me twice as long as usual to get ready that morning because of the painful stiffness in my right shoulder. I'd forgotten you shouldn't go tenpin bowling unless you've got the upper body fitness levels of an Olympic shot putter.

The first house was at the head of a cul-de-sac that spiralled round like a nautilus shell. I tried the doorbell of the neat semi, but got no response. I peered through the picture window into the lounge, which was furnished in spartan style, with no signs of current occupation. The clincher was the fact that there was no TV or video in sight. It looked as if my conservatory buyers had moved and were renting out their house. Most people who let their homes furnished tuck their expensive but highly portable electrical goods away into storage in case the letting agency don't do their homework properly and let the house to people of less than sterling honesty. Strangely, a couple of the houses I'd visited the previous evening had had a similar air of absence.

Round the back, there was more evidence of the missing conservatory than in the others I'd seen, where the concrete bases they'd been built on had simply looked like unfinished patios. Here, there was a square of red glazed quarry tiles extending out beyond the patio doors. Round the edge of the square was a little wall, two bricks deep, except for a door-sized gap. And the walls showed the now familiar traces of the mortar that had attached the extension to the house.

I'd noticed a car parked in the drive of the other half of the semi, so I made my way back round to the front and rang the doorbell, which serenaded me with an electronic 'Yellow Rose of Texas'. The woman who opened the door looked more like the Dandelion Clock of Cheshire. She had a halo of fluffy white hair that looked like it had been defying hairdressers for more than half a century. Grey-blue eyes loomed hazily through the thick lenses of gold-rimmed glasses as she sized me up. 'Yes?' she demanded.

'I'm sorry to bother you,' I lied. 'But I was wondering if you could help me. I represent the company who sold next door their conservatory ...'

Before I could complete my sentence, the woman cut in. 'We don't want a conservatory. And we've already got double glazing and a burglar alarm.' The door started to close.

'I'm not selling anything,' I yelped, offended by her assumption. Great start to the day. Mistaken for a double-glazing canvasser. 'I'm just trying to track down the people who used to live next door.'

She stopped with the door still open a crack. 'You're not selling anything?'

'Cross my heart and hope to die. I just wanted to pick your brains, that's all.' I used the reassuring voice. The same one that usually works on guard dogs.

The door slowly opened again. I made a great show of consulting the file I was carrying in my bag. 'It says here the conservatory was installed back in March.'

'That would be about right,' she interrupted. 'It went up the week before Easter, and it was gone a week later. It just disappeared overnight.' History had just been made. I'd dropped lucky at the first attempt.

'Overnight?'

'That was the really peculiar thing. One day it was there, the next day it wasn't. They must have taken it down during the night. We never heard or saw a thing. We just assumed there must have been some dispute about it. You know, perhaps she didn't like it, or she didn't pay or something? But then, you'd know all about that, if you represent the firm,' she added with a belated note of caution.

'You know how it is, I'm not allowed to discuss things like that,' I said. 'But I am trying to track them down. Robinson, my file says.'

She leaned against the door jamb, settling herself in for a good gossip. It was all right for her. I was between the cold north wind and the door. I jerked up the collar of my jacket and hated her quietly. 'She wasn't what you'd call sociable. Not one for joining in, you might say. I invited her in for coffee or drinks several times and she never came once. And I wasn't the only one. We're very friendly here in the Grove, but she kept herself to herself.'

I was slightly puzzled by the constant reference to the woman alone. The form in the file was in two names – Maureen and William Robinson. 'What about her husband?' I asked.

The woman raised her eyebrows. 'Husband? I'd have said he was somebody else's husband, myself.'

I sighed mentally. 'How long had you known Mrs Robinson?' I asked.

'Well, she only moved in in December,' the woman said. 'She was hardly here at all that first month, what with Christmas and everything. Most weeks she was away three or four nights. And she was always out during the day. She often didn't get home till gone eight. Then she moved out a couple of days after the conservatory went. My husband said she probably had to move suddenly, on account of her work, and maybe took the conservatory with her to a new house.'

'Her work?'

'She told my Harry that she was a freelance computer expert. It takes her all over the world, you know. She said that's why she'd always rented the house out. There's been a string of tenants in there ever since we moved in five years ago. She told Harry this was the first time she'd actually had the chance to live in the house herself.' There was a note of pride in her voice that her Harry had managed to get so much out of their mysterious neighbour.

'Can you describe her to me, Mrs—?'

She considered. 'Green. Carole Green, with an e, on the Carole, not the Green. Well, she was taller than you.' Not hard. Five three isn't exactly Amazonian. 'Not much, though. Late twenties, I'd say. She had dark brown hair, in a full page-boy, really thick and glossy her hair was. Always nicely made up.

And she was a nice dresser, you never saw her scruffy.'

'And the man you mentioned?'

'There was more than one, you know. Most nights when she was here, a car would pull up in the garage later on, about eleven. A couple of times, I saw them drive off the next morning. The first one had a blue Sierra, but he only lasted a couple of weeks. The next one had a silver Vauxhall Cavalier.' She seemed very positive about the cars and I commented on it. 'My Harry's in the motor trade,' she informed me. 'I might not have noticed the men, but I noticed the cars.'

'And you haven't seen her since she moved out?'

The woman shook her head. 'Not hide nor hair. Then the house was rented out again a fortnight after she moved. A young couple, just moved up from Kent. They left a month ago, bought a place of their own over towards Widnes. Lovely couple, they were. Don and Diane. Beautiful baby girl, Danni.'

I almost pitied them. I bet they'd not thought fast enough to get out of the little social events of the Grove. I couldn't think of anything else to ask, so I made my excuses and left. I considered trying the other neighbours, but I didn't see how anyone could have succeeded where Carole with an e had failed.

Scarborough Walk was only a mile away as the crow flies. Clearly the crow has never inspired a town planner. Only a Minotaur fresh from the Cretan labyrinth would feel at home in the newer parts of Warrington. I negotiated yet another roundabout with my street map on my knees and entered yet another new development. Whitby Way encircled a dozen Walks, Closes and Groves like the covered wagons pulled up to repel the Indians. It was about as hard to breach. Eventually, second time round, I spotted the entrance to the development. Cleverly designed to look like a dead end, in fact it led straight into a maze that I managed to unravel by driving at 10 m.p.h. with one eye on the map. Sometimes I wonder how I cope with a job as glamorous, exciting and risky as this.

Again, there was no conservatory. The couple who lived there now had only been renting it for a couple of months, so the harried mother with the hyperactive toddler wasn't able to tell me anything about the people who'd actually bought the conservatory. But the woman next door but one had missed her way. She should have been on the *News of the World*'s investigative desk. By the time I escaped, I knew more than I could ever have dreamed possible about the inhabitants of Scarborough Walk. I even knew about the two couples who had moved out in 1988 after their wife-swapping had turned into a permanent transfer. However, I didn't know much about the former inhabitants of number six. They'd bought the house the previous November, and had moved out at the end of February because he'd got a job out in the Middle East somewhere and she'd gone with him. She'd been a nurse on permanent night duty, at one of the Liverpool hospitals, she thought. He'd been something in personnel. She'd had a blonde urchin cut, just like that Sally Webster on *Coronation Street*. He'd been tall, dark and handsome. She'd had some kind of little car, he'd had some kind of big car. He often worked late. They went out a lot when they weren't working. The perfect description to put out to Interpol.

The next house still had its conservatory. It also still had a satisfied customer, which I was grateful for. I really didn't need to be mistaken for the customer services department of Colonial Conservatories. I ploughed on through the list, and when I reached the end, I reckoned I was entitled to a treat for having spent so task-orientated a day. Four o'clock and I was back in Manchester, sitting in my favourite curry shop in Strangeways, tucking into a bowl of karahi lamb.

As I scoffed, I popped the earpiece of my miniature tape recorder in place and played back the verbal notes I'd made after each of my visits. Five out of the eight were victims of MCS (Missing Conservatory Syndrome, I'd christened it). The only common factor I could isolate was that, in each case, the couple concerned had only lived in the house for a few months after buying it, then they'd moved out and let the place via an agency. I couldn't make sense of it at all. Who were all these people? Two brunettes, one auburn, two blondes. Two with glasses, three without. All working women. Two drove red Fiestas, one went everywhere by taxi, one drove a white Metro, one drove 'something small'. All the men were on the tall side and dark, ranging from 'handsome' to 'nowt special'. A description that would cover about half the male population. Again, two wore glasses, three didn't. They all drove standard businessmen's cars – a couple had metallic Cavaliers, one had a red Sierra, one had a blue Sierra, one changed his car from 'a big red one' to 'a big white one'. Not a single lead as to the whereabouts of any of them.

I had to admit I was completely baffled. I dictated my virtually non-existent conclusions, then checked in with Shelley. I answered half a dozen queries, discovered there was nothing urgent waiting for me, so I hit the supermarket. I fancied some more treats to reward me for the ironing pile that faced me at home. I had no intention of including myself in Richard's plans for the evening. I can think of more pleasurable ways of getting hearing damage than boogying on down to a double wicked hip hop rap band from Mostyn called PMT, or something similar. There's nothing like a quiet night in.

4

And that's exactly what I got. Nothing like a quiet night in. I'd gone back to the office after a quick hit on Sainsbury's and dropped off my cassette for Shelley to input in the morning. I was sure the thought that it was for Ted Barlow would make her fingers fly. Then I'd finally managed to find the peace and quiet to develop my surveillance films from PharmAce Supplies. As I stared at the film, I wished I hadn't. On the other hand, if you're going to have a major downer, I suppose it's as well to have it at the end of a day that's already been less than wonderful, rather than spoil a perfectly good one.

Where there ought to have been identifiable images of PharmAce's senior lab technician slipping in and out of the building in the middle of the night (timing superimposed on the pictures by my super-duper Nikon), there was only a foggy blur. Something had gone badly wrong. Since the commonest cause of fogged film is a camera problem, what I then had to do was to run a film through the camera I'd been using that night, and develop it to see if I could pinpoint the problem. That took another hour, and all it demonstrated was that there was nothing wrong with the camera. Which left either a faulty film or human error. And the chances were, whether I liked it or not, that human error was the reason. Which meant I was stuck with the prospect of another Saturday night in the back of the van with my eye glued to a long lens. Sometimes I really do wonder if I did the right thing when I gave up my law degree after the second year to come and work with Bill. Then I look at what my former fellow students are doing now, and I begin to be grateful I made the jump.

I binned the useless film, locked up and drove home in time to listen to *The Archers* on the waterproof radio in the shower.

It was a birthday present from Richard; I can't help feeling there was a bit of Indian giving involved, considering how often I have to tune it back to Radio 4 from Key 103. I don't know why he can't just use his own bathroom for his ablutions. I'm not being as unreasonable as that sounds; although we've been lovers for over a year now, we don't actually live together as such. When Richard first crashed into my life – or rather, my car – he was living in a nasty rented flat in Chorlton. He claimed he liked a neighbourhood where he was surrounded by students, feminists and Green Party supporters, but when I pointed out that for much the same outlay he could have a spacious two-bedroomed bungalow three minutes' drive from his favourite Chinese restaurant, he instantly saw the advantages. The fact that it's next door to my own mirror-image bungalow was merely a bonus.

Of course, he wanted to knock the walls down and turn the pair into a kind of open-plan ranch-house. So I persuaded Chris to come round and deliver herself of the professional architect's opinion that if you removed the walls Richard wanted rid of, both houses would fall down. Instead, she designed a beautiful conservatory that runs the length of both properties, linking them along the back. That way, we have the best of both worlds. It removes most of the causes of friction, with the result that we spend our time together having fun rather than rows. I preserve my personal space, while Richard can be as rowdy as he likes with his rock band friends and his visiting son. It's not that I don't like Davy, the six-year-old who seems to be the only good thing that came out of Richard's disastrous marriage. It's just that, having reached the age of twenty-seven unencumbered (or enriched, according to some) by a child, I don't want to live with someone else's.

I was almost sorry that Richard was out working, since I could have done with a bit of cheering up. I got out of the shower, towelling my auburn hair as dry as I could get it. I couldn't be bothered blow-drying it. I pulled on an old jogging suit which was when I remembered my shopping was still in the car. I was dragging the carriers out of the hatchback of my Nova when a hand on my back made my heart bump wildly in my chest. I whirled round, going straight into the 'ready to attack' Thai boxing position. In inner-city neighbourhoods like ours, you don't take chances.

'Hang about, Bruce Lee, it's only me,' Richard said, backing off, raising his palms in a placatory gesture. 'Jesus, Brannigan, hold your fire,' he added, as I moved menacingly towards him. I bared my teeth and growled deep in my throat, just the way my coach Karen trains us to do. Richard looked momentarily terrified, then he gave that Cute Smile of his, the one that got me into this in the first place, the smile that still, I'm ashamed to admit, turns me into a slushy Mills and Boon heroine. I stopped growling and straightened up, slightly sheepishly. 'I've told you before, sneak up on me outside and you risk a full set of broken ribs,' I grouched. 'Now you're here, give me a hand with this.'

The effort of carrying two carrier bags and a case of Miller Lite was clearly too much for the poor lamb, who immediately slumped on one of my living-room sofas. 'I thought you were doing your brains in to the sound of young black Manchester tonight?' I said.

'They decided they weren't ready to expose themselves to the fearless scrutiny of the music press,' he said. 'So they've put me off till next week. By which time, I hope one of them's had a brain transplant. You know, Brannigan, sometimes I wish the guy who invented the drum machine had been strangled at birth. He'd have saved the world a lot of brain ache.' Richard shrugged his jacket off, kicked off his shoes and put his feet up.

'Haven't you got someone else to mither,' I asked politely.

'Nope. I haven't even got any deadlines to meet. So I thought I might go and pick up a Chinese, bring it back here and litter your lounge with beansprouts out of sheer badness.'

'Fine. As long as you promise you will not insinuate a single shirt into my ironing basket.'

'Promise,' he said.

An hour and a half later, I pressed my last pair of trousers. 'Thank God,' I sighed.

No response from the sofa. It wasn't surprising. He was on

his third joint and it would have been hard to hear World War Three over the soundtrack of the Motley Crue video he was inflicting on me. What did penetrate, however, was the high-pitched electronic bleep of my phone. I grabbed the phone and the TV remote, hitting the mute button as I switched the phone to 'talk'. That got a reaction. 'Hey,' he protested, then subsided immediately as he registered that I was using the phone.

'Hello,' I said. Never give your name or number when you answer the phone, especially if you've got an ex-directory number. In these days of phones with last number re-dial buttons, you never know who you're talking to. I have a friend who discovered the name and number of her husband's mistress that way. I know I've got nothing to fear on that score, but I like to develop habits of caution. You never know when they'll come in necessary.

'Kate? It's Alexis.' She sounded the kind of pissed off she gets when she's trying to put together a story against the clock and the news editor is standing behind her chair breathing down her neck. But the time was all wrong for her deadlines.

'Oh, hi. How's tricks?' I said.

'Is this a good time?'

'Good as any. I've eaten, I'm still under the limit and I still have my clothes on,' I told her.

'We need your help, Kate. I don't like to ask, but I don't know who else would know where to begin.'

This was no pick-your-brains business call. When Alexis wants my help with a story, she doesn't apologize. She knows that kind of professional help is a two-way street. 'Tell me the score, I'll tell you if I can help.'

'You know that piece of land we're supposed to be buying? The one I showed you the pix of yesterday? Yeah?'

'Yeah,' I soothed. She sounded like she was about to explode.

'Well, you're not going to believe this. Chris went up there today to do some measurements. She figured that if she's going to be designing these houses, she needs to have a feel for the lie of the land so the properties can blend in with the flow of the landscape, right?'

'Right. So what's the problem?'

'The problem is, she gets up there to find a couple of surveyors marking out the plots. Well, she's a bit confused, you know, because as far as we know none of the other self-builders we're working with have asked anyone to start work yet, on account of we haven't completed on it yet. So, she parks up in the Land Rover and watches them for half an hour or so. Then it dawns on her that the plots they're marking out are different altogether from the plots we've been sold. So she goes over to them and gets into conversation. You know Chris, she's not like me. I'd have been out there gripping them by the throat demanding to know what the hell they thought they were up to.' Alexis paused for breath, but not long enough for me to respond.

'But not Chris. She lets them tell her all about the land and how they're marking out the plots for the people who have bought them. Half a dozen have been bought by a local small builder, the rest by individuals, they tell her. Well, Chris is more than a little bewildered, on account of what they are telling her is completely at odds with the situation as we know it. So she tells them who she is and what she's doing there and asks them if they've got any proof of what they're saying, which of course they don't have, but they tell her the name of the solicitor who's acting for the purchasers.'

This time, I managed to get in, 'I'm with you so far,' before the tide of Alexis's narrative swept back in. Richard was looking at me very curiously. He's not accustomed to hearing me take such a minor role in a telephone conversation.

'So Chris drives down to this solicitor's in Ramsbottom. She manages to convince their conveyancing partner that this is urgent, so he gives her five minutes. When she explains the situation, he says the land was sold by a builder and that the sales were all completed two days ago.' Alexis stopped short, as if what she'd said should make everything clear.

'I'm sorry, Alexis, I suspect I'm being really stupid here, but what exactly do you mean?'

'I mean the land's already been sold!' she howled. 'We handed over five grand for a piece of land that had already been sold. I just don't understand how it could have happened!

And I don't even know where to start trying to find out.' The anguish in her voice was heartbreaking. I knew how much she and Chris wanted this project to work, for all sorts of reasons. Now, it looked as if the money they'd saved to get their feet on the first rung of the ladder had been thrown away.

'OK, OK, I'll look into it,' I soothed. 'But I'm going to need some more info from you. What was the name of the solicitor in Ramsbottom that Chris saw?'

'Just a minute, I'll pass you over to Chris. She's got all the details. Thanks, Kate. I knew I could count on you.'

There was a brief pause, then a very subdued Chris came on the line. Her voice sounded like she'd been crying. 'Kate? Oh God, I can't believe this is happening to us. I just don't understand it, any of it.' Then she proceeded to repeat everything Alexis had already told me.

I listened patiently, then said, 'What was the name of the solicitor's you went to see in Ramsbottom?'

'Chapman and Gardner. I spoke to the conveyancing partner, Tim Pascoe. I asked him the name of the person who had sold the land, but he wouldn't tell me. So I said, was it T.R. Harris, and he gave me one of those lawyer's looks and said he couldn't comment, only he said it in that kind of way that means yes, you're right.'

I looked at the names I'd scribbled on my pad. 'So who exactly is T.R. Harris?'

'T.R. Harris is the builder who was supposedly selling the land to us.' There was a note of exasperation in her voice, which I couldn't help feeling was a bit unfair. After all, I'm not a fully paid up member of the Psychic Society.

'And your solicitor is?'

'Martin Cheetham.' She rattled off the address and phone number.

'He your usual solicitor?' I asked.

'No. He specializes in conveyancing. One of the hacks on the *Chronicle* was interviewing him about how the new conveyancing protocol is working out, and they got talking, and they got on to the topic of builders catching a cold because they'd bought land speculatively and the bottom had fallen out of the market, and this hack said how one of his colleagues, i.e. Alexis, was looking for a chunk big enough for ten people to do a self-build scheme, and Cheetham said he knew of a colleague who had a client who was a builder who had just the thing, so we went to see Cheetham, and he said this T.R. Harris had bought this land and couldn't afford to develop it himself so he was selling it off.' Chris talks in sentences longer than the law lords.

'And did you ever meet this builder?'

'Of course. T.R. Harris, call me Tom, Mr Nice Guy. He met us all out there, walked the land out with us, divided it up into plots and gave us this sob story about how desperate he was to keep his business afloat, how he had half a dozen sites where the workers were depending on him to pay their wages, so could we please see our way to coughing up five thousand apiece as a deposit to secure the land, otherwise he was going to have to keep on trying to find other buyers, which would be a real pity since it obviously suited our needs so well and he liked the idea of the land being used for a self-build if only because he wouldn't have the heartache of watching some other builder make a nice little earner out of such a prime site that he'd been really sick to have to let go. He was so convincing, Kate, it never crossed our minds that he was lying, and he obviously fooled Cheetham as well. Can you do something?' I couldn't ignore the pleading note in her voice, even supposing I'd wanted to.

'I don't really understand what's happened, but of course I'll do what I can to help. At the very least, we should be able to get your money back, though I think you'll have to kiss goodbye to that particular piece of land.'

Chris groaned. 'Don't, Kate. I know you're right, but I really don't want to think about it, we'd set our hearts on that site, it was just perfect, and I'd already got this really clear picture in my mind's eye of what the houses were going to look like.' I could imagine. Eat your heart out, Portmeirion.

'I'll take a look at it tomorrow, promise. But I need something from you. You'll have to give me a couple of letters of authority so that your solicitor and anybody else official will talk to me.

Could Alexis drop them off on her way to work tomorrow morning?'

We sorted out the details of what the letters should say, and I only had to listen to the tale once more before I managed to get off the phone. Then, of course, I had to go through it all for Richard.

'Somebody's been bang out of order here,' he said, outraged. He summed up my feelings exactly. It was the next bit I wasn't so happy about. 'You're going to have to get this one sorted out double urgent, aren't you?'

Sometimes, it's hard to escape the feeling that the whole world's ganging up on you.

5

I gave Alexis her second shock of the week next morning when she dropped off the letters of authority. It was just before seven when I heard her key in my front door. Her feet literally left the floor when she walked through the kitchen doorway and saw me sitting on a high stool with a glass of orange juice.

'Shit!' she yelled. I thought her black hair was standing on end with fright till I realized I was just unfamiliar with how untamed it looks first thing. She runs a hand through it approximately twice a minute. By late afternoon, it usually manages to look less like it's been dragged through a hedge backwards then sideways.

'Ssh,' I admonished her. 'You'll wake Sleeping Beauty.'

'You're up!' she exclaimed. 'Not only are you up, your mouth's moving. Hold the front page!'

'Very funny. I can do mornings when I have to,' I said defensively. 'I happen to have a breakfast meeting.'

'Excuse me while I vomit,' Alexis muttered. 'I can't take yuppies without a caffeine inoculation. And I see that being conscious hasn't stretched to making a pot of coffee.'

'I'm saving myself for the Portland,' I said. 'Help yourself to an instant. It's still better than that muck they serve in your canteen.' I plucked the letters from her hand, tucked them in my bag and left her deliberating between the Blend 37 and the Alta Rica.

Josh was already deep in the *Financial Times* when I got to the Portland, even though I was four minutes early. Eyeing him up across the restaurant in his immaculate dark blue suit, gleaming white shirt and strident silk tie, I was glad I'd taken the trouble to get suited up myself in my Marks & Spencer olive green with a cream high-necked blouse. Very businesslike.

He was too engrossed to notice till I was standing between the light and his paper.

He tore himself away from the mating habits of multinational companies and gave me the hundred-watt smile, all twinkles, dimples and sincerity. It makes Robert Redford, whom he resembles slightly, look like an amateur. I'm convinced Josh developed it in front of the mirror for susceptible female clients, and now it's become a habit whenever a woman comes within three feet of him. The charm comes without patronage, however. He's one of those men who doesn't have a problem with the notion that women are equals. Except the ones he has relationships with. Them he treats like brainless bimbos. This makes for a quick turnover, since the ones who have a brain can't take it for more than a couple of months, and the ones who haven't bore him rigid after six weeks.

In spite of keeping his emotions in his underpants, when it comes to business he's one of the best financial consultants in Manchester. He's a walking database on anything relating to insurance, investments, trust funds, tax shelters and the Financial Services Act. Anything he doesn't know, he knows where to find out. We met when I was still a law student, eking out my grant by doing odd jobs for Bill. My first ever undercover was in Josh's office, posing as a temp to track down the person who was using the computer to divert one pound out of each client account into his own unit trust account. Because our relationship started on a professional footing, Josh never came on to me and it's stayed that way. Now, I take him out for a slap-up dinner every couple of months as a thank you for running credit checks for me. The rest of the work and advice, like this, he bills us for at his usual extortionate hourly rate, so I got straight to the point.

I outlined the problem facing Ted Barlow while we scoffed our bowls of fruit and cereal. Josh asked a couple of questions, then the scrambled eggs and bacon arrived. He frowned in concentration as he ate. I wasn't sure if that was because he was thinking about Ted's problem or appreciating the subtle pleasures of the scrambled eggs, but I decided not to interrupt anyway. Besides, I was enjoying the rare pleasure of hot food so early in the day.

Then he sat back, mopped his lips with the napkin and poured a fresh cup of coffee. 'There's obviously some kind of fraud going on here,' he said. With anyone else, I'd have made some sarcastic crack about stating the obvious, but Josh did his degree at Cambridge and he likes to establish the ground under his feet before he builds up the speculation, so I managed to keep my mouth zipped.

'Mmm,' I said.

'I would say that the chances are the bank has a pretty shrewd idea of what that fraud is. They obviously think, however, that your Mr Barlow is the villain of the piece, and that is why they have taken the steps they've taken, and why they are refusing to discuss their detailed reasons with him. They don't want to alert him to the fact that they have worked out for themselves what he is up to, so they have shrouded it in generalizations.' He paused and spread a cold triangle of toast thickly with butter. The way he was chugging the cholesterol, I didn't feel at all confident he'd live long enough to retire at forty. I don't know how he stays so trim. I suspect there's a portrait of an elephant in his attic.

'I'm not sure I follow you,' I admitted.

'Sorry. I'll give you an example I came across a little time ago. I have a client who owns a double-glazing firm. They had a similar experience to that of your Mr Barlow – the bank closed down their credit and a few days later, the police were all over them. It turns out that there had been a spate of burglaries around the North West that all followed the same pattern. They were all houses that had a drive at the side with access to the rear of the house. The neighbours would see a double-glazing firm's van turn up. The workmen would start removing the ground floor windows, while one of them was removing the household valuables through the back or side of the house and loading them into the van. The neighbours, of course, thought the family were simply having replacement windows installed. They might wonder why the workmen disappeared at lunch-time and failed to return, leaving plastic sheeting over the window holes and the old windows sitting in the drive, but no one wondered enough to do anything about it.

'The common factor that all those houses shared, it eventually transpired, was that they had all been canvassed by the same double-glazing firm in the weeks previous to the burglary. And of course, the canvassers had established whether both husband and wife were working, thus uncovering which houses were empty during the day. The police suspected my client and paid a visit to his bankers. They, of course, were only too aware that after a grim spell my client's account had started to look very healthy again, and that much of his recent incomings had been in cash. After the police visit, they put two and two together and regrettably made a pig's ear of it. Partly the fault of my client, who had omitted to mention his recent investment in a couple of amusement arcades.' Josh's sardonic tone told me all I needed to know about his opinion of slot machines as investments.

'It was, of course, all sorted out in the fullness of time. The burglaries were the brainchild of a couple of former employees, who paid backhanders to unemployed youths of their acquaintance to go and get jobs as canvassers with this double-glazing firm and report back to them. However, my client had an extremely sticky time in the interim. That experience leads me to suspect the bank think your Mr Barlow is the brains behind whatever is going on here. You said they mentioned a high default rate on remortgages?'

'That's about all they did say,' I replied. 'More toast?' Josh nodded. I waved the toast rack plaintively at a passing waitress and waited for Josh's next pearl of wisdom.

'If I were you, that's where I'd start looking.' He sat back with the air of a conjuror who has just completed some amazing feat. I wasn't impressed, and I guess it showed.

He sighed. 'Kate, if I were you, I'd ask my friendly financial wizard to run a credit check on all those good people who have taken out remortgages and whose conservatories have now vanished.'

I still wasn't getting it. 'But what would that show?' I asked.

'I don't know,' Josh admitted. He didn't know? I waited for

the sky to fall, but incredibly it didn't. 'But whatever happens, you'll know a lot more about them than you do now. And I have that curious tingling in my stomach that tells me that's the right place to look.'

I trust Josh's tingle. The last time I had personal experience of it, I quadrupled my savings by buying shares in a company he had a good feeling about. The truly convincing thing was that he told me to offload them a week before they crashed spectacularly following the arrest of their chairman for fraud. So I said, 'OK. Go ahead. I'll fax you the names and addresses this morning.'

'Splendid,' he said. I wasn't sure if he was addressing me or the waitress placing a rack of fresh toast in front of him.

As he attacked the toast, I asked, 'When will you have the info for me?'

'I'll fax it across to you as soon as I get it myself. Probably tomorrow. Mark it for Julia's attention when you send the details over. I'm hopelessly tied up today, but it's just routine, she can do it standing on her head. What I will also do is have a quiet word with a guy I know in Royal Pennine Bank's fraud section. No names, no pack drill, but he might be able to shed some light as to the general principle of the thing.'

'Thanks, Josh. That'll be a big help.' I gave my watch a surreptitious glance. Seven minutes till we got into the next billable hour. 'So how's your love life?' I hazarded.

Martin Cheetham's office was in the old Corn Exchange, a beautiful golden sandstone building that, in aerial photographs, looks like a wedge of cheese, the windows pocking the surface like dozens of crumbly holes. The old exchange floor is now a sort of indoor flea market in bric-à-brac, antiques, books and records, while the rest of the building has been turned into offices. There are still a few of the traditional occupants – watch menders, electric razor repairers – but because of the unusual layout, the rest range from pressure groups who rent a cubbyhole to small legal firms who can rent a suite of offices that fit their needs exactly.

The office I was looking for was round the back. The reception room was small to the point of poky, but at least the receptionist had a fabulous view of Manchester Cathedral. I hoped she was into bullshit Gothic. She was in her late forties, the motherly type. Within three minutes, I was clutching a cup of tea and a promise that Mr Cheetham would be able to squeeze me in within the half-hour. She had waved away my apologies for not having an appointment. I couldn't understand how she kept her job, with all this being polite to the punters.

One of the reasons I wasn't sorry to quit my law degree was that after two years, I began to realize I'd stand all the way from Manchester to London rather than sit next to a lawyer on a train. There are, of course, notable exceptions, lovely people upon whose competence and honesty I'd stake my life. Unfortunately, Martin Cheetham wasn't one of them. For a start, I couldn't see how anyone could run an efficient practice when their paperwork was stacked chaotically everywhere. On the floor, on the desk, on the filing cabinets, even on top of the computer monitor. For all I could tell, there could be clients lurking underneath there somewhere. He waved me to one of the two surfaces in the room that wasn't stacked with bumf. I sat on the uncomfortable office chair, while he headed for the other, a luxurious black leather all-singing, all-dancing swivel recliner. I suppose that since most conveyancing specialists see very little of their clients he didn't place a high priority on their comfort. He obviously wasn't a fan of the cathedral either, since his chair faced into the room.

While he took his time with Alexis's letter, I took the chance to study him. He was around 5′ 8″, slim without being skinny. He was in shirt sleeves, the jacket of a chain-store suit on a hanger suspended from the side of a filing cabinet. He had dark, almost black hair, cut short but stylish, and soulful, liquid dark eyes. He had that skin that looks sallow and unhealthy if it goes without sun for more than a month or so, though right now he looked in the peak of health. He obviously lived on his nerves, for his neat, small feet and hands were twitching and tapping as he read the letter of authority. Eventually, he steepled his fingers and gave me a cautious smile. 'I'm not exactly sure how you think I can help, Miss Brannigan,' he said. 'I am,' I told him. 'What I have to do in the first instance is to track down T.R. Harris, the builder. Now, it was through you that Miss Lee and Miss Appleby heard this land was available. So, I think you must know something about Mr T.R. Harris. Also, I figure you must have an address for him since you handled the matter for Miss Lee and Miss Appleby and presumably had some correspondence with him.'

Cheetham's smile flickered again. 'I'm sorry to disappoint you, but I know very little about Mr Harris. I knew about the land because I saw it advertised in one of the local papers. And before you ask, I'm sorry, I can't remember which one. I see several every week and I don't keep back numbers.' It looked like they were the only bits of pulped tree he didn't keep. 'I have a client who is looking for something similar,' he continued, 'but when I made further inquiries, I realized this particular area was too large for him. I happened to mention it to Miss Lee's colleague, and matters proceeded from there.'

'So you'd never met Harris before?'

'I've never met Mr Harris at all,' he corrected me. 'I communicated with his solicitor, a Mr Graves.' He got up and chose a pile of papers, seemingly at random. He riffled through them and extracted a bundle fastened with a paper clip. He dumped them in front of me, covering the body text of the letter with a blank sheet. 'That's Mr Graves' address and phone number.'

I took out my pad and noted the details on the letterhead. 'Had you actually exchanged contracts, then?'

Cheetham's eyes shifted away from mine. 'Yes. That's when the deposits were handed over, of course.'

'And you were quite convinced that everything was above board?'

He grabbed the papers back and headed for the haven behind his desk. 'Of course. I mean, I wouldn't have proceeded unless I had been. What are you getting at, exactly, Miss Brannigan?' His left leg was jittering like a jelly on a spindrier.

I wasn't entirely sure. But the feeling that Martin Cheetham wasn't to be trusted was growing stronger by the minute. Maybe he was up to something, maybe he was just terrified I was going to make him look negligent, or maybe he just had the misfortune to be born looking shifty. 'And you've no idea where I can find Mr Harris?' I asked.

He shook his head and said, 'Absolutely not. No idea whatsoever.'

'I'm a bit surprised,' I said. 'I'd have thought that his address would have appeared on the contracts.'

Cheetham's fingers drummed that neat little riff from the '1812 Overture' on the bundle of papers. 'Of course, of course, how stupid of me, I didn't even think of that,' he gabbled. Again, he flicked through his papers. I waited patiently, saying nothing. 'I'm sorry, this shocking business has really unsettled me. Here we are. How foolish of me. T.R. Harris, 134 Bolton High Road, Ramsbottom.'

I wrote it down, then got to my feet. I didn't feel like someone who's had a full and frank exchange of views, but I could see I wasn't going to get any further with Cheetham unless I had specific questions. And at least I could go for Harris and his solicitor now.

I took a short cut down the back stairs, a rickety wooden flight that always makes me feel like I've stepped into a timewarp. My spirits descended as I did. I still had some conservatories to check out south-west of the city, and I was about as keen on that idea as I was on fronting up T.R. Harris's brief. But at least I was getting paid for that. The thought lifted my spirits slightly, but not as much as the hunk I clapped eyes on as I yanked open the street door. He was jumping out of a Transit van that he'd abandoned on the double yellows, and he was gorgeous. He wore tight jeans and a white t-shirt – on a freezing October day, for God's sake! – stained with plaster and brick dust. He had that solid, muscular build that gives me ideas that nice feminists aren't supposed to even know about, never mind entertain. His hair was light brown and wavy, like Richard Gere's used to be before he found Buddha. His eyes were dark and glittery, his nose straight, his mouth firm. He looked slightly dangerous, as if he didn't give a shit.

He sure as hell didn't give a shit about me, for he looked straight through me as he slammed the van door shut and headed past me into the Corn Exchange. Probably going to terrify someone daft enough not to have paid his bill. He had that determined air of a man in pursuit of what's owed to him. Ah well, you lose some and you lose some. I checked out the van and made a mental note. Renew-Vations, with a Stockport phone number. You never know when you're going to need a wall built. Say across a conservatory ...

6

I stopped by the house to pick up my sports bag. I figured if I was on that side of town anyway, I might as well stop in at the Thai boxing gym and see if there was anyone around to share a quick work-out. It would be better for me than lunch, and besides, after the breakfast I'd had, I needed to do something that would make me feel good about my body. Alexis was long gone, and Richard appeared to have returned to his own home. There was a message on the answering machine from Shelley, so I called in. Sometimes she really winds me up. I mean, I was going to check in anyway, but she'd managed to get her message in first and make me feel like some schoolkid dogging it.

'Mortensen and Brannigan, how may I help you?' she greeted me in the worst mid-Atlantic style. That wasn't my idea, I swear. I don't think it was Bill's either.

'Brannigan, how may I help you?' I said.

'Hi, Kate. Where are you?'

'I'm passing through my living room between tasks,' I replied. 'What's the problem?'

'Brian Chalmers of PharmAce called. He says he needs to talk to you. Asap, not lad.' M & B code for 'As soon as possible, not life and death'.

'Right. I have to go over to Urmston anyway, so I'll come back via Trafford Park and see him. Can you fix up for me to see him around two? I'll call in for an exact time.'

'Fine. And Ted Barlow rang to ask if you'd made any progress.'

'Tell him I'm pursuing preliminary inquiries and I'll get back to him when I have something solid to report. And are you?'

'Am I what?' Shelley sounded genuinely baffled. That must have been a novel experience for her.

'Making any progress.'

'As I'm always having to remind my two children,' heavy emphasis on the 'children', 'there's nothing clever about rudeness.'

'I'll consider my legs well and truly smacked. But are you?'

'That's for me to know and for you to find out. Goodbye, Kate.' I didn't even have time for the goodbye before the line went dead.

It was just before twelve when I managed to find someone who could give me any useful information about my missing conservatories. But when I did, it was worth the wait. Diane Shipley was every private investigator's dream. She lived at the head of Sutcliffe Court, her bungalow commanding a view of the whole close. With a corner of my brain, I had noted the raised flower beds and the ramp leading up to the front door, but it still didn't stop me having my eyes at the wrong level when the door opened. I made the adjustment and found myself staring down into a face like a hawk; short, salt and pepper hair, dark beady eyes, deep set and hooded, narrow nose the shape of a puffin's beak, and, incongruously, a wide and humorous mouth. The woman was in a wheelchair, and it didn't seem to bother her in the slightest.

I delivered my usual spiel about the house next door's conservatory, and her face relaxed into a smile. 'You mean Rachel Brown's conservatory?' she inquired.

I checked my list. 'I've got Rowena and Derek Brown,' I said.

'Ah,' said the woman. 'Dirty work at the crossroads. You'd better come in. My name's Diane Shipley, by the way.'

I introduced myself as I followed her down the hall. We turned left into an unusual room. It ran the whole depth of the house, with windows on three walls, giving a sensation of light and air. It was painted white, with cork-tiled flooring. The walls were decorated with beautifully detailed drawings of flowers and plants. Across one corner was a draughtsman's table, set at the perfect height for her chair. 'I illustrate children's books for a living,' she said. 'The other stuff I do for fun,' she added, gesturing at the walls. 'In case you were wondering, I had a riding accident eight years ago. Dead from the waist down.'

I swallowed. 'Right. Em, sorry about that.'

She grinned. 'That's not why I told you. I find that if I don't, people only concentrate on half of what I'm saying because they're so busy wondering about my disability. I prefer a hundred per cent attention. Now, how can I help you?'

I trotted out the old familiar questions. But this time, I got some proper answers. 'When I'm working, I tend to do a fair bit of staring out of the window. And when I see people in the court, I must confess I watch them. I look at the way their bodies move, the shapes they make. It helps when I'm drawing action. So, yes, I noticed quite a lot about Rachel.'

'Can you describe her?'

Diane wheeled herself across to a set of map drawers. 'I can do better than that,' she said, opening one and taking out an A4 file. She shuffled through the sheets of paper inside, extracted a couple and held them out to me. Curious, I took them from her. They were a series of drawings of a head, some quite detailed, others little more than a quick cartoon of a few lines. They captured a woman with small, neat features, sharp chin, face wider across the eyes. Her hair was shoulder-length, wavy. 'It was streaked,' Diane said, following my eyes. 'I wondered a couple of times if it might be a wig. It always looked the same. Never looked like she'd just been to the hairdresser. If it was a wig, though, it was a good one. You couldn't tell, not even face to face.'

'How well did you know her?' I asked.

'At first, not at all. She didn't spend that much time here. It was May when she moved in, and really, she was only here perhaps three or four nights a week, Monday to Friday. She was never here at weekends. Then, one evening in June, she came over. It was about half past nine, I'd guess. She said she had a gas leak and she was waiting for the emergency engineers. She told me she was nervous of staying in, especially since they had told her not to turn any lights on. So I invited her in and gave her a drink. White wine. I had a bottle open already.'

I loved it. A witness who could tell me what she'd had to

drink four months before. 'And did she tell you anything about herself?'

'Yes and no. She told me her name, and I remarked on the coincidence. She said yes, she had noticed when she exchanged contracts to buy the house that she had the same name as the vendors, but she'd got used to that kind of coincidence with a name like Brown. I was a little surprised, because I had no idea that Rowena and Derek had actually sold the house.'

I had that feeling you get when you walk into a theatre halfway through the first act of a new play. What she was saying made perfect sense, but it was meaningless unless you'd seen the first twenty minutes. 'I'm sorry, you're going to have to run that past me a little more slowly. I mean, surely you realized they'd sold the house when they stopped living there and a new person moved in?'

It was her turn to give me the baffled look. 'But Derek and Ro haven't lived in the house for four years. Derek is an engineer in the oil industry, and he was away two weeks in four, so Ro and I got to be really good friends. Then, four years ago, Derek was offered a five-year contract in Mexico with a company house thrown in. So they decided to rent out their house over here on a series of short-term lets. When Rachel moved in, I thought she was just another tenant till she told me otherwise.'

'But surely you must have realized the house was up for sale? I mean, even if there wasn't an estate agent's board up, you can't have missed them showing people round,' I remarked.

'Funny you should say that. It's exactly what I thought. But Rachel told me that she'd seen it advertised in the *Evening Chronicle*, and that she'd viewed it the next day. Perhaps I was out shopping, or she came after dark one evening when I wasn't working. Anyway, I saw no reason to doubt what she was telling me. Why lie about it, for heaven's sake? It's not as if renting a house is shameful!' A laugh bubbled up in Diane's throat.

'Was she on her own, or was she living with someone?' I asked.

'She had a boyfriend. But he was never there unless she was. And he wasn't always there even if she was. I tended to see him leave, rather than arrive, but a couple of times, I saw him pay off a taxi around eleven o'clock at night.'

'Did he leave with Rachel in the mornings?' I couldn't see how this all fitted together, but I was determined to make the most of a co-operative witness.

Diane didn't even pause for thought. 'They left together. That's why I don't have any drawings of him. She was always between me and him, and he always got in the passenger side of the car, so I never really got a clear view of him. He was stylish, though. Even at a distance I could see he dressed well. He even wore a Panama hat on sunny mornings. Can you believe it, a Panama hat in Urmston?'

Like cordon bleu in a motorway service station, it was a hard one to get my head round. 'So tell me about the conservatory.'

This time she did take a moment to think. 'It must have been towards the end of July,' she said slowly but without hesitation. 'I was away on holiday from the first to the fifteenth of August. The conservatory went up a couple of days before I left. Then, when I came back from Italy, they'd all gone. The conservatory, Rachel Brown and her boyfriend. Six weeks ago, a new batch of tenants arrived. But I still don't know if Rachel has let the house, or indeed if Rachel ever bought it in the first place. All I know is that the chaps in there now rented it through the same agency that Derek and Ro used, DKL Estates. They've got an office in Stretford, but I think their head office is in Warrington.'

I was impressed. 'You're very well informed,' I said.

'It's my legs that don't work, not my brain. I like to make sure it stays that way. Some people call me nosy. I prefer to think of it as a healthy curiosity. What are you, anyway? Some kind of bailiff? And don't give me that stuff about being a representative of the conservatory company. You're far too smart for that. Besides, there's obviously been something very odd going on there. You're not just following up who you've sold conservatories to.'

I could have carried on bluffing, but I couldn't see the point. Diane deserved some kind of quid pro quo. 'I'm a private investigator,' I said. 'My partner and I investigate white-collar crime.'

'And this is the case of the missing conservatories, eh? Wonderful! You have made my week, Kate Brannigan.'

As I drove off towards Trafford Park, I began to suspect that Diane Shipley might just have made mine.

Brian Chalmers of PharmAce was less than thrilled when I told him the results of my work both inside and outside his factory and warehouse. He was furious with himself for employing a senior lab technician whose loyalty lay to his bank account rather than his boss. Unfortunately, because of my cock-up with the surveillance film, he didn't have any evidence other than my word, which wasn't enough for him to drag the guy into his office and fire him on the spot. So, since he had to take his anger out on someone, I got the lab technician's kicking. And because the client is always right (at least while he's actually in the room) I had to bite the bullet and stand on for the bollocking.

I let him rant for a good ten minutes, then offered to repeat the surveillance exercise over the weekend at a reduced rate. That took the wind out of his sails, as it was meant to. Unfortunately, as I left Chalmers' office, I passed one of the technicians I had dealt with during my short spell working undercover at PharmAce but, although he looked at me as if he ought to know me, he passed by without greeting me. Looked like I'd been lucky. The phenomenon of not recognizing people out of context had worked in my favour. After all, what would a temporary stock clerk be doing in the managing director's office, all suited up?

It was just before three when I pulled up outside the Thai boxing gym. My head felt like it was full of cogs and wheels all spinning out of sync, trying to assimilate everything that Diane Shipley had told me and make it fit what I'd been told at the other houses. None of it really made any sense so far. I know from bitter experience that when my mind is churning and fizzing, there's nothing better than some hard physical exercise. Which for me these days means Thai kick-boxing.

It started off as purely utilitarian. My friend Dennis the burglar pointed out to me that I needed self-defence skills. He wasn't so much thinking about the job I do as the neighbourhood where I live. He persuaded me to come along to the club where his adored teenage daughter is the junior champion. When I saw the outside of the building, a horrible, breezeblock construction like an overgrown Scout hut, I was deeply unimpressed. But inside, it's clean, warm and well-lit. And the women's coach, Karen, is a former world champion who gave up serious competition to have a family. One of the wildest sights in our club is watching her three-year-old toddling round the ring throwing kicks at people twice his size, and causing them a lot of grief.

I was in luck, for Karen was in the tiny cubicle she calls an office, desperate for an excuse to avoid doing the paperwork. She was in luck too, for I was so bagged off at the verbal beating I'd had from Brian Chalmers that I gave her the most challenging work-out I'd ever managed.

Left to their own devices, the tumblers in my brain started to slot into place. By the time we'd finished trading blows, I knew where I had to look next on the trail of the missing conservatories.

7

Since the Land Registry keeps office hours rather than super-market ones, I couldn't have done anything more that after-noon, even supposing they didn't insist that you make a prior appointment to look at the registers. The real blow was that Ted had inconsiderately sold his conservatories to properties that were covered by two separate offices; the Warrington ones came under Birkenhead, the Stockport ones under Lytham St Anne's, an arrangement about as logical as having London covered by Southampton. Just to confuse things even more, the Lytham registry is in Birkenhead House ... Ever get the impression they really don't want you to exercise your rights to examine their dusty tomes? However, I did manage to get an appointment in Birkenhead for the Monday morning. When I read over the list of addresses, the woman I spoke to sounded positively gleeful. It's a joy to deal with people who love their work. After sorting that out, I felt I could pursue Alexis's dodgy builder with a clear conscience.

I went home to change into something a little less threatening than a business suit. While I was there, I tried to ring T.R. Harris's solicitor, Mr Graves. The number rang out without response. The idleness of some of the legal profession never ceases to amaze me. Twenty past four and everyone had knocked off for the day. Maybe Thursday was early closing day in Ramsbottom. I couldn't find T.R. Harris in the phone book, which was annoying but not too surprising, given the habits of builders.

My hair was still damp from my shower at the gym, so I gave it a quick blast with the hair dryer. I decided a couple of months ago to let it grow. Now it's reached my shoulders, but instead of growing longer, it just seems to get wilder. And I've noticed a couple of grey hairs in among the auburn. Some hair colours go grey gracefully, but auburn ain't one of them. So far, there are few enough to pull out, but I suspect it won't be long before I have to hit the henna, like my mother before me. Muttering under my breath, I chose a pair of russet trousers, a cream polo-neck angora and lambswool jumper and a tweedy jacket. Now the nights were drawing in, it was time for my favourite winter footwear, my dark tan cowboy boots that might have seen better days but fit like a pair of gloves. Just the thing for a trip to the horrid, nasty, windy, wet, dark countryside. If you have to abandon the city, you might at least be dressed for it. Remembering the lack of street lights out there, I slipped a small torch in my bag.

As I drove across town towards the motorway, I decided that I needed to track down the farmer who had sold the land to T.R. Harris in the first place. But on the way, I decided to check out Harris's premises. I wanted to know where I could lay hands on him once I had my ammunition.

134 Bolton High Road wasn't the builder's yard I'd been expecting. It was a corner shop, still open for the sale of bread, chocolate, cigarettes and anything else the forgetful had omitted to lay in for the evening's viewing. An old-fashioned bell on a coiled spring jangled as I opened the door. The teenage lad behind the counter looked up from his motor-bike magazine and gave me the once-over reserved for anyone who hadn't been crossing the threshold on a regular basis for the last fifteen years.

'I'm looking for a builder,' I said.

'Sorry, love, we don't sell them. There's no demand, you see.' He struggled to keep a straight face, but failed.

'I'm demanding,' I said. I waited for him to think of the reply. He only took a few seconds. 'I bet you are, love. Can I help?'

'A builder called Harris. T. R. Harris. This is the address I've got for him. Do you act as an accommodation address for people?'

He shook his head. 'Me mam won't stand on for it. She says people who won't use their own address must be up to no good. Tom Harris, the guy you're looking for, he rented one of the offices upstairs for a couple of months. Paid cash, an' all.'

'So you don't live over the shop, then?'

'No.' He closed his magazine and leaned back against the cigarette shelves, happy to have a break in routine. 'Me mam told me dad it was dead common, made him buy the house next door. He turned the upstairs here into offices. Brian Burley, the insurance broker, he's got two offices and a share of the bathroom and kitchenette. He's been here five years, ever since me dad did them up. But the other office, that's had loads of people through it. I'm not surprised. You couldn't swing a rat in there, never mind a cat.'

'So, Tom Harris isn't here any longer?' I asked.

'Nah. He was paid up to the end of last week, and we ain't seen him since. He said he just needed an office while he sorted out a couple of deals over here. He said he was from down south, but he didn't sound it. Didn't sound local neither. Anyway, what're you after him for? He stood you up, or something?' He couldn't help himself, and he was cute enough to get away with it. Give him a few years and he'd be lethal. God help the women of Ramsbottom.

'I need to talk to him, that's all. Any chance of a look round upstairs? See if he left anything that might give me an idea where he moved on to?' I gave him my sultriest smile.

'You'll not find so much as a fingerprint up there,' the lad told me, disappointed. 'Me mam bottomed it on Sunday. And when she cleans, she cleans.'

I could imagine. There didn't seem a lot of point in pushing it, and if Harris had paid in cash, there wasn't likely to be any other clue as to his whereabouts. 'Did you know him at all,' I asked.

'I saw him going in and out, but he didn't have no time for the likes of me. Fancied himself, know what I mean? Thought he was hard.'

'What did he look like?' I asked.

'A builder. Nowt special. Brown hair, big muscles, quite tall. He drove a white Transit, it said 'T.R. Harris Builders' along the side. Here, you're not the cops, are you?' he asked, a sudden note of apprehension mixing with excitement.

I shook my head. 'Just trying to track him down for a friend he promised to do some work for. D'you know if he hung out in any of the local pubs?'

The lad shrugged. 'Dunno. Sorry.' He looked as if he meant it, too. I bought a pound of Cox's Orange Pippins to stave off the hunger pains and hit the road.

Some days things get clearer as time wears on. Other days, it just gets more and more murky. This one looked like a gold-fish bowl that hasn't been cleaned since Christmas. The address I'd carefully copied down from Graves' letterhead that Martin Cheetham had showed me wasn't the office of a solicitor. It wasn't any kind of office at all, to be precise. It was the Farmer's Arms. The pub was about quarter of a mile from the nearest house, the last building on a narrow road up to the moors where Alexis and Chris had hoped to build their dream home. In spite of its relative isolation, the pub seemed to be doing good business. The car park was more than half full, and the stonework had been recently cleaned.

Inside, it had been refurbished in the 'country pub' style of the big breweries. Exposed stone and beams, stained-glass panels in the interior doors, wooden chairs with floral chintz cushions, quarry-tiled floor and an unrivalled choice of fizzy keg beers that all taste the same. There must have been getting on for sixty people in, but the room was big enough for there still to be a sense of space. Two middle-aged women and a man in his late twenties were working the bar efficiently.

I perched on a stool at the bar and didn't have long to wait for my St Clement's. I watched the clientele for ten minutes or so. They sounded relatively local, and were mostly in their twenties and thirties. Beside me at the bar was the kind of group I imagined T.R. Harris would feel one of the lads with. But first I had to solve the problem of the moody address for his solicitor.

I waited for a lull, then signalled one of the barmaids. 'Same again, love?' she asked.

I nodded, and as she poured, I said, 'I'm a bit confused. Is this 493 Moor Lane?'

It took a bit of consultation with bar staff and customers, but eventually, consensus was reached. 493 it was. 'I've been given this as the address for a bloke called Graves,' I told them. For some reason, the men at the bar convulsed with laughter.

The barmaid pursed her lips and said, 'You've got to excuse them. They're not right in the head. The reason they're laughing is, the pub car park backs on to the churchyard. We're always having a to-do with the vicar, because idiots that know no better go and sit on the gravestones with their pints in the summer.'

I was beginning to feel really pissed off with T.R. Harris and his merry dance. Wearily, I said, 'So there's no one here by the name of Graves? And you don't let rooms, or have any offices upstairs?'

The barmaid shook her head. 'Sorry, love. Somebody's been having you on.'

I forced a smile. 'No problem. I don't suppose any of you know a builder called Tom Harris? Bought some land up the road from here?'

There were smiles and nods of recognition all around me. 'That's the fella that bought Harry Cartwright's twelve-acre field,' one said. 'The man from nowhere,' another added.

'Why do you say that?' I asked.

'Why are you asking?' he countered.

'I'm trying to get hold of him in connection with the land that he bought.'

'He doesn't own it any more. He sold it last week,' the barmaid said. 'And we haven't seen him since.'

'How long has he been coming in here?' I asked.

'Since he first started negotiating with Harry about the land. Must be about three months ago, I'd guess,' one of the men said. 'Good company. Had some wild stories to tell.'

'What kind of wild stories?' I asked.

They all laughed uproariously again. Maybe I should audition for the Comedy Store. 'Not the kind you tell when there are ladies present,' one of them wheezed through his laughter.

I couldn't believe I was putting myself through this out of friendship. Alexis was going to owe me a lifetime of favours after this. I took a deep breath and said, 'I don't suppose any of you knows where his yard is? Or where he lives?'

They muttered among themselves and shook their heads dubiously. 'He never said,' one of them told me. 'He rented an office above the corner shop on Bolton High Road, maybe they'd know.'

'I've tried there. No joy, I'm afraid. You lads are my last hope.' I batted my eyelashes, God help me. The appeal to chivalry often works with the kind of assholes who sit around in pubs telling each other mucky stories to compensate for the lack of anything remotely exciting in their own squalid little lives.

Depressingly, it worked. Again, they went into a muttering huddle. 'You want to talk to Gary,' the spokesman eventually announced confidently.

Not if he's anything like you lot, I thought. I smiled sweetly and said, 'Gary?'

'Gary Adams,' he said in that irritated tone that men reserve for women they think are slow or stupid. 'Gary cleared the land for Tom Harris. When he bought it, half of it was copse, all overgrown with brambles and gorse between the trees. Gary's got all the equipment, see? He does all that kind of work round here.'

I kept the smile nailed on. 'And where will I find Gary?' I said, almost without moving my lips.

Watches were studied, frowns were exchanged. Exasperated, the barmaid said, 'He lives at 31 Montrose Bank. That's through the centre of the village, up the hill and third left. You'll probably find him in his garage, rebuilding that daft big American car of his.' I thanked her and left, managing to keep the smile in place for as long as the lads could see me. My face muscles felt like they'd just done a Jane Fonda work-out.

As predicted, Gary was in the garage tacked on to a neat stone cottage. The up-and-over door was open, revealing a drop-head vintage Cadillac. The bonnet was up, and the man I took to be Gary Adams was leaning into the engine. As I approached, I could see him doing something terribly brutal-looking with a wrench the size of a wrestler's forearm. I cleared my throat and instructed the muscles to do the smile again. Reluctantly, they obeyed. Gary glanced up, surprised. He was in his mid-thirties, with a haircut that looked like it came right out of National Service.

'Gary?' I said.

He straightened up, placed the wrench lovingly on the engine block, and frowned. 'That's right. Who wants to know?'

Time for another fairy story. 'My name's Brannigan. Kate Brannigan. I'm an architect. A friend of mine bought some land from Tom Harris, and she needs to get in touch with him about another deal. The lads at the Farmer's Arms reckoned you might know where I can find him.'

Gary gave a knowing smile as he wiped his hands on his oily overalls. 'Owes you money, does he?'

'Not exactly,' I said. 'But I need to speak to him. Why? Does he owe you?'

Gary shook his head. 'I made sure of that. His kind, they're ten a penny. Ask you to do a job, you do it, you tell them what they owe, they ignore you. So, I made him pay up in cash. Half before, half after. Glad I did, an' all, looking at the way he's sunk without trace since he sold them plots on.'

'What made you think he was dodgy?'

Gary shrugged. 'I didn't know him, that's all. He wasn't from round here. And he obviously wasn't stopping, neither.'

This was like drawing teeth. Sometimes I think I might have been better suited to a career in psychotherapy. The punters might not want to talk to you either, but at least you get to sit in a warm, comfy office while you're doing it. 'What makes you say that?' I asked.

'When you're in business and you're planning to stop somewhere, you get a local bank account, don't you? Stands to reason,' he said triumphantly.

'And Tom Harris didn't?'

'I saw his chequebook. He was going to give me a cheque for the advance on the work, but I said no way, I wanted cash. But I got a good enough look at it to see that it wasn't a local bank that he had his account with.'

I tried to hide the deep breath. 'Which bank was it?' I inquired, resisting the temptation to kick-box him to within an inch of his life.

'Northshires Bank, in Buxton. That isn't even in *Lancashire*. And the account wasn't in his name, either. It was some business or other.' I opened my mouth and a smile twitched at the corner of Gary's mouth as he anticipated me. 'I didn't pay attention to the name. I just noticed that it wasn't Tom Harris.'

'Thanks, Gary,' I said. 'You've been a big help. I don't suppose you'd know anybody else who might know where I can get hold of Tom Harris?'

'It's really important, is it?' he asked. I nodded. 'Harry Cartwright's the farmer who sold him the land. He might know.'

'Where's his farm?' I asked.

Gary shook his head with the half-smile of a man who's dealing with a crazy lady. 'How good are you with Dobermans? And if you get past them, he'll have his shotgun ready and waiting. He's not an easy man, Harry.' I must have looked like I was going to burst into tears. I imagine he thought they were tears of despair; they were really tears of frustration. 'Tell you what,' he said. 'I'll come with you. Give me a minute to get out of my overalls, and phone the old bugger to let him know we're coming. He's known me long enough to talk before he shoots.'

I walked back to the car and turned the heater up full. I hate the country.

8

Within ten minutes of leaving Gary's, we were driving up an unmetalled track. I stopped at a five-barred gate festooned with barbed wire, and Gary jumped out to open it. When he closed it behind me, he sprinted for the car. He'd barely slammed the door behind him when a pair of huge Dobermans hurled themselves at the passenger side of the car, barking and slavering hysterically. Gary grinned, which convinced me he wasn't the full shilling. 'Bet you're glad you brought me along,' he said.

I slammed the car into gear and continued up the track. Half a mile on, my headlights picked out a low stone building in the gathering rural gloom. The roof appeared to sag in the middle, and the window frames looked so rotten that I couldn't help thinking the first winter gales would have the glass halfway across the farmyard. I could tell it was a farmyard by the smell of manure. I drove as close as I could to the door, but before I could cut the engine, an elderly man appeared in the doorway. As confidently predicted by Gary, he was brandishing an over-and-under double-barrelled shotgun. Just then, the dogs arrived and started a cacophony of barking that made my fillings hurt. I *really* love the country.

'What now?' I demanded of Gary.

The old man approached. He wore a greasy cardigan over a collarless shirt that might have started its life the colour of an oily rag, but I doubted it. He walked right up to the car and stared through the window, the gun barrels pointing ominously through the glass. My opinion of T.R. Harris's bottle had just gone up a hundred per cent. Having satisfied himself that my passenger really was Gary, Cartwright stepped back a few feet and whistled to the dogs. They dropped at his feet like logs.

Gary said, 'It's OK, you can get out.' He opened his door and climbed out. Warily, I followed.

I moved close enough to get a whiff of the old man. It was enough to make me pray we could conduct our business out in the farmyard. Cartwright said, 'Gary says you're after Tom Harris. What I did with him was all legal, all above-board.'

'I know that, Mr Cartwright. I just need to speak to Tom, and no one seems to know where I can find him. I hoped maybe you would know.'

He tucked his gun under one arm and fumbled in the deep pocket of his grimy corduroy trousers and produced a document which he waved under my nose. 'That's all I know,' he said.

I reached for it, but he snatched it back. 'You can look but you mustn't touch,' he said, just like a five-year-old. I held my breath and moved close enough to read it. It was an agreement between Henry George Cartwright of Stubbleystall Farm and Thomas Richard Harris of 134 Bolton High Road, Ramsbottom. I didn't have to read any further. I had more bells ringing in my head than Oxford on May morning. I smiled politely, thanked Harry Cartwright and got back in my car. Looking bewildered, Gary folded himself in beside me and we shot back down the track again.

Thomas Richard Harris. Tom, Dick and Harry. If Thomas Richard Harris was a straight name, I was Marie of Romania.

By eleven on Friday morning, I was stir crazy. Shelley was thrilled that I was stymied on our two paying jobs, the conservatories and the pharmaceuticals, and she wasn't about to let me bunk off and follow the clues to Alexis's con man. I was trapped in an office with a woman who wanted me to do paperwork, and I had no excuse to get away. By ten, all my files were up to date. By eleven, my case notes were not only written but polished to the point where I could have joined a writers' group and read them out. At five past eleven, I rebelled. Clutching the Ted Barlow file, I sailed through the outer office, telling Shelley I was following a new lead. It led me all the way to the Cornerhouse coffee shop, where I browsed through the file as I sipped a cappuccino. As I ploughed through my interview notes yet again, it hit me. There was something I could do while I was waiting for my Monday morning appointment at the Land Registry.

DKL Estates, the estate agents Diane Shipley had mentioned, was a shopfront opposite Chorlton Baths. DKL looked reasonably prosperous, but I realized almost immediately that there was a good reason for that. They specialized in renting, and in selling the kind of first-time-buyer properties that shift even at the bottom of a recession. There are always people desperate to climb on to the property ladder, not to mention the poor sods trading down. It looked to me as if they'd also got a significant number of ex-council houses on their books, which took a bit of courage. Their gamble seemed to have paid off in terms of customers, though. One woman walked in just ahead of me, but there were already a couple of other serious browsers. I joined them in their study of properties for sale.

The woman I had followed in selected a couple of sets of details, then approached the young man behind the desk that sat at an angle to the room. He looked as if he should be in a classroom swotting for his GCSEs. I know they say you should worry when the policemen start looking younger, but estate agents? She asked in a low, cultivated voice if she might arrange to view both properties. I was surprised; she was wearing a knitted Italian suit that couldn't have cost less than three hundred pounds, her shoes looked like they'd come from Bally or Ravel, the handbag was a Tula, and I'd have put money on the mac being a four hundred pound Aquascutum. Put it another way, she didn't look like a terraced house in Whalley Range was her idea of a des. res. Maybe she was looking for a nice little investment.

As I studied her, the lad behind the desk was phoning to fix her up with viewing appointments. I took in the grooming: the polished nails, the immaculately styled dark brown hair, the expert make-up that accentuated her dark eyes. I had to admire her style, even though it's one I've no desire to aspire to.

I'd stared too long, however. The woman must have felt my eyes on her, for she turned her head sharply and caught my gaze. Her eyes seemed to open wider and her eyebrows climbed. Abruptly, she turned on her heel and walked quickly out of the agency. I was gobsmacked. I didn't know her from a hole in the ground, but she clearly knew me. Or maybe I should say, she clearly knew who I was.

The lad looked up from his pad and realized his customer was halfway out of the door. 'Madam,' he wailed. 'Madam, if you'll just give me a minute ...' She ignored him and kept walking without a backward glance.

'How bizarre,' I said, approaching the desk. 'Do you always have that effect on women?'

'It takes all sorts,' he said with a cynical resignation that would have been depressing in a man ten years his senior. 'At least she took the details with her. If she wants to view, she can always phone. Maybe she remembered an appointment.'

I agreed. Privately, I was dredging my memory of recent cases, trying to see if I could place the elegant brunette. I gave up after a few seconds when the lad asked if he could help me. 'I'd like to talk to whoever's in charge,' I said.

He smiled. 'Can you tell me what it's in connection with? I might be able to help.'

I took a business card out of my wallet, the one that says Mortensen and Brannigan: Security Consultants. 'I don't mean to appear rude, but it's a confidential matter,' I told him.

He looked slightly disconcerted, which made me wonder what little scam DKL were up to. He pushed his chair back and said, 'If you'd care to wait a moment?' as he reversed across the room and through a door in the far corner. He emerged less than a minute later, looking slightly shaken. 'If you'd care to go through, Mrs Lieberman will see you now.'

I flashed him a quick, reassuring smile, then opened the door. As I entered the back office, a woman I put in her late forties rose from a typist's chair behind an L-shaped desk. On one leg of the desk, an Apple Mac stood, its monitor showing a full page mock-up of some house details. Mrs Lieberman extended a well-manicured hand displaying a few grands' worth of gold, sapphires and diamonds. 'Miss Brannigan? I'm Rachel Lieberman. Do sit down. How may I help you?' I instantly realized who had taught the young man in the front office his style.

I gave her the quick once-over as I settled into a comfortable chair. Linen suit over a soft sueded silk blouse. Her brown hair, with the odd thread of silver, was swept up into a cottage loaf above a sharp-featured face that was just beginning to blur around the jawline. Her brown eyes looked shrewd, emphasized by the slight wrinkles that appeared as she studied me right back. 'It's to do with a matter I'm looking into on behalf of a client. I'm sorry to arrive without an appointment, but I was in the area, so I thought I'd drop by on the off-chance of catching you,' I started. She looked as if she didn't believe a word of it, a smile twitching at one corner of her mouth. 'I wonder if you can clear something up for me. I realise that your main office is in Warrington, but are you actually the owner of DKL, or do you manage this branch?'

'I own the company, Miss Brannigan.' Her voice had had most of the northern accent polished off. 'I have done since my husband died three years ago. Daniel Kohn Lieberman, hence the name of the company. What, if anything, does that have to do with your client?'

'Nothing, Mrs Lieberman, except that I shouldn't imagine a manager would have the authority to release the information I'm after. Mind you, a mere employee probably wouldn't grasp the importance of it, either.' I tried that on for size. I hoped she was a woman who'd respond to flattery. If not, that left me with nothing but threats, and I hate to threaten anyone in daylight hours. It takes so much more energy.

'And what exactly is this information?' she asked, leaning forward in her chair and fiddling with a gold pen.

'I'd like to level with you, if I may. My company specializes in white-collar crime, and I'm investigating a serious fraud. We're looking at a six-figure rip-off here, probably more like a million. I suspect that the perpetrators may be using properties on a short-term lease for their particular scheme.' Mrs Lieberman was listening, her head cocked on one side. So far, no reaction was making it through to the surface. I soldiered on.

'One of the addresses I'm looking at was rented through your agency. What I'm trying to do here is to find a common factor.

The thing is, I'm beginning to think the renting of the houses is a key factor in the way the fraud is organized, and I hoped that if I gave you the addresses of the other houses I suspect have been involved, then you could check for me and see if they are on your books.' I paused. I wanted some feedback. I'd never have made a politician.

Mrs Lieberman straightened up in her chair and drew her lower lip under her teeth. 'And that's all you want to know? Whether or not they're on my books?'

'Not quite all, I'm afraid. Whether they are now or have ever been on your books is the first step. Once we've established that, I want to ask you the names of the owners.'

She shook her head. 'Out of the question. I'm sure you'll appreciate that. We're looking at very confidential matters here. There are only a few agencies that specialize in rental properties in this area, and we are by far the biggest. I act as agent for almost three hundred rental properties, the bulk of them on short-term leases. So you can imagine how important it is that my clients know they can trust me. I can't possibly start giving you their names. And I can't believe you really expected me to. I'm sure you don't release information like that about your clients.'

'Touché. But surely you can tell me if a particular property is on your books? Then when you call up the details on your screen, you might notice a pattern emerging.'

'What sort of a pattern did you have in mind, Miss Brannigan?'

I sighed. 'That's what I don't know, Mrs Lieberman. So far, all I have to go on is that I think most of the addresses involved in this scam have been rented. In one case that I'm sure about, I know that the couple who rented the house shared the surname of the couple who actually owned it.'

Rachel Lieberman leaned back in her chair and gave me the once-over again. I felt like a newly discovered species of plant – strange, exotic and possibly poisonous. After what seemed to me to be a very long time, she nodded to herself, as if satisfied.

'I'll tell you what I'll do, Miss Brannigan. If you give me the addresses you're interested in, I'll look through my records and see what I can come up with. Frankly, I have to say, I think it'll be a waste of time, but then I wasn't doing anything this evening anyway. I'll call you and let you know. Will Monday morning do, or would you prefer me to ring you at home over the weekend?'

I grinned. Deep down, Mrs Lieberman was a woman after my own heart.

I spent the afternoon with Ted Barlow, doing the boring stuff of checking back through all his records, making notes of ex-salesmen who'd been sacked, and learning exactly how a conservatory is installed. I glanced at the dashboard clock as I got back behind the wheel of my Nova. Just after seven. I figured I'd be quicker picking up the motorway than going home by the more direct crosstown route. A few minutes later, I was doing eighty in the middle lane, the Pet Shop Boys blasting out of all four speakers. The huge arc of Barton Bridge glittered against the sky, sweeping the motorway over the dark ribbon of the Manchester Ship Canal. As the bridge approached, I moved over to the inside lane, positioning myself to change motorways at the exit on the far side. I was singing 'Where the streets have no name' at full belt when I automatically registered a white Ford Transit coming up outside me in the middle lane.

I paid no attention to the van as it drew level then slightly ahead. Then, suddenly, his nose was turning in front of me. My brain tripped into slow motion. Everything seemed to last forever. All I could see out of the side of my car was the white side of the van, closing in on me fast. I could see the bottom edge of some logo or sign, but not enough to identify any of the letters. I could hear screaming, then I realized it was my own voice.

The nightmare was happening. The van swiped into me, crushing the door of my car against my right side. At the same time, the car skidded sideways into the crash barrier. I could hear the scream of metal on metal, I could feel the rise in temperature from the friction heat, I could see the barrier buckle, I could hear myself sobbing 'Don't break, bastard thing, don't break!'

The front of my car seemed to be sandwiched between the struts of the crash barrier. I was tilted forward at a crazy angle. Below me, I could see the lights twinkling on the black water of the Ship Canal. The cassette player was silent. So was the engine. All I could hear was the creaking of the stressed metal of the crash barrier. I tried to open the driver's door, but my right arm was clamped in place by the crushed door. I tried to wriggle round to open it with my left arm, but it was no use. I was trapped. I was hanging in space, a hundred feet above the empty depths of the canal. And the Ford Transit was long gone.

9

I came to a very important decision sitting in a cubicle in the casualty department of Manchester Royal Infirmary. Time for a yuppie phone. I mean, have you been in a casualty department lately? Because I was a road traffic accident, I was whizzed straight through the waiting area on a trolley and deposited in a cubicle. Not that that meant I was going to be attended to any more quickly, oh no. I realized pretty soon I was supposed to regard this as my very own personal waiting room. And me not even a private patient!

I stuck my head out of the curtains after about ten minutes and asked a passing nurse where I could find a phone. She barked back at me, 'Stay where you are, doctor will be with you as soon as she can.' I sometimes wonder if the words that people hear are the same ones that come out of my mouth.

I tried again a few minutes later. Different nurse. 'Excuse me, I was supposed to be meeting someone before I had this accident, and he'll be worried.' Not bloody likely, I thought. Not while we're in the same calendar month. 'I really need to phone him,' I pleaded. I didn't want sympathy, nor to allay his non-existent worries. I simply didn't feel up to walking the half-mile home or coping with a taxi. Yes, all right, I admit it, I was shaken up. To hell with the tough guy private eye image. I was trembling, my body felt like a 5' 3" bruise, and I just wanted to pull the covers over my head.

The second nurse had clearly graduated from the same charm school. 'Doctor is very busy. She doesn't have time to wait for you to come back from the phone.'

'But doctor isn't here,' I said. 'I'm not convinced that doctor is even in this hospital.'

'Please wait in the cubicle,' she ordered as she swept off. That was when I realized that my resistance to a mobile phone was a classic case of cutting off my nose to spite my face. Never mind that they always ring at the least convenient moment. Never mind that even the lightest ones are heavy enough to turn your handbag into an offensive weapon or wreck the line of your jacket. At least they can summon knights in shining armour. I'll rephrase that. At least they can summon rock journalists with customized hot pink Volkswagen Beetle convertibles.

They let me at a phone about an hour and a half later, when they'd finally got round to examining me, X-raying me and prodding all the most painful bits. The doctor informed me that I had deep bruising to my spine, ribs, right arm, and right leg, and some superficial cuts to my right hand, where the starburst from the driver's window had landed. Oh, and shock, of course. They gave me some pain killers and told me I'd be fine in a few days.

I went through to the waiting room, hoping Richard wouldn't be long. A uniformed constable walked over and sat down beside me. 'Miss Brannigan?' he said.

'That's right.' I was beyond surprise. The pain killers had started to work.

'It's about the accident. A few questions, I'm afraid.'

I closed my eyes and took a deep breath. That was my first mistake. My ribs had decided to go off duty for the night and I ended up doubled over in a gasping cough. Of course, that was precisely the moment Richard chose to arrive. The first I knew of it was the yell. 'Oi, you, leave her alone! Jesus, don't you think she's been through enough tonight?' Then he was crouched in front of me, gazing up into my eyes, genuine fear and concern in his face. 'Brannigan,' he murmured. 'You're not fit to be let out on your own, you know that?'

If I hadn't feared it would kill me, I'd have laughed. This, from the man who gets to the corner shop and forgets what he went out for? All of a sudden, I felt very emotional. Must have been the combination of the shock and the drugs. I felt a hot tear trickle down my nose. 'Thanks for coming,' I said in a shaky voice.

Richard patted my shoulder softly, then straightened up. 'Can't you see she's in a state?' he demanded. I twisted my head round to look at the constable, a young lad who was scarlet with embarrassment. The rest of the waiting room were avidly following the drama, momentarily forgetting their own pain.

'I'm sorry, sir,' the cop mumbled. 'But I need to get some details of the accident from Miss Brannigan. So we can take appropriate action.'

Richard appeared to relax slightly. Uh-oh, I thought. 'And you can't wait till morning? You have to harass an innocent woman? What's your problem, pal? Got no real criminals out there in the naked city tonight?'

The constable looked hunted. His eyes flickered round the room, desperately seeking a Tardis. I took pity. 'Richard, leave it. Just take me home, please. If the constable needs some details, he can follow us there.'

Richard shrugged. 'OK, Brannigan. Let's roll.'

We were halfway to the door when the cop caught up with us. 'Em, excuse me, I don't actually have your address.'

Richard said 'Four', I said 'Two' then we chorused 'Coverley Close'. The copper looked completely bemused.

'Em, can I ask you to take me with you, sir? I'm afraid I haven't any transport here.' The poor lad looked mortified. He looked even more mortified folded into the back seat of Richard's Beetle, helmet on his knees.

By the time I had dragged my weary body up the path, I was seriously considering a jacuzzi as well as a mobile phone. I certainly wasn't in the mood for a police interview. But I wanted to get it over with.

We got name, address, date of birth and occupation (security consultant) out of the way while Richard brewed up. The constable looked utterly bewildered when Richard dumped the tray on my coffee table, announced that I was out of milk and wandered off into the conservatory. As Richard came back clutching half a bottle of milk, I put the young copper out of his misery.

'The conservatory runs across the back of both houses,' I

explained. 'That way, we don't get under each other's feet.'

'She means she gets out of washing my dishes and my socks,' Richard said, settling down on the couch beside me. I winced as he leaned into me, and he pulled away quickly. 'Sorry, Brannigan,' he added, stroking my good arm.

I outlined what had happened on Barton Bridge. I have to admit it was satisfying to see both Richard and the copper turn pale as I gave them the details. 'And then the fire brigade arrived and cut me free. Just about the time I should have been eating my first crispy prawn wonton,' I added, for Richard's benefit.

The constable cleared his throat. 'Did you see the driver of the van at all, miss?'

'No. I wasn't paying attention till it was too late. Far as I was concerned, it was just a van overtaking me.'

'And did the van have any identification?'

'There was something, but I couldn't see what. It was higher than the top of my window. I could just catch the bottom couple of inches. And I didn't get his number, either. I was too occupied with the thought of plunging into the Ship Canal. I mean, have you seen the state of the water in there?'

The constable looked even greener. He took a deep breath. 'And was it your impression that this was a deliberate attempt to run you off the road?'

The $64,000 question. I tried to look innocent. It wasn't that I felt like being a hero and sorting it all out myself. I just couldn't cope with a long interrogation right then. Besides, that would mean giving them the kind of confidential client information that we're supposed to guard with our lives, and I couldn't do that without consulting Bill. 'Officer, I can't imagine why anyone would want to do that,' I said. 'I mean, this is Manchester, not LA. I suppose I was in the guy's blind spot. If he was tired, or he'd had a few too many on the way home from work, he probably didn't even register I was there. Then when he hit me, he panicked, especially if he'd had a drink. I don't think it's anything more sinister than that.'

He fell for it. 'Right.' He closed his notebook and got to his feet, replacing his helmet. 'I'm really sorry to have bothered you when you weren't feeling too good. But we want to catch this joker, and we had to see what you could tell us that might help.'

'That's all right, officer. We all have our jobs to do,' I said sweetly. Richard looked as if he was going to puke. 'See the nice officer out, Richard, would you?'

Richard returned. 'We all have our jobs to do,' he mimicked. 'Dear God, Brannigan, where do you dig that shit up from? OK, you fooled the sheriff, but you can't fool the Lone Ranger. What really went down there tonight?'

'Wonderful,' I muttered. 'The feds aren't allowed to interrogate Tonto, oh God no. But you get to ask all the questions you want, huh?'

He smiled and shrugged. 'I love you. I'm entitled.'

'If you really loved me, you'd run me a bath,' I told him. 'Then I'll tell you all about it.'

Ten minutes later, I was soaking in the luxuriant bubbles of Van Cleef & Arpel's First. When I say luxuriant, I mean it. Richard has a heavy hand with the bubble bath. I reckoned there was at least a fiver's worth of foam bath surrounding me. I was decent enough to have starred in a forties Hollywood extravaganza.

Richard sat on the closed toilet lid, smoking a joint that smelled heavily loaded to me. His glasses had steamed up, so he'd shoved them up on his head like flying goggles. His hazel eyes peered short-sightedly at me. 'So, Brannigan. What really happened out there tonight?' he asked the mirror above my head.

'Somebody was either trying to frighten me off or see me off.' There wasn't any point in dressing it up.

'Shit,' Richard breathed. 'Do you know who?'

'I couldn't swear it in a court of law, but I've got a good idea. I've just turned over a fraud at a pharmaceutical company running into a hundred grand or so. They use white Ford Transits with a logo quite high up on the side. I think that probably covers it, don't you?' I stretched gingerly, then wished I hadn't. The next few days were not going to be fun.

'So what are you going to do about it?' Richard asked. I'll say this for him: he doesn't come on like macho man where my work is concerned. He doesn't like the fact that I have to take risks, but he generally keeps his mouth shut on the subject.

'Tomorrow I'm going to get one of our leg men to go over there and take a look at their rolling stock. And I'm going to get him to keep the place under surveillance until we get the pics we need. And you, my sweet darling, are going to take me for a day out in Buxton.'

'Buxton? What's in Buxton?'

'Lots of lovely things. You'll like it. But right now, what I'm going to do is lie in this bath till the hot water runs out, then I'm going to crawl into bed.'

'Fair enough. D'you want supper in bed? If you do, I'll nip out for a Chinese.'

The words were poetry to my ears. I wasn't convinced that I could handle anything as complicated as chopsticks, but there was only Richard to see. And if he ever threatened to tell, I was sure I could find something to blackmail him into silence with. After all, I know he's got a Barry Manilow CD.

I woke in the same position I'd gone to sleep in. When I tried to move, I understood why. Inch by agonizing inch, I got myself out of bed and on to my feet. Making it to the bathroom was hell on legs. I'd just made it back to the hall when Richard appeared at the other end, hair awry, duvet trailing behind him. He rubbed the sleep out of his eyes, muttered 'You OK?' and reached for his glasses. When he'd put them on and looked at me, he couldn't stifle a snort of laughter. 'I'm sorry,' he gasped. 'I really am. But you look like Half Man, Half Biscuit. One side's flesh coloured, the other side's all brown and purple. Wild!'

I looked down. He was right. At least he'd found it funny rather than repulsive. 'You really know how to make a woman feel special,' I muttered. It was kind of him to have slept on my sofa rather than going back to his own house. I was about to thank him when I saw the havoc he'd managed to wreak in my kitchen with one Chinese takeaway. It looked like the entire

People's Army had marched through on their stomachs. I didn't have the energy or the mobility to do anything about it, so I tried to blank it while I poured a cup of coffee from yesterday's jug and waited for the microwave to do its magic.

By the time I'd got my first cup down, Richard was back, showered and shaved. I was just beginning to realize how much my accident had frightened and upset him. He knows how much I hate fuss, so he was trying desperately to disguise the fact that he was running round like a mother hen. I know it's disaster for the image, but I was touched, I have to admit it.

'What's the plan for today, then?' he asked. 'You still want to go to Buxton?'

'How are you fixed?' I asked.

'I can be free. Couple of calls to make, is all.'

'Can you drive me round to the Turkish? And pick me up an hour later?'

The Turkish is bliss. It's part of the Hathersage Road Public Baths, a magnificent Victorian edifice about ten minutes walk from my flat. If walking's your thing. Because it's owned by the city council, there's never been any money to gut it and refurbish it, so it's still filled with the glories of its Victorian heyday. The original green, yellow and blue tiles adorn the walls. They still have the old-fashioned wrap-round showers: as well as water coming at you from above, hot water hits you from the pipes that surround you on three sides as well. The only concession to the last decade of the twentieth century is the plastic loungers that complement the original marble benches in the steam room. Like I say, it's always bliss. But that particular Saturday morning was more blissful than most.

I came out an hour later feeling almost human. Richard was only five minutes late in collecting me, which approaches an all-time record. Back home, I called the garage who had towed the remains of my Nova away, and my insurance company. Next, I left a message on the office answering machine asking Shelley to sort out the best possible deal on a mobile phone for me first thing Monday morning.

Finally, I rang Brian Chalmers of PharmAce. 'Sorry to bother you at home, Brian, but have any of your vans been in an accident over the last twenty-four hours?'

'I don't think so. Why do you ask?'

'I thought I saw one in a crash on the motorway last night. I reckoned you might need a witness. Can you check for me?'

He obviously wondered why on earth I was so interested, but I'd just plugged a leak that was costing him a fortune, so he decided to humour me.

He got back to me ten minutes later. 'None of our vans has reported any accidents last night,' he said. 'However, one of our Transits was stolen from the depot on Thursday night. So I suppose it's possible that was the van you saw.'

Thursday night. Just after I'd talked to Chalmers at Pharm-Ace's office. The only thing I needed now was proof. Perhaps after we'd fronted up the errant lab technician, we could persuade him to confess. By then, maybe I'd be fit enough to make his kidneys feel the way mine felt.

We were just about to leave when the phone rang again. 'Leave it,' Richard shouted from halfway down the hall. But I can't help myself. I waited till the answering machine clicked in.

'This is Rachel Lieberman calling Kate Brannigan on Saturday . . .' was broadcast before I got to the phone.

'Mrs Lieberman?' I gasped. 'Sorry, I was just walking through the door. Did you manage to go through those details?'

'There is a pattern, Miss Brannigan. All but one of those properties are now or have been on our books. They are all rented out on short-term leases of between three and six months. And in every case, the tenants have shared the surname of the real owners.'

I nearly took a deep breath to calm my nerves before I remembered that wasn't part of my current repertoire. 'Thank you very much, Mrs Lieberman,' I said. 'You have no idea how much I appreciate it.'

'You're welcome. I enjoy a challenge now and again,' she replied, a warmth in her voice I hadn't heard before. 'It may not mean much, however. These are common names – Smith,

Johnson, Brown; it's not such a big coincidence. By the way, I don't know if you're interested, but after I'd worked through these details I checked out recent rentals. There are three other properties where the same pattern seems to be repeated. One was rented three months ago, the other two months ago and the third three weeks ago.'

I closed my eyes and sent up a prayer of thanks. 'I'm interested, Mrs Lieberman. I don't suppose . . .'

She cut me off. 'Miss Brannigan, I like to think I've got good judgement. I faxed the addresses to your office overnight. I'm not happy with the idea that my business is being used, however innocently, in any kind of fraud. Keep me posted, won't you?'

Keep her posted? I could find myself sending Chanukah cards this year!

10

I didn't get much chance to mull over what Rachel Lieberman had told me. I find I have some difficulty in concentrating when Edward the Second and the Red Hot Polkas are being played at a volume that makes my fillings vibrate. I know this is a measure of my personal inadequacy, but we all have to live with our little weaknesses. And it was keeping the chauffeur happy. I decided to put my new information in the section of my brain marked 'pending'. Besides, until I'd been to the Land Registry, and collated all the information from there, from Ted's records and the material Josh's Julia had faxed to the office the previous afternoon, I didn't want to fall in love with any theories that might distort my judgement.

We made it to Buxton before lunch with only a couple of wrong turnings. I'm not quite sure what I expected, but it wasn't what I got. There's a grandiose little opera house with a conservatory that some spiritual ancestor of Ted Barlow's had installed. I'd have loved to have heard the salesman's pitch. 'Now, Mr and Mrs Councillor, if I could show you a way to enhance the touristic value of your opera house for less than the product of a penny rate, I take it that would be something you would be pleased to go along with?' There's also a magnificent Georgian crescent that ought to blow your socks off, but it's been allowed to run to seed, rather like an alcoholic duchess who's been at the cooking sherry. Frankly, I couldn't see what all the fuss was about. If this was the jewel in the crown of the Peak District, I wasn't keen on seeing the armpit. I guess growing up in Oxford spoiled me for any architecture in the grand style that isn't kept in tip-top condition.

Like Oxford, Buxton is a victim of its own publicity. Everyone knows Oxford because of the university; what they don't realize is that it's really much more like Detroit. It's the motor car that puts money in the pockets of Oxford's shopkeepers, not the privileged inhabitants of the colleges. Walking round Buxton, it didn't take me long to figure out that it isn't culture or the spa that keeps the wheels of commerce turning there. It's limestone.

Richard was as enamoured of the place as I was. Before we'd walked the length of the rather dismal main street, he'd already started grumbling. 'I don't know why the hell you had to drag me here,' he muttered. 'I mean, look at it. What a dump. And it's raining.'

'I think you'll find the rain isn't just falling on Buxton,' I said.

'I wouldn't bank on it,' he replied gloomily. 'It's a damn sight colder than it was in Manchester. I don't see why it shouldn't be a damn sight wetter too.' He stopped and stared with hostility at the steamed-up window of a chip shop. 'What the hell are we doing here, Brannigan?'

'I'm just doing what you told me,' I said sweetly.

'What *I* told you? How d'you figure that one out? I never said let's go and find the most horrible tourist attraction in the North West and spend the day wandering round it in the rain.' He does a good line in outrage, does Richard. Before he got into his stride and started ranting for England, I relented.

I slipped my arm through his, more for support than to show solidarity. 'The guy who ripped off Alexis and Chris has some connection with Buxton,' I explained. 'He used a hooky name to pull off the scam, and the only clue I've got on him is that his bank account is in Buxton.' Richard's mouth opened, but I carried on relentlessly. 'And before you remind me that your bank account is still in Fulham, let me point out that this guy is supposedly a builder and the account in question appears to be a business account.'

'So what do we do? Wander round Buxton asking people if they know any iffy builders who might have ripped off our friends? Oh, and here's the big clue. We know which bank he keeps his overdraft in! I mean, do we even know what this guy looks like?'

'Alexis says he's in his late twenties, early thirties. Wavy brown hair, medium height, regular features. According to another witness, brown hair, big muscles, fancies himself, drives a white Transit,' I said.

'A white Transit?' Richard interrupted. 'Jesus! You don't think it was him that tried to run you off the road last night?'

'Behave,' I told him. 'Half the tradesmen in the world drive Transits, and half of them are white. You can't go round suspecting every plumber, joiner or glazier in Greater Manchester. Whoever this guy is, he hasn't got the remotest notion that I'm even interested in him, never mind that I'm after him for fraud.'

'Sorry,' Richard said. 'So what do we do, then?'

'The first thing we do is we buy a local paper and then we find a nice place to have lunch, and while you're stuffing your greedy little face, I will study the paper and see who the local builders are. Then, after lunch, we will behave like tourists and do a tour of Buxton. Only, instead of taking in the sights, we'll be taking in the builders' yards.'

'But there won't be anyone there on a Saturday afternoon,' Richard objected.

'I know that,' I said through tight lips. 'But there will be neighbours. You know. The sort of net-twitchers who can tell you what people drive, what they look like and whether vans marked "T.R. Harris, Builders" ever find their way into the yard.'

Richard groaned. 'And I'm missing Man United and Arsenal for this.

'I'll buy lunch,' I promised. He pulled a doubtful face. 'And dinner.' He brightened up.

We ended up in a pub near the opera house that looked like it had been single-handedly responsible for Laura Ashley's profits last year. The chairs were upholstered in a fabric that matched the wallpaper, and the mahogany-stained wood of the furniture was a perfect match for the big free-standing oval bar in the centre of the big room. In spite of the décor, however, they were still clearly not catering for anything other than a local clientele. Richard complained bitterly because their idea of designer beer was a bottle of brown ale. He ended up nursing a pint of lager, then insisted on sitting in a side bar with a view of the door so if anyone he knew came in he could swap his drink for my vodka and grapefruit juice. Humouring him, I settled for a view of the rest of the room. Luckily, the food was good. Wonderful sandwiches, stunning chips. Proper chips, big fat brown ones like my Granny Brannigan used to make in a chip pan so old and well-used that it was black. And the campaign to keep Richard happy got a boost when he discovered Sticky Toffee Pudding on the sweet menu.

After his second helping, we were ready to make a move. I staggered upstairs to the ladies while Richard attempted to scrape the pattern off the plate. Coming back down the wide staircase, I got the kind of surprise that makes people miss their footing and end up looking like human pretzels in hallways. It also has the unfortunate side effect of attracting an enormous amount of attention. Luckily, because of my brush with permanent disability the night before, I was clutching the banister tightly.

I moved gingerly down the last few stairs and slipped round the back of the oval bar where I could study my prey rather less obviously. Halfway down the stairs may well be a nice place to sit, but it sure as hell is an appalling place to do a stake-out. I edged round the bar, getting a couple of strange looks from the barman, till I could see them in the mirror without them being able to get a clear view of me.

Over at a small table in the bay window, Martin Cheetham was deep in earnest conversation with someone I'd seen before. The hunk with the van who'd looked straight through me outside the Corn Exchange after I'd interviewed Cheetham. Today, they were both out of their working clothes. Cheetham wore a pair of cords and an Aran sweater, while his companion looked even hunkier than before in a blue rugby shirt tucked into a pair of Levis. There was a black leather blouson slung over the arm of his chair. Whatever they were talking about, Cheetham wasn't happy. He kept leaning forward, clutching his glass of beer tightly. His body was like a textbook illustration of tension.

By contrast, his companion looked as relaxed as a man on his holidays. He leaned back in his seat, casually smoking a slim cigar. He kept flashing smiles at Cheetham which didn't reassure him one little bit. They'd have reassured me if I'd been on the receiving end, no messing. He was seriously sexy.

Unfortunately, it was beginning to look as if he might just be seriously villainous too. Here was Martin Cheetham, the man who had offered the land deal to Alexis and Chris, sitting drinking and talking with a guy in Buxton that I had pegged as a builder. And Alexis and Chris had been cheated out of their money on a deal arranged by the same Martin Cheetham with T.R. Harris, a builder with Buxton connections. I tried to remember the name on the van the hunk had parked outside the Corn Exchange, but the brain cell that had been taking care of the information appeared to be one of the ones that perished on Barton Bridge.

I realized that watching the pair of them wasn't really getting me anywhere. I needed to be able to hear their conversation. I gave the layout of the room some attention. Obviously, I didn't want Cheetham to see me. Of course, if he was innocent of any shady dealing, he'd have no problem with my presence. But I was beginning to have serious suspicions about his role in the business, so I wasn't about to take the chance.

I figured that if I cut across the room behind Cheetham, I could slide along an empty banquette till I was just behind him. From there, I should be able to hear something of their conversation. It wouldn't require much in the way of stealth, which was just as well, given the condition of my body. I made it across the room, but as I was edging towards the end of the banquette the hunk caught sight of me. He was instantly alert, sitting up and leaning forward to say something to Cheetham. The solicitor immediately swivelled round in his chair. I was well and truly blown.

Bowing to the inevitable (not a position that comes naturally to me), I got up and walked towards them. Cheetham's face registered momentary panic, and he cast a look over his shoulder to his companion, who flicked an alert look at me and said something inaudible to Cheetham. Cheetham ran a nervous hand through his dark hair then took a step towards me. 'Miss Brannigan, what a surprise, let me buy you a drink,' he said without drawing breath. He stepped to his left, blocking the way past him.

In total frustration, I watched his companion turn on his heel and practically run out of the bar. I gave Cheetham the hard stare. There was a sheen of sweat on his forehead, and the colour had vanished from under his tan, leaving him looking like he'd suddenly developed cirrhosis. 'I was hoping you'd introduce me to your friend,' I said, making the best of a bad job.

His smile barely made it to his lips, never mind his dark eyes. 'Er, no, sorry, he had to rush.' He picked up his glass and took a swift sip. 'Do let me buy you a drink, Miss Brannigan,' he pleaded.

'No thanks. I was just leaving myself. Do you have a lot of friends in the building trade, Mr Cheetham?'

He looked as if he wanted to burst into tears. 'The building trade? I'm sorry, I'm not at all sure that I understand you.'

'Your friend. The one who just left? He's a builder, isn't he?'

He gave a nervous laugh. It sounded like a spaniel choking on a duck feather. From the look on his face, he realized it hadn't really worked either. He shifted gear and tried for the throwaway approach. 'You must be mistaken. John's a lorry driver. He works for one of the quarry companies.'

'You're sure about that, are you?' I asked.

'Well,' he said, recovering his poise, 'I've known him and his family for years, and if he's not a lorry driver, he's done a good job of fooling the lot of us. I was at university with his sister.' It was a great performance.

I had no evidence. All I had were a lot of suspicions and one or two coincidences. It wasn't nearly enough to harass a member of the Law Society. 'I'll be seeing you around,' I said, trying to make it sound like a threat rather than a promise. I stalked off, the effect rather spoiled by the limp.

I found Richard waiting crossly on the pavement outside the pub. 'At last!' he sighed. 'Do you need to go to a chemist for some laxatives, or were you just enjoying the *Buxton Advertiser* so much you didn't notice the time? I've been standing here like patience on a flaming monument.'

'Did you happen to notice a guy tearing out of the pub a few minutes ago? Black leather jacket, brown hair, moody looking?' I asked, ignoring his complaints.

'Hasn't realized he's too old for the James Dean impersonation? That the one?'

'That's right. I don't suppose you noticed where he went?'

'He took off across the park,' Richard said, waving a hand in the vague direction of the Pavilion Gardens. 'Why? Did he do a runner without paying for his butty or something?'

'I think that was our man. T.R. Harris himself. Shit! If I could only remember the name on his van!' I snarled.

Richard looked blank. 'But he wasn't driving a van.'

'He was the last time I saw him. It was some dreadful pun of a name,' I muttered, opening the paper again and scanning the ads.

'Bricks and Motor? Mean and Roofless?' Richard wittered on as I continued my fruitless scrutiny.

Then an advert caught my eye. 'Doing up your house? Don't touch a thing till you've called us. Cliff Scott & Sons.' Then, in bold capitals, 'Renovations our speciality.' I let out a sigh of satisfaction. 'Renew-Vations,' I announced triumphantly.

'Yeah, right,' Richard said, giving me the kind of uneasy look we normally reserve for those in the later stages of dementia.

The look didn't go away as I marched back into the pub and asked for their phone book. While I was waiting, I noticed Cheetham had been joined by a stylish and attractive brunette with a clutch of carrier bags. Judging by the logos, she hadn't been to Safeway for a frozen chicken. She was stroking Cheetham's thigh proprietorially while he appeared to be conducting an inquisition about the carrier bags. Then the phone book arrived and I had to drag my attention away from them. Surprise, surprise. Renew-Vations didn't have a listing. Back to Plan A.

Amazingly enough, Richard was still standing on the pavement when I emerged from the pub for a second time. He had the look of a man who has decided that happiness lies along the line of least resistance. 'What now, my love,' he sang in a bad imitation of Shirley Bassey as he attempted to sweep me into his arms. I dodged, wincing, and he instantly stopped. 'Sorry, Brannigan, I keep forgetting you're one of the walking wounded.'

I didn't need reminding. I was beginning to feel tired and a bit shaky. To be honest, I was glad of the chance to sit in the car while Richard drove me round the builders' yards I'd marked. Again, we drew a blank. There was no sign of a van marked Renew-Vations. Or, come to that, T.R. Harris. Questioning local residents established that six out of nine builders drove white Transits. Four of them answered the general description of Tom Harris. When I asked where they banked, I got some very strange looks and not a lot of help.

By four o'clock, I was worn out. But I wasn't ready to give up, in spite of Richard's heavy hints about it being time to go home.

'I've got an idea,' I said as we drove back towards the town centre. 'Why don't we find ourselves a nice little hotel and book in for the night? That way, you won't have to drive me back here tomorrow.'

'You what?' he exploded. 'Spend a *night* in this dump? You have got to be kidding, Brannigan. I'd rather go to a Richard Clayderman concert.'

'That could be arranged,' I muttered. 'Look, I've got a gut feeling about this guy. I need to find out his name and where he lives. I'm not going to be able to do that in Manchester.'

'So wait for a weekday when there are some builders around in their yards and the builders' merchants are open,' Richard said reasonably.

'The only problem is that I'm doing this job as a favour for Alexis. Bill's back from the Channel Islands on Monday morning, and he's not going to be thrilled if I'm off doing a freebie instead of the jobs I'm paid for. I'd really like to try and get this cleared up tomorrow. Besides, I've got to go to the Land Registry on Monday,' I added, laying on the pathos.

Richard scowled. 'OK, Brannigan, you win.'

Had he ever doubted I would?

11

It was a whole new adventure in pain, finding a hotel room in Buxton acceptable to Richard. For a start, it had to have a colour television and a phone in the bedroom. It had to have a proper bar, not a poxy built-in cocktail bar like darts and snooker players have in one corner of the lounge. It also had to feel like part of the twentieth century, which ruled most of them out. His final insistence was that it had a lift, on account of I was injured, couldn't they see that? After he'd ranted at the woman in the Tourist Information Office about the plight of the disabled, we finally ended up in an extremely pleasant establishment overlooking the park. At least, they were pleasant as we booked in. I had this horrible feeling that by the time we left, relations would be a lot more strained. When Richard gets one on him, the staff at Buckingham Palace would be hard pressed to meet his demands.

I headed straight for the bath to ease my aching limbs, while Richard turned on the TV and collapsed on the bed, complaining about the lack of a) a remote control and b) satellite television. I have to confess I wasn't sorry. My head was splitting, and I didn't think I could put up with his usual channel hopping or MTV at full volume without giving way to the urge to commit GBH. I closed the bathroom door so I didn't have to listen to his comments on the football match reports, and subsided thankfully into the hot water while I attempted to order my thoughts.

First, the conservatories. Thanks to Rachel Lieberman, I now knew that the houses where the conservatories had disappeared had all been rented. It seemed that the people who had rented them shared their surname with the real owners. Was there any significance in the fact that they'd all been rented through DKL? Or was it simply that DKL was one of the few agencies around who specialized in rental property? What I didn't understand was where the conservatories had gone, or how the con with the second mortgages had been worked. After all, these days, financial institutions are a little bit fussier than they used to be about who they lend money to. The other problem was that I didn't have the first idea of who was pulling the scam. Maybe there was something I wasn't understanding, but the more I found out, the more it seemed to me that there wasn't necessarily any connection between Ted Barlow and the criminals. But until I figured out how it worked, I couldn't see a way of finding out who was behind it. It was enormously frustrating. Perhaps it would all become clearer after I'd been to the Land Registry and studied the stuff Julia had dug up.

Next, PharmAce. I felt reasonably certain that Paul Kingsley, the freelance operative I'd laid on for tonight, would come up with the necessary photographs. But after the previous night's run-in on the bridge, I felt a more personal interest in the case. If it had been a PharmAce van that had tried to cut short my promising career, then I wanted to know who had done it so someone could make him feel as shaky if not as sore as I was feeling.

And finally, the case of the bent builder. I had a gut feeling about 'John'. There were too many coincidences piling up. Besides, there was a matter of professional pride at stake here. I reckoned I'd always managed to impress Alexis with my skills, largely because she only ever saw the end result. I didn't want her to start seeing the feet of clay.

However, I still didn't have any bright ideas about how to find the elusive 'John', alias 'T.R. Harris', and the bath was starting to cool off. Gingerly, I pushed myself up till I was perched on the end of the bath, then I swung my legs over the edge and on to the floor. I wrapped myself in a generous bath sheet and joined my beloved, who was now pouring scorn on a mindless game show.

I snuggled up to him and he paused in his stream of invective long enough to say, 'Have they got a Chinese in Buxton?'

'Try looking in the paper. Or the phone book. Or ring reception.'

The last suggestion obviously required the least effort. While he made the receptionist's day, I staggered back to the bathroom and struggled into my clothes, wishing I'd thought to bring an overnight bag. Luckily, my handbag always contains a tiny bottle of foundation and a functional compact with eyeshadows, blusher, mascara and lipstick, so I managed to hide the black shadows under my eyes and the bruise on my jaw.

By the time I'd finished, Richard was raring to go. I couldn't help feeling it was a little early for dinner and said so. 'I'm hungry,' Richard said. I raised my eyebrows. He smiled sheepishly. 'The receptionist said there's a pub that does live music on a Saturday night. Local bands, that sort of thing. I thought you'd probably want an early night, and I thought I might drop by later and see if there was anything worth listening to.'

Which translated as, 'This trip looks like a wash-out. If one of us can get something out of it, it won't have been a complete waste of time.' One of the ways rock journos like Richard get their stories is to maintain good relations with the record company A & R men. They're the ones who sign up new acts and build them into the next U2. So Richard's always on the look-out for U3 so he can tip the wink to one of his mates.

'No problem,' I sighed. 'Let's go and eat.' It was easier to give in, especially since I didn't think waiting till later would improve my appetite. The reaction to the accident seemed to have set in, and I was secretly grateful at the thought of an early night without having to worry about entertaining Richard.

The Chinese restaurant was in the main street, above a travel agency. Considering it was half past six on a Saturday night, the place was surprisingly busy. At least a dozen tables were occupied. We both took that as an indication that the food must be reasonable. I should have known better. All the other signs said the opposite. The fish tank was filled with goldfish rather than koi carp, the tables were already set with spoon and fork, there wasn't a Chinese character in sight on the menu, which was heavy on the sweet and sour and the chop suey. I've never fancied chop suey, not since someone told me with malice aforethought that it's Chinese for 'mixed bits'. Besides, it's not even a proper Chinese dish, just something they invented to keep the Yanks happy.

Richard grunted in outrage as he read the menu. As the waiter returned with our two halves of lager, Richard opened his wallet and pulled out a heavily creased piece of paper which he unfolded and waved under the waiter's nose. The waiter studied the Chinese characters gravely. At least he seemed to recognize Richard's favourite half-dozen Dim Sum dishes. A while ago, he persuaded the manager of his regular restaurant in town to write them down for him in case of emergency. This was clearly an emergency. The waiter cleared his throat, carefully folded up the paper and handed it back to Richard.

'No Dim Sum,' he said.

'Why not? I've shown you what I want,' Richard protested.

'No Dim Sum. Bamboo not hygienic,' the waiter retorted. He walked off before Richard could find his voice.

'Bamboo not hygienic?' Richard finally echoed, incredulity personified. 'I have now heard everything. Dear God, Brannigan, what have you got me into this time?'

I managed to pacify him long enough to order, which was my next mistake. They didn't do salt and pepper ribs, but barbecue ribs were on the menu. They were orange. I don't mean glossy reddish brown. I mean orange, as in Jaffa. The taste defied description. Even Richard was stunned into silence. He took a swig of tea to get rid of it, and nearly gagged. After a cautious sip, I understood why. Clearly unaccustomed to people wanting Chinese tea, they'd served us a pot of very weak yet stewed tea-bag.

I thought it couldn't get worse, but it did. When the main courses arrived, I thought Richard was going to burst a blood vessel. The sweet and sour pork consisted of a mound of perfectly spherical balls topped with a lurid red sauce that I'd bet contained enough E numbers to render half the population of Buxton hyperactive. The chicken in black bean sauce looked as if it had been knitted, and the fillet steak Cantonese appeared to have escaped from the Mister Minit heel bar. The waiter refused to understand that we wanted chopsticks and bowls.

The final indignity came when I took the lid off the fried rice. It was pink. I swear to God, it was pink. Richard just sat staring at it all, as if it was a bad joke and the real food would arrive in a minute.

I took a deep breath, and said, 'Just try to think of it as one of those things we do for love.'

'Does that mean if I threw it at the waiter, you'd think I didn't love you any more?' Richard growled.

'Not exactly. But I don't think it's going to get any better and I don't feel strong enough to cope with you shredding the waiter just as an act of revenge. Let's just eat what we can and go.' Normally, I'd have been the first to complain, but I didn't have the energy. Besides, I couldn't face the thought of trailing round Buxton trying to find somewhere half-decent to eat.

I think Richard saw the exhaustion in my face, since he caved in without a performance for once. We both picked at the food for a few minutes, then demanded the bill frostily. The waiter appeared oblivious to our dissatisfaction until Richard subtracted the ten per cent service charge from the bill. This was clearly a novel experience, and one that the waiter wasn't standing on for.

I couldn't handle the aggravation, so I walked downstairs to the street while Richard was explaining in words of several syllables to the waiter why he had no intention of paying a shilling for service. I was leaning against the door jamb, wondering how long I'd have to wait to see another human being, when the patron saint of gumshoes looked down on me and decided it was time I got something approaching an even break.

A white Transit van came down a side street facing me and turned on to the main street. Following my current obsession, I made a mental note of the name on the panels bolted on to the side of the van. 'B. Lomax, Builder', I read. His was one of the yards I'd visited that afternoon. The van drew up, and I heard the driver's door open and close, though I couldn't see anything since the van was between us. I guessed that the driver was heading for the pizzeria I'd noticed on the opposite side of the street.

Just then, Richard emerged, a grim smile on his face. 'Crack it?' I asked.

'I got him to knock a couple of quid off as well, on account of the ribs had triggered off an allergy and given you an asthma attack.'

I don't have asthma. As far as I am aware, I'm allergic to nothing except bullshit. I pointed this out to Richard as we walked back to the car. 'So?' replied. 'They don't know that, do they? And besides . . .'

'Shut up!' I interrupted, guessing what was coming next. 'I do *not* need to be told that I look shitty enough to be suffering from an asthma attack.'

'Please yourself,' he said.

I eased myself into the car, then screeched in excitement. 'It's him, Richard, it's him!' I shouted, digging Richard in the ribs more savagely than I intended.

'Who?' he yelped.

'The guy I'm looking for,' I yelled, unable to take my eyes off the man who had come out carrying three pizzas which he was carefully placing on the passenger seat of the white Transit. It was the man I'd seen with Cheetham, the same man I'd seen in the Renew-Vations van, the man I strongly suspected was also T.R. Harris.

'That's the guy that came horsing out of the pub at lunch-time,' Richard said, on the ball as ever.

'I know. I think he's the guy who ripped off Alexis and Chris,' I told him.

'So let's see where he goes,' Richard said. He waited till our man climbed back into the driver's seat before starting the distinctive Beetle engine. A hot pink VW convertible wasn't the car I'd have chosen to tail someone in, but then I didn't have a choice.

'Keep as far back as you can,' I cautioned him.

We stayed where we were as the van pulled out and drove slowly towards a mini-roundabout, where the driver paused momentarily. As he turned right, Richard released the clutch and shot off in pursuit. When we turned, we could just see the tail-lights of the van rounding the bend ahead. Moments later, we came round the bend to see the van turning at the traffic lights. 'Go for it,' I shouted at Richard as the lights changed to amber.

He stamped on the accelerator and hauled on the steering wheel, cornering with a shriek of rubber. Thank God for low profile tyres and customized Beetles. The van was still in sight, and we followed it sedately through another set of lights and up a hill. Then it pulled into a drive. I let my breath out in a sigh of relief. It's harder than most people think to tail another vehicle. A good thirty per cent of the time you lose them completely.

'Well done. But don't slow down,' I told Richard. 'Just pull up round the next corner.'

He drew up a few seconds later and I was out of the car before he'd switched off the engine. The aches and pains I'd forgotten in the excitement of the chase suddenly reasserted themselves. I winced as I straightened up and tottered back down the street, which gave Richard the chance to catch up with me.

'What d'you think you're doing?' he demanded. 'You should be in bed, not tearing round the back streets of Buxton.'

'I just want to check the house out.'

'You've done enough for one night,' Richard replied. 'Come on, Kate, don't be silly. You're supposed to be taking it easy. Alexis wouldn't expect any more.'

I shook off his restraining hand. 'I've got to make sure I know which house it is,' I said. 'I'm not about to do anything more adventurous than that.' Which was nothing less than the truth. At least for the time being.

Forty minutes later, I was striding openly up the drive of 'Hazledene'. That's a tip I learned very early on in this game. Never skulk, creep or sidle when you can boldly go. There's nothing less suspicious than someone who looks as if they know where they're going and have a perfect right to be there. Luckily, the drive was tarmacked, so there was no chance of anyone in the house hearing me crunch gravel underfoot.

Richard had delivered me back to the hotel after we'd strolled past the residence of B. Lomax, Builder. I'd told him I was going to settle down with the TV then have an early night. I hadn't specified when, or that that was all on my agenda. However, he'd trotted off happily to check out the local bands, kindly leaving his car keys behind in anticipation of finding something he might enjoy drinking. I gave him fifteen minutes to get clear, then I drove back to the side street near Lomax's.

The house was solid, four-square and looked as if it would still be standing after the nuclear holocaust. I suppose it needed to be like that to survive Buxton winters. I'll say this for the Victorians; they really knew how to build things to last. I bet designers get down on their hands and knees every morning and give thanks for the death of that particular tradition. The drive was lined on one side with a solid privet hedge and tall trees that looked as if they'd been there as long as the grey stones of the house. As I neared the house, I moved closer to the hedge, letting myself be absorbed into its shadow.

A black BMW 3-series sat on the curve of drive that swept round the front of the house. The van was parked round the side, blocking the doors of a large detached wooden garage. There were no lights showing at the front of the house, except for a stained-glass lantern above the sturdy front door. I moved as cautiously as my stiffness would allow, keeping the van between me and the house. When I reached the end of the van's cabin, I could see a couple of patches of light spilling out on to the lawn at the back of the house.

It was almost spookily silent. The hum of traffic was so distant I had to make a conscious effort to hear it. I slipped back to the side of the van and carefully took my mini flashlight out of my bag and shone it on the side of the van. It was impossible to tell what was behind the bolt-on plywood panel. However, I was a Girl Guide. I'd also taken the precaution of raiding the tool box in Richard's boot. The small wrench I'd selected was perfect for the job.

Unfortunately, I wasn't. The top set of bolts were just too high for me. And there was nothing immediately obvious to stand on. So I made the best of a bad job and undid the four bolts along the bottom edge of the panel. They came off smoothly. The fact that they weren't rusted on seemed suspicious to me.

I pushed a screwdriver under the edge of the panel and levered it away an inch or so. By twisting my head round and angling the torch under the panel, I could just make out the 'Renew-Vations' logo along the side of the van. Bingo! I made a note of the phone number, then screwed the bolts back in place. Even that small effort was enough to have me breaking out in a sweat. I really felt like going back to the hotel and crawling into bed, but I didn't want to waste the opportunity of having a good nose around while my man was otherwise engaged with a pizza and a couple of guests.

I slipped back down to the front of the van and studied the garage. The van was parked about two feet away from the double doors. They were held shut by a heavy bolt with a padlock. I've never been very good at picking locks, in spite of the expert tuition of my friend Dennis the burglar, and I didn't really feel up to it. Then I realized that if I stood on the bumper of the van, I might just be able to see through the grimy windows at the top of the doors. That would at least tell me whether or not it was worth going into my master cracksman routine.

I eased myself up and leaned forward against the doors, which gave a creak that nearly gave me a coronary. I held my breath, but nothing stirred. I gritted my teeth and raised the torch above my head, so it was shining through the glass and into the garage.

My hunch about the garage had been right. But I didn't have to indulge in any breaking and entering to see all the proof I needed.

12

I waited till Richard was halfway through his second cup of coffee before I gave him the good news. 'You can go back to Manchester if you like,' I said, nonchalantly buttering a slice of toast.

'Do what?' he spluttered.

'You can go back to Manchester if you like.' I glanced at my watch. 'In fact, if you shoot off in the next half-hour, you'll probably be back in time for your football match,' I added, smiling sweetly. I've never understood why Richard feels the need to run around a muddy field with a bunch of his fellow overgrown schoolboys every Sunday morning. I keep telling him he doesn't need an excuse to go to the pub at Sunday lunchtime, but he's adamant that this ritual is a vital part of his life. He'd been grumbling about missing his game ever since I'd pitched him into staying over in Buxton.

'But what about this guy? Lomax, or Harris, or whatever he's called. I thought you had it all to do?'

'I decided that since it's Alexis's business, she can come over and help me with the legwork. And I didn't think spending a Sunday in Buxton with Alexis was your idea of a good time,' I said solicitously.

The waitress arrived with his full English breakfast and my scrambled eggs just then, so we had a pause while he scoffed one of his fried eggs before it congealed. 'So what exactly is Alexis going to do that I can't?' he asked suspiciously. 'I'm not sure I trust the pair of you let loose together. I mean, if this is the guy that ripped off Alexis, isn't she going to go apeshit when she sees him? And you're in no fit state to take anybody on right now.'

I was touched. It was worrying. A year before, I'd have bitten the head off any man who suggested I might not be up to looking after myself. Now, I was touched. Definitely worrying. 'It'll be fine,' I said. 'After we had that lucky break last night, I realized there wasn't anything more I could do till Alexis had positively ID'd the guy.' I hadn't told Richard about my little excursion. Judging by his concern for my health, it was probably just as well.

He looked doubtful. 'I don't know,' he said through a mouthful of sausage. 'You drag me over to this God-forsaken hole, you make me eat the worst Chinese I've ever had in my life, with the possible exception of the one in Saltcoats where there was a prawn in the banana fritter, you send me off to endure the most derivative and listless music I've heard since Billy Joel's last album, then you tell me you're replacing me with an evening paper hackette! What's a man to think?'

'Just be grateful I'm not making you stay here for Sunday lunch, pal,' I replied with a grin. 'Look, I'll be fine. I promise not to take any risks.' That was a promise I could make with hand on heart. After all, I'd already taken all the risks I needed to take where T.R. Harris was concerned.

'All right,' he said. 'As long as you promise me one other thing?' I raised my eyebrows in a question. 'Promise me you'll force Alexis to take several risks. Preferably of the potentially fatal kind.' I told you he pretends they hate each other.

'Pig,' I said mildly. 'If Alexis heard you say that, she'd be cut to the quick.'

'Heard him say what?' Alexis boomed threateningly as she pulled out a chair and threw herself into it, waving at the waitress. 'Good morning, children,' she greeted us. 'Full English,' she added to the waitress.

'Kate's in no state for anything strenuous—'

'Lucky Kate!' Alexis interrupted Richard, ducking her head in a louche wink.

'So I said if anyone's got to take any physical risks, it had better be you,' he concluded, on his dignity.

'Well, of course, it stands to reason,' Alexis replied. 'First sign of danger, you're off over the nearest distant horizon, leaving us women to deal with the physical risks.'

I thought he was going to choke. 'You'd better get a move on if you're going to make it back in time for the match,' I said, treading on Alexis's toe under the table.

Richard glanced at his watch, said 'Shit!' and shovelled the rest of his breakfast down in record time. Then he pushed back his chair, got to his feet, downed a cup of tea in a oner and planted a greasy kiss somewhere in the region of my mouth. 'See you tonight, Brannigan,' he said, then headed for the door.

'Typical male,' Alexis called after him. 'When the going gets tough, the tough get going.'

'The only reason it's safe to leave things in your hands is that all the real work's been done already,' Richard shouted back.

By now, we had more viewers than BSkyB TV. The rest of the breakfasters were agog. 'Shut up,' I muttered through clenched teeth at Alexis. I waved goodbye to Richard, and he left, giving me a smile and a wink. 'Honestly,' I complained. 'What are you like? And don't tell me he started it, because you're each as bad as the other. Thank God we're not trying to do some quiet, unobtrusive undercover!'

'Sorry,' Alexis said unrepentantly. 'Anyway, now the Gary Lineker of the Press corps has departed, tell me all about it! You only gave me the bare bones over the phone.' She lit a cigarette and squinted at me through the smoke.

I started to tell her how I'd tracked down T.R. Harris, but she interrupted me impatiently. 'Not my stuff,' she said. 'You! Tell me how you are? I mean, I don't want to make you feel even worse, but you don't look like a woman who should be chasing the guys in the black hats all over Derbyshire. God, Kate, you shouldn't have been running around after Harris yesterday! You should have been in bed, recovering.'

I shook my head. 'With Richard ministering to my every need? Have you any idea what my kitchen would look like after he'd had a free rein in there for twenty-four hours?' I shuddered. 'No thanks. Besides, I was quite glad to have something to take my mind off what happened. Knowing there's someone out there who either wants to kill you or wants to warn you off so badly they're prepared to risk killing you isn't very relaxing.'

'Any idea who's behind it?' Alexis asked. She couldn't help herself. Once she'd established she was a caring friend, she just had to go into journo mode.

'I think it might have a connection to a job I'm working on. I should have a better idea in a day or two. Don't worry, you'll be the first to know when there's anything fit to print,' I reassured her.

'That's not why I was asking,' Alexis scolded. 'Aren't you worried that they'll have another go?'

'I suppose they might. But no one followed us yesterday. I've put a new face on the job in question, and I should be able to get it cleared up tomorrow. I feel like I've done everything I can to minimize the risk.'

The waitress arrived and dumped a steaming plateful in front of Alexis. It was the second time that morning I'd had to look at enough fried food to feed a Romanian orphanage for a week, and I began to feel faintly queasy. 'So, tell me about T.R. Harris,' Alexis prompted as she ground out her cigarette.

I filled her in on my search for the missing builder. 'And when I shone my torch in the garage window, there it was,' I ended up.

'The other panel?' Alexis asked.

'The same. The one that says "T.R. Harris, Builder". Of course, I still need you to ID the guy, but I reckon that's just a formality.'

'So Cheetham set the whole thing up?' Alexis demanded. 'I'll kill the little shit when I get my hands on him.'

'I'm still not sure exactly what his role in the whole thing was,' I said. 'He's obviously in it up to the eyeballs, but I'm not sure who's been pushing who.'

'Does it matter? The pair of them are crooks! Let me tell you, they're both going to regret the day they crossed me and Chris!' Alexis fumed. She ran a hand through her hair angrily then lit a cigarette, sucking the smoke deep into her lungs.

'We'll cross that bridge when we come to it,' I soothed. 'First things first. We've got to make sure we've got the right guy, that there's not some innocent explanation for what I've seen.'

'Oh yes? Like what?' Alexis scoffed. 'Like Cheetham is secretly working undercover for the Fraud Squad?'

'No, like B. Lomax, Builder, is renting out his garage to T.R. Harris, Builder. Like B. Lomax, Builder, is an old friend of Martin Cheetham's who introduced them to each other, and Cheetham, like you, is an innocent dupe.' That shut her up long enough for me to explain I was going to check out of my room.

Back upstairs, I dialled Paul Kingsley's home number. It was a call that could comfortably have waited till later in the day, but I was desperate to know if the surveillance had worked out. Paul answered on the third ring. Luckily, he didn't sound like a man who's just been roused from sleep. 'How did it go?' I asked after we'd got the pleasantries out of the way.

'Just as you predicted it would,' he said, unable to keep the disappointment from showing. They can't help themselves, can they? 'Our man turned up about nine o'clock, loaded up his hatchback with boxes and took off into the night.'

'Did he seem at all suspicious?' I asked.

'He drove all round the car park before he parked up by the loading bay. Then he did the circuit on foot,' Paul said.

'I take it he didn't spot you?' It was a safe bet. Paul's a good operator. He's a commercial photographer who thinks it's great fun to do the odd job for us. I think it makes him feel like James Bond, and he's probably got more professional pride in his work than those of us who do it for a full-time living.

Paul chuckled. 'Nah. They've got these industrial-sized rubbish bins. I was inside one.' See what I mean? There's no way I'd have spent an evening communing with maggots in the line of duty. Apart, of course, from the occasional journalistic piss-up Richard drags me along to.

'And you got pics?'

'I did. I popped back to my darkroom to dev and print them later. I've got great shots of him prowling round, loading up, then transferring the gear to an unmarked Renault van at Knutsford motorway services,' Paul said proudly.

'You managed to follow him?' I was impressed. It was more than I'd achieved.

'I got lucky,' he admitted. 'I had to wait till he was out of sight before I could get out of the bin, and I'd left my car round the back of the warehouse next door. But he was headed the same direction as I was going, and I was obviously luckier with the lights. I pulled up at a junction in Stretford, and there he was, right in front of me. So I stayed with him, and snapped the handover. And I got the van's number, so you can find out who's handling the stuff at the other end.'

'Great job,' I said, meaning it. 'Can you do me a favour? Can you drop the prints in tomorrow at the office and tell Shelley what they're about? I won't be in first thing, but I'll get to it later in the day.'

'No problem. Oh, and Kate?'

'Mmm?'

'Thanks for thinking of me,' he said, sounding sincere. I'll never understand men. Stand them in a dustbin for hours and you've made their Saturday night.

Alexis was pacing up and down the hall, doing that agitated flicking of the filter when there's no loose ash that smokers do when they're feeling twitchier than nicotine can soothe. When she saw me, she stopped pacing and started rattling her car keys, unnerving the poor receptionist who was trying to do my bill.

Reluctantly, I climbed into Alexis's car. Journalists seem to need to take the office with them in all its horror wherever they go. Alexis's Peugeot contained more old newspapers than the average chip shop could use in a week. The ashtray had been full since a month after she bought the car last year. The parcel shelf was home to a clutch of old notebooks that slid back and forwards every time she cornered, and there was a portable computer terminal that lived under the passenger seat and bruised the passenger's heels every time Alexis braked. I'd be ashamed to let anyone in my car if it was like that, but journalists always seem strangely proud of their mobile rubbish dumps.

First, we went to the local cop shop and checked out the electoral roll. There were two residents at that address, Brian and Eleanor Lomax. His wife, I presumed. Next, we slowly drove past the house. The black BMW had gone, but the van was still parked outside. I told Alexis to park up, and she turned the car round in the side street and drove back towards Lomax's house. She stopped about one hundred yards away from the house. We could see the front door and the drive, though we couldn't actually see the van.

Alexis, as much a veteran of the stake-out as me, pulled a paperback out of her handbag and settled back in her seat to read, secure in the knowledge that any movement round the house would instantly register in her peripheral vision. Me, I sucked peppermints and listened to the radio.

It was a couple of hours before there was any sign of life. We both spotted him at the same moment. Alexis sat up in her seat and chucked her book into the back seat. Brian Lomax had appeared round the side of the house and was walking down the drive. He wore the familiar black leather blouson and jeans, this time with a cream polo-neck sweater. At the end of the drive, he turned right, down the hill and towards the traffic lights.

'That him?' I asked. Nothing like the obvious question.

Alexis nodded grimly. 'T.R. Harris. I'd know the bastard anywhere.' She turned the ignition key and the Peugeot coughed into life.

'Wait a minute!' I said sharply. 'Where are you going?'

'I'm going to follow him,' Alexis said sharply. 'And then I'm going to front him up.' She shoved the car into gear.

I pulled it out again. 'No you're not,' I told her.

'I bloody am!' Alexis exploded. 'That bastard is walking around with five grand of our money, and I want it back.'

'Look, cool it,' I commanded. Alexis obviously recognized I meant it, for she subsided, showing her feelings by revving the engine at irregular intervals. 'Now you know his name and where he lives, you can lay your hands on him any time you want to. And so can the cops.'

Alexis shook her head. 'No cops. I want our money back, and if the guy's in custody, he's not earning. All I want is to front him up and get our money back.'

'Fronting him up isn't going to get your money back. He'll just laugh at you. And even if you go round with some of your less pleasant associates, I'm not convinced he's the kind of guy who'd be scared into handing the money over.'

'So what do you suggest? I just lie down and die?'

'No. I know it's a bit radical, but why don't you sue him? As long as you don't use Cheetham, that is,' I added, trying to get her to lighten up a bit.

'Because it'll take forever,' Alexis wailed.

'It doesn't have to. You get your solicitor to write a letter demanding payment, and if he doesn't cough up, you get her or him to issue a Statutory Demand, which means Lomax has to pay up within a certain time or you petition for bankruptcy. And since what he's done is illegal, he's not likely to quibble about repaying your money as soon as you start making legal noises,' I explained.

Alexis sighed. 'OK, you win. But on one condition.'

'What's that?'

'That you keep tabs on him for a day or two. I want to know his haunts, where he works out of, who he works with, just in case he decides to go to ground. I'll pay you, of course. Put it on an official footing.'

It was my turn to sigh. 'You've picked the worst possible week. I'm up to my eyeballs with vanishing conservatories and hooky drugs.'

'I won't institute proceedings till I know where we can lay hands on him if he's not home,' Alexis said obstinately.

My exertions of the previous day and a half had finally caught up with me. I didn't have the energy left to argue, so I caved in. 'OK. Put the car in gear. I'll get to it as soon as I can.'

13

The Birkenhead Land Registry's address is Old Market House, Hamilton Square. Sounds almost romantic, doesn't it? I pictured a mellow stone building, Georgian, with perhaps a portico. Wood panelling, maybe, with grey stooped figures shuffling past in a Dickensian hush. Fat chance. Negotiating the one-way system brought me to a modern dark red brick building, seven storeys tall with plenty of windows overlooking breathtaking views of the entrance to the Mersey tunnel.

I found a space in the car park for the Fiesta I'd hired to replace my wrecked Nova and tagged on to a group of women heading for the building. They were having the Monday morning chatter to each other about the weekend, obviously familiar with each other's routines. The leading pair stopped at the entrance to the building and keyed a number into a security lock. The women swept on into the building. One of them held the door open for me. That was when I noticed the sign informing me that the public entrance was at the front of the building. One of the great truisms of our business is that the more security a building has, the easier it is to penetrate. I caught the door and stood uncertainly for a moment. It was tempting to waltz in the back door and have a good wander round, just for the hell of it. But prudence won over my sense of adventure and I reluctantly let the door swing closed. I was too busy to spend a day down the police station explaining why I'd hacked into the Land Registry computer network.

I walked round to the front of the building, distinguishable from the back only by the double doors. I entered a cheerless foyer with a security booth and banks of stainless-steel lift doors. The Scouse security officers were as efficient as if they'd been privatized. Name and purpose of visit, who visiting, where car parked, car registration number. Then they note your arrival time and issue a security pass. If I were a dedicated hacker, I could see half a dozen ways to get my hands on one of their terminals.

Again, I restrained my more piratical instincts and went across the hall to Inquiries. It was like a dentist's waiting room, complete with year-old magazines sitting on a low table. The chairs were the cloth-upholstered sort two grades up from those hideous orange plastic ones you get down the Social Security. Everything was a bit scuffed, as if it was last redecorated before Thatcher came to power. I walked over to a high counter in the corner of the room. It was empty except for a cash register and a computer monitor and keyboard. I craned my neck round to read 'Welcome to the Land Registry Computer System' in amber letters on the black screen.

The sign on the desk said, 'Please ring for attention'. They obviously brought the sign with them from the old building, since it's probably the only thing in the whole place made of wood. It's certainly the only thing made of wood with gilt lettering on it. I rang the bell and waited for a desiccated old man in a frock coat to shuffle through the door.

That'll teach me to make my mind up in advance of the facts. It took less than a minute for a young woman to appear who, frankly, wasn't my idea of a civil servant. For a start, she wouldn't have looked out of place at one of Richard's gigs in her fashionably baggy Aran sweater and jeans. For another, she looked like she enjoyed her work. And she didn't behave as if having to deal with members of the public was a major pain for her. All very novel.

'I wonder if you can help me,' I said. 'My name's Brannigan, Kate Brannigan. I rang last week with a list of addresses that I needed copies of the register for.'

The woman smiled. 'That's right. It was me you spoke to. I've got the copies ready, if you don't mind waiting a minute?'

'Fine,' I said. As she disappeared back through the door, I allowed myself a grim smile of satisfaction. No doubt this was where the wait began. I helped myself to one of the elderly magazines and sat down. I was only one paragraph into the fascinating tale of a soap star's brush with death on the motorway when she returned with a thick bundle of documents.

'Here you are,' she announced. 'Seven sets of copies of the register. It's not often we get asked for so many, except by conveyancing experts. And in so many different locations,' she added, obviously fishing.

I dumped the magazine and went back to the counter. 'I suppose it made life a lot more complicated for you when they changed the rules to allow anyone to examine any entry in the register,' I parried.

'I don't know about complicated,' she said. 'But it's made it a lot more interesting. I only ever used to talk to solicitors and their secretaries, and occasionally people who wanted copies of their own entries. Now we get all sorts coming in. Often, they want to check the register on their neighbours' properties because they think they might be in breach of some covenant or other, like no caravans, or no garden bonfires. A right lot of Percy Sugdens, some of them are,' she added with a giggle.

She turned to the cash register. I'd taken the precaution of hitting the hole in the wall with the company cashpoint card, so I wasn't flummoxed by her demand any more than she was by my request for a VAT receipt. I made a mental note to ask Shelley to keep a running total of Ted Barlow's account and to bill him as soon as it went five hundred pounds over the retainer he'd given us. I didn't want us to end up working for nothing if I couldn't clear up the scam fast enough to keep his business afloat.

I picked up my copies of the register entries and squeezed them into the back pocket of my handbag. Then, a thought occurred to me. 'I wonder if you could clear something up for me?' I said.

'If I can, I'd be happy to,' the young woman said, giving me a bright smile that appeared to be completely natural. She obviously wasn't destined to last long in the Civil Service.

'What's the actual process here? And how long does it take between details being sent to you and them being entered into the register? I was thinking particularly of land that's being

registered for the first time and has then been split into parcels.'
If anyone could help me work out Martin Cheetham's role in
the double-sale scam, it had to be the Land Registry.

'Right,' she said, dragging the word out into three distinct
Scouse syllables. 'What happens is this. Every morning, a Day
Listing gets put on the computer. That lists all the title numbers
that are the subject of alteration, inquiry, registration or anything else. Once a title number has appeared on the Day Listing,
it stays listed until it has been entered into the full register. At
any one time there are about 140,000 properties on the Listing,
so it takes a little time to get round to them all.'

Suddenly, I began to understand how the Land Registry got
its reputation for being as slow as a tortoise on valium. Before
they started their computerization, it must have been a nightmare. 'So what sort of time scale are we looking at?' I asked.

'It depends,' she said. 'We've got about half a million records
on computer, which has speeded things up a bit, except when
the system crashes.'

'So, allowing for that, how long does it take for changes to
make their way on to the register?'

'For a change of ownership, we've got it down to about four
weeks. A first registration takes about eleven weeks, and for a
transfer of part, it's about fifteen weeks,' she said.

Light was beginning to glimmer, very faintly. 'So if someone
was registering a piece of land for the first time, then almost
immediately registering the division of that land into plots and
the sale of those plots, the whole thing could take six months?'

'In theory, yes,' she admitted, looking slightly uncomfortable.

'So if someone tried to sell the same plot twice, they might
be able to get away with it?'

She shook her head vehemently. 'Absolutely not. Don't
forget, it would be on the Day Listing. As soon as the second
purchaser's solicitor instigated a search, they would be told
that the file was already active, which would ring alarm bells
and put any transaction on hold.'

'I see,' I said, smiling my thanks. 'You've been very helpful.'
'No problem. Any time.' She returned the smile.

I walked back to the car in thoughtful mood. I was pretty convinced now that I knew how Alexis and Chris had been ripped off. The root of the scam lay in the difference between registered and unregistered land. I dredged my memory for all I'd ever learned about land, which wasn't that much, since land comes in the final year of a law-degree course. I suspect that might have been one of the factors in my decision to duck out after my second year. But sometimes, like now, that last year would have come in handy.

The ownership of about a third of the land in the North West of England has never been registered. If you think about it, it's only in relatively recent times that there was any need for registration, when we all became economically and socially mobile, as the academics put it. In the olden days before the Second World War, if you were buying a property or a piece of land, you usually knew the person who was selling it. Probably, they'd been your employer, or had sat in the front pew of the local church all your life. Some form of independent registration only became an issue when you were buying from a stranger and you had no proof of their reputation; they just might not actually *own* London Bridge, after all. Since the Land Registry really got going in the thirties, most transactions have been registered in what was supposed to be a slow but sure process. Ho, ho.

In practice, before compulsory registration was introduced in the late sixties and seventies, a lot of properties still changed ownership on a handshake and the exchange of a fistful of title deeds for a fistful of readies. And, since those properties haven't changed hands again since then, they're still not registered. This doesn't just apply to farmland that's been in families for generations; there are whole chunks of rented terraced housing in Manchester where ownership has remained the same for thirty or forty years. In terms of the Registry, it just doesn't exist. Frankly, I think it'd be an enormous improvement if it didn't exist in reality either.

Anyway, when someone like Brian Lomax pitches a farmer like Harry Cartwright into selling him a chunk of land, all the paperwork goes off to the Land Registry. And I'm not talking pristine forms and word processor-generated contracts. I'm talking dirty bits of paper covered in spidery writing and sealing wax. When it got to the Land Registry, I now knew, it would go on the Day Listing and be given a provisional title number. When Lomax then split the land into plots and sold them, the buyers' solicitors would carry out searches with the Land Registry to see if Lomax really owned it, and the individual plots would be given a number. So far, all very straight.

What happened next was what had done the damage. Lomax had obviously sold the land twice over in short order. But for the scheme to work, there had to be a crooked solicitor handling the second, moody purchase of the land, a solicitor who wouldn't consult the Land Registry's Day Listing, a solicitor who would lie to his clients about the title to the land. And that solicitor was Martin Cheetham.

The problem, as I saw it, was that it was a lot of risk to take for so small a profit. When the people who had been ripped off realized what had happened, they'd be on to the Law Society with their complaints faster than a speeding bullet. Which might well mean the end of Martin Cheetham's career as a solicitor, and all for a half share of fifty grand. Unless ... I had a horrible thought. What if they hadn't just sold the land twice, but had sold it three or four times over? What if there was a queue of punters who didn't even know yet that they'd been conned? After all, it was only by coincidence that Chris had happened upon the surveyors. If they hadn't been there, Chris, Alexis and all their self-build cronies probably would have handed over the rest of the cash. The mind boggled! I began to wonder if getting Alexis's money back was going to be quite so easy after all. If Lomax and Cheetham had any sense, they'd be planning to do a runner any day now before it all came on top.

And there was very little I could do about it. Apart from anything else, I had to sort out Ted Barlow's problem before he went bankrupt. I pulled into a Happy Eater and ordered a brunch of hash browns, omelette and beans while I studied the register entries for the seven properties which had lost their conservatories. I'd also taken the precaution of dropping by the office to pick up the stuff from Josh and from Rachel Lieberman. Taken together, an interesting picture began to emerge. Unfortunately, it was more like a Jackson Pollock than a David Hockney.

Firstly, all the houses in question had been rented from DKL. All the tenants in question shared their surname with the owners of the house. All the title deeds showed that there was a charge against the property. Unfortunately they didn't tell me how much, although the dates of these existing charges corresponded roughly to the dates the conservatories had been bought, and in all cases the charge was held by the finance company that was a subsidiary of Ted Barlow's bank. Surprise, surprise. Interestingly, Josh's searches had revealed that all the owners had good to excellent credit ratings, which explained why Ted's bank's finance company had been so ready to grant them the remortgages. What it didn't explain was how those remortgages came to be granted to someone other than the owner.

Somehow, the remortgages held the key. What I needed to find out fast was how big they were. If those charges were anything like you'd expect from a one hundred per cent remortgage, then things would begin to fall into place. Bearing in mind that each of the houses had been owned by its present owners for at least four years, then the houses had been bought for significantly less than they were now worth. Given that the mortgages had presumably been paid for at least four years, the amount now outstanding should be considerably less than the current value of the house. I wandered across to the phone-booth and dialled Josh. Luckily I got straight through.

'Just a quickie,' I said. 'How do I find out the amount outstanding on a mortgage?'

'You can't,' he said.

I was overcome with the desire to kick someone.

'Oh shit,' I moaned.

'But I probably can,' he added smugly.

Then I knew I wanted to kick someone, only he wasn't within range.

'As a finance broker I can ring up the charge holder and tell them I have a client who's looking to make a second loan against his property, can they tell me how much their outstanding charge is so that I can check whether there's enough equity left in the property. Is this to do with your conservatory scam?'

'Yes. It's slowly beginning to make sense,' I told him.

'I'll ask Julia to do it this afternoon,' he said.

I decided not to kick him after all. 'She's already got the names and addresses, hasn't she?'

I arranged to call back in the afternoon. I was still cross and frustrated because I didn't fully understand how the con was working. But I did have one thing going for me. Rachel Lieberman had given me the addresses of three other properties that fitted the bill. Looking at the dates on the previous sales that had turned into missing conservatories, the scammers seemed to work a production-line system. They were getting the loans through at the rate of about one a month, so, given that it can take up to three months for the money to come through from finance companies, they must have been working three properties at any given time, each at various stages of the operation. Dear God! They really were serious about this!

It was three weeks since the last one had gone down, so by my reckoning, we were due for another any day now. I had a good idea where, a rough idea when. And I had an excellent idea how to discover exactly what was going on. All it should take was a phone call.

14

I sat in the back of a bright yellow van, headphones clamped to my ears. My friend Dennis sat next to me, looking for inspiration in the pages of an Elmore Leonard. To anyone wandering along this Stockport cul-de-sac, it looked like a British Telecom van. The inside would have completely confounded them. Instead of racks of tools, spare parts and cable, there were a couple of leather car seats, the kind you get in top-of-the-range Volvos or Mercs, and a table, all bolted to the floor. There was a portable colour TV and a video fixed to the top of a fridge. There was also a hatch in the floor. The van belongs to Sammy, one of Dennis's mates. I don't want to know what he uses it for on a regular basis. I know for sure it isn't anything to do with telecommunications.

Dennis O'Brien and I have been friends now for years. I know he's a criminal, and he knows I put criminals out of business. But in spite of, or maybe because of, that we've each got a lot of respect for the other. I respect him because in his own way he's a highly skilled craftsman who sticks rigidly to his own rules and values. They might not be the same as mine, but who's to say mine are any better? After all, this society that puts burglars behind bars is the same society that helps the really big bandits like Robert Maxwell thrive.

I owe Dennis a lot. My martial arts skills, my knowledge of lock-picking, and the part of Mortensen and Brannigan's income that depends on being able to think like a burglar so you can construct a security system that will defeat the real thing. He likes having me around because he thinks I'm a good role model for his teenage daughter. There's no accounting for tastes.

After I got back from the Land Registry, I'd rung Dennis on

his mobile phone. It's a fascinating thing, the mobile phone. In London, when one starts ringing in a pub, chances are it's someone in the City on the receiving end. In Manchester, it's a bob to a gold clock it's a villain. It's a mystery to me how they get past the credit-worthiness checks that the airtime companies run. Now I think about it, they've probably got their very own airtime company, Criminal Communications, or Funny Phones, just for bad lads. With absolutely no directory enquiries service.

Anyway, I caught Dennis at a good time, so I invited him to find Sammy and help me out. I didn't even have to mention money before he agreed. He's nice like that, is Dennis. Unlike me, he doesn't think a friend in need is a pain in the arse. Which is why I was sitting in a fake Telecom van while Sammy was planting Mortensen and Brannigan's bugs in the three-bedroomed semi that Brian and Mary Wright were renting through DKL Estates.

Normally, when we use surveillance equipment, we place it ourselves. It's seldom a problem, since more often than not we're being paid by the person who is in charge of the place we're bugging. It usually arises because a boss suspects one of their subordinates of a) flogging information to a competitor; b) embezzling money or goods from the firm; or c) just a bit of good, old-fashioned internecine warfare against the boss. In those cases, we just wander in after closing time and drape the place in all the electronic surveillance a body could want. Sometimes, however, we have to be a little more discreet. While Bill and I have an agreement that we won't do things that are outrageously illegal, we occasionally find ourselves technically a little bit on the wrong side of the law when acquiring information. In situations like that, one of us insinuates ourself into the building in question by some subterfuge or other. Personally, I always find the most effective one is to claim to be the woman who's come to refill the tampon dispensers. Not a lot of security guards want to look too closely inside your boxes.

However, in this case, none of the usual ploys would work. And I didn't really want either Brian or Mary Wright to see me, since I'd be the person hanging round the street checking out the surveillance tapes. Hence Sammy's van. I'd given him a quick crash course in how to take apart the phone sockets and install the simple bug I'd decided to use. It consisted of a phone tap and a tiny voice-activated mike that would pick up the conversation in the room itself. The bug had a range of about one hundred and fifty metres, though reception in the metal-walled van wasn't as good as it would be once I'd transferred my receiver into the unobtrusive rented Fiesta where I could leave it sitting on the parcel shelf.

Sammy had marched up the path in his Telecom overalls ten minutes ago, and the woman who answered the door had let him in without even asking to see the carefully forged ID card he always carries. Perhaps she'd tried to dial out in the five minutes since I'd fiddled with her phone at the junction box round the corner. The reason I know about all these exotic things is that I once had a fling with a Telecom engineer. He came to install a second line in my bungalow for my computer modem and fax machine and stayed for a month. He had wonderfully dexterous fingers, and, as a bonus, he taught me everything I'd ever need to know about the British telephone system. Unfortunately, he felt the need to tell me it five times over. When he started telling me for the sixth time about new developments in fibre optic technology, I knew he'd have to go or I'd be risking a murder charge.

What I was waiting for now was the sound of Sammy's voice over my headphones. As soon as I was receiving him loud and clear, I'd nip back to the junction box, restore the telephone to full working order, and leave the receiver in my car wired up to a very clever tape recorder that a sound engineer friend of Richard's built for me. It links the mechanisms of six Walkmans to a signal-activated mike/receiver. When the bug's signal comes in, the first tape starts running. When the counter mechanism hits a certain number, it sets tape two running and switches off tape one. And so on. So, it gives a minimum of six hours recording time when you're not actually there listening in.

Five minutes later, I heard, 'Two sugars, love,' booming in

my ears. Thanks to Sammy, I was all wired up and ready to roll. Half an hour later, I was back in the office, ready to debrief Bill. He was, of course, horrified about my brush with death on Barton Bridge. Together we went through Paul's photos and the report from his surveillance of PharmAce, Bill muttering into his thick blond beard about the temerity of anyone who would mess with his partner.

'Paul's done a good job there. You did absolutely the right thing, laying him on like that,' he rumbled, shuffling the pics together into a neat pile. 'I'll go and see them this afternoon.' He got to his feet, shouting, 'Shelley? Get Brian Chalmers at PharmAce and tell him I'm on my way to see him.'

'Wait a minute,' I protested, angry at what felt like Bill pulling rank. 'I'd planned to take those pictures over myself.'

'I'm sure you did,' he said. 'And I don't have a problem with the way you've handled things. But I want someone with Chalmers when he fronts up the lab technician. And I'd rather it was me if only to show this creep that he's up against more than a one-woman show. If it was him that ran you off the road, he's got to be made to realize that there's no point in trying to write you off because it's not just you who knows what he's up to. Besides, we need a lot more information about this stolen van, and you've got enough on your plate right now with your missing conservatories.'

I couldn't find any good reason for arguing with Bill. Personally, if I had his six foot plus towering over me, I'd admit to just about anything to get him to back off. So I left him to it. On my way out the door, I picked up the hand-held computer scanner which had been his monthly contribution to the office gadget mountain back in June. At last, I had found a use for it. As I crossed the outer office, Shelley said, 'Ted Barlow's been on. That's the second time today. He's really starting to get desperate. He says he can pay his staff this week's wages, but he's not sure about next week. He wants to know if he should warn them or whether you think you'll have sorted it out by then.'

I sighed. 'I'm doing my best, Shelley,' I said.

'Can't you do it a bit faster, Kate? Ted's scared he's going to lose his business.'

'Shelley, I'm dancing as fast as I can, OK,' I snapped, and stomped into my office. I'm ashamed to admit that I slammed the door. Unfortunately, I used the muscles that were still solid as a rock from the accident, so I lost out on comfort as well as dignity. Just to put the tin lid on it, the vibration of the door caused the last three leaves on the rubber plant to fall off. I threw the plant in the bin and made a note to stop by the florist in the morning. I'd had nine weeks out of that rubber plant, which was approaching a record for me and the chlorophyll kingdom.

I picked up the phone, dialled Josh's number and asked for Julia. I've never actually met her but her voice conjures up this image of a bright-eyed blonde with her hair in a neat bun, a Country Casuals suit and the hips of a girl raised on the Pony Club. The nearest I ever got to that was reading *Bunty*.

'Hello, Kate,' she enthused down the phone at me. 'Fabulous little challenge, darling!' I swear she really does say 'darling'.

'Any joy?' I asked gruffly. For some reason Julia always brings out the peasant in me.

'I only tried three of them,' she said. 'With the charges all being held by the same finance company, I had to be a little bit cautious. However, the interesting thing is that, in each case, what we're looking at is a hundred percent remortgage. The people I spoke to all said the same thing. "There's not a shilling of equity left for your client." So there you have it, Kate.'

I could have kissed her. But she'd probably have mis-understood and taken my name off her database. I thanked her prettily, just like my mother always told me to, put down the phone and yelled 'Yo!' in satisfaction. The way things were heading, I was going to make Shelley a very happy woman.

I booted up my computer and entered my notes. Then I used the scanner on the Land Registry documents and saved them all to disc. It wasn't as easy as it was supposed to be, since the scanner had the unhelpful tendency to turn things into gobbledygook unless I kept my hand steady as a rock. I felt virtuous enough after all that to ring Richard and suggest a movie that evening. 'Sorry, Brannigan,' he said. 'I'm going to a rave.'

Richard may be four years older than me, but at times he makes me feel like my Granny Brannigan. Except that my Irish Granny B would probably love the idea of an all-night party where you can dance as much as you want. She'd even feel at home with the smell of the Vicks Vapor Rub that the ravers massage each other with in their bizarre search to improve the high of the designer drug cocktails they swallow. 'Why?' I asked.

I could picture the shrug. 'I need to keep in touch. Besides, they've got this new DJ. He's only thirteen and I want to take a look.' Thirteen. Dear God, the Little Jimmy Osmond of Acid House. 'You can come if you want,' he added.

'I think I'll pass, Richard. Nothing personal, but frankly I'd rather go on a stake-out.' At least I could choose the music. At least I'd be able to recognize what I was hearing as music.

I left the office just after four, picked up a pizza from the local trattoria and headed back out to Stockport in the Little Rascal. I parked round the corner from the target house, strolled round to the Fiesta and checked out the tape machine. The third was rolling, and I had a quick listen on the headphones. Blue Peter, by the sound of it. That's the trouble with Elint (electronic intelligence, or bugs to you). It has as much discrimination as a hooker on smack. I restrained myself from listening in to the rest of the Blue Peter tape, helped myself to the two I'd made earlier, and locked up the Fiesta.

Back in the van, I munched my pizza and listened to the tapes. The first one featured ten minutes of small talk with Sammy, a phone call to the hairdresser, a phone call to a friend who whined for twenty minutes about her business, her ex and her garage bill. Then the TV had gone on, its tinny sound an interesting contrast to the live voices I'd been hearing. An Australian soap, then a pre-teen comedy drama, then cartoons. I whizzed through the programmes on double speed, ear cocked for any more real conversations amongst the Mickey Mouse squeaks. Nothing.

Bored, I went back to the Fiesta and listened in again. By

now, we were on to *Granada Reports*. Why couldn't my target have been one of these quiet, refined people who don't feel the need of some kind of audio wallpaper? I reset the recording machine with fresh tapes and decided to give my eaves-dropping another hour before heading home. I reminded myself that I had a right to some free time of my own. Besides, I was feeling cold and stiff and I was longing to get to grips with my latest computer game purchase. *Civilization* promised to be the most enthralling strategy game I'd played for a long time, taking the player from the dawn of man to the space age. So far, I hadn't been able to get much further than settlements of tent dwellers who'd just discovered the wheel before the barbarians came along and clobbered us.

I was trying to work out an approach that would be more fruitful when everything changed. The noise in my ears sud-denly stopped altogether. For a few heart-stopping seconds I thought she'd discovered the bug. Then I heard a dialling tone and the click of numbers being keyed in. Maybe I'd be able to identify the number when I had the chance to analyse the tape at more length. The phone at the other end rang three times before it was picked up. An answering machine clicked and a man's voice said, 'I'm sorry, I'm not taking calls right now. Leave your message after the bleep, and we'll talk soon.' The voice was cool, with a suggestive edge that made me smile rather than squirm.

After the tone, the woman said, 'Hi, it's me. It's just before seven. I'm going round to my mother's, then I'll be at Colin and Sandra's. See you there. Love you. Bye.' There was a click as she put the phone down. I scrambled out of the car and hurried down the street towards the van. The last thing I wanted was for her to become suspicious of the Fiesta.

I had just shut myself into an atmosphere of stale pizza when a square of light from the front door spilt over the drive of my target's house. The light disappeared as she shut the door and opened the garage. I concentrated on the features. The hair might change, the clothes might change, the height might change with the shoes, but the face wasn't going to, especially the profile. I registered small, neat features, sharp chin, face wider across the eyes. Just like Diane Shipley's sketch. A couple of minutes later, a white Metro emerged and drove past me, heading south towards Hazel Grove. I'd gambled when I parked that if she was going to drive off anywhere, she'd be heading north into Manchester. Wrong again. I did as quick a three-point turn as I could manage, which wasn't fast enough. By the time I reached the end of the road, she was gone. There was just enough traffic around to make it impossible to guess which set of distant tail lights were hers.

There was nothing else for it. I'd just have to go home and bring my own unique blend of civilization to some unsuspecting barbarian tribe. Maybe this time I should develop map-making ahead of ceremonial burial . . .?

When I got home, my answering machine was flashing. I pressed the playback button. 'Kate, Bill here. I've just got back from PharmAce. We need to talk. This is the number where you can reach me this evening after seven.'

He rattled off a Didsbury number, which I failed to recognize. Hardly surprising. Bill changes his girlfriends as often as Rod Stewart in his bachelor days. When I dialled the number, true to form, a woman's voice answered. While I waited for her to fetch Bill, I conjured up the image her voice generated.

'Twenty-five, Home Counties, graduate, blonde, smokes,' I said when Bill answered.

'Well done, Sherlock. You're two years too generous, though,' he said.

'You said we need to talk. Will the phone do, or shall I come over and meet you for a drink?' I asked maliciously.

'The phone will do nicely,' he said. 'First, the good news. Brian Chalmers is delighted, and has sacked the senior technician on the spot, with no reference. And tomorrow I'm meeting someone from Knutsford CID to see if they'd like to pursue the company receiving the stolen goods.'

'Fine,' I said. 'And the bad news?'

'It wasn't a PharmAce van that ran you off the road. They had a call today from the police in Devon. The van that was stolen from PharmAce was written off in some village on Dartmoor on Friday morning after being used in a supermarket robbery down there. So it couldn't have rammed you on Friday night. Kate, whoever had a go at you on Barton Bridge is still out there.'

15

I could get used to being waited on hand and foot at breakfast. What I couldn't handle is the early rising that seems to go hand in hand with business briefings over the bacon butties. The following morning, I was back in the dining room of the Portland at Josh's invitation. 'I've got someone I want you to meet,' he'd said mysteriously on the phone, refusing to be drawn further.

I approached with caution, since I could see Josh's companion was a woman. I hoped he hadn't dragged me out of bed to tell me he was getting married. That was news I couldn't handle on an empty stomach. I saw Josh spot me and say something to his companion, who glanced over her shoulder at me. She didn't look Josh's type. For a start, she looked in her middle thirties, which made her at least ten years too old. The most striking thing about her was her hair, the colour of polished conkers, hanging down her back in a thick plait.

When I reached the table, Josh half-stood and said, 'Kate! I'm glad you could make it. Della, this is Kate Brannigan, the private investigator I told you about.'

A potential client, then, I thought. I smiled. Josh continued, 'Kate, this is Detective Chief Inspector Della Prentice. She's just been transferred to the Regional Crime Squad. We were at Cambridge together, and I thought the pair of you ought to meet.'

I tried not to look as gobsmacked as I felt. There aren't a lot of women who make it to the rank of DCI, especially not at the sharp end of crime. Della Prentice smiled and extended her hand. 'Pleased to meet you, Kate,' she said. 'At the risk of making your heart sink, Josh has told me a lot about you.'

'I wish I could say the same about you,' I replied, shaking a dry, firm hand. I sat down with a bit of a bump. I didn't expect to be dragged out of bed at sparrowfart to meet a copper. Especially not a ranking woman officer. I gave her the quick once-over. Deep-set greenish eyes, good skin, the kind of strong bones that look lumpy in teenagers but become more attractive with every year that passes after the age of thirty.

'He tries to keep me under wraps because I know where the bodies are buried,' she said, as she gave me the same scrutiny. 'I could tell you a tale ...'

Josh cleared his throat and said hastily, 'Della's something of an expert in the kind of fraud you seem to be dealing with in your conservatory case,' he said. 'I rather thought she might be of some help to you.'

'I've just done eighteen months with the West Yorkshire Fraud Squad,' Della said. 'Now I've been transferred to the RCS to be the operational head of a fraud task force.'

'How are you finding it?' I asked.

'It's always a bit of an uphill struggle, learning to work with a new team.' Of course. She wouldn't have climbed that far up the ladder if she hadn't been something of a diplomat.

'Made five times worse because you're a woman?' I asked.

'Something like that.'

'I can imagine. Plenty of that dumb insolence, literal interpretation of orders and no respect till they decide you've earned it.'

Della's twisted smile said it all. 'What we're doing is working with banks and other financial institutions on the kind of small-scale fraud that doesn't warrant the attentions of the Serious Fraud Office. Usually, it involves forgery or the kind of deception where people assume someone else's identity for the purposes of obtaining goods or cash.'

'At the risk of sounding like the punters I meet at parties, that must be fascinating,' I said.

She smiled. 'It can be very satisfying to put together the pieces of the jigsaw.'

'Yes, you get a better class of villain in your line of work than your colleagues who get lumbered with the ram raiders and the drug dealers,' I said. 'For me, it's a little out of the usual run of things. I'm more accustomed to poking about in computers' memories than fronting people up.'

Della leaned back in her chair. 'Now, that really *must* be fascinating. No, I mean it. I'd love to have the time to learn more about computers. Mind if I smoke?' I shook my head. She took out a pack of Silk Cut and a Zippo lighter. As she lit up she said, 'Josh tells me you've got a problem with defaulting mortgagees. Maybe we could do each other a bit of good here. I might be able to shed some light for you and, frankly, if you can stand it up, I could really use the collar.'

I liked Della Prentice's candour. And she came vouched for by Josh, which in my book was the seal of professionalism. So I took a deep breath and said, 'This is off the record. Agreed?' I had no authority from Ted to involve the police. Added to which, as yet, I had no real evidence that a crime had been committed, only a lot of circumstantial coincidences.

A waitress appeared and we ordered our breakfasts before Della could reply. When she'd gone, she said, 'Off the record.'

I gave Della the bare bones. To her credit, she heard me out in silence. Most of the questions she asked afterwards were sensible and to the point, just as I'd expected. 'The banks have got their own investigators, you know,' she said at last. 'I'm surprised they haven't been digging around in this one themselves.'

'I don't know that they haven't been,' I said. 'But if they have, they've been going at it from a different angle. They're probably trying to prove Ted Barlow is bent, whereas I'm trying to establish the exact opposite.'

She nodded. 'I don't mean to sound like I'm teaching you to suck eggs, but I suppose you have considered that your client might be at it?'

'It was the first thing I thought of. But people who know him say he lacks the imagination or the inclination to be that bent. Besides, he's telling the truth about the missing conservatories. Even I can see they were installed originally, and if he was behind it himself, he wouldn't have to bother with that,' I explained.

Della considered while she lit another cigarette. Then she

said, 'He might have been doing that to cover his own back when it all came on top. And who better than him to find a new home for the conservatories? After all, he could just recycle them. And he could simply be employing you to make it look good to the bank – and to us, if we're called in eventually by the bank's security crew.'

I shook my head. 'It's not Ted. I know it's possible to find an explanation that points the finger at him. But the clincher for me is that he just doesn't match the descriptions I've got of the man who spends the night at these houses.'

'It's an unusual one, Kate,' she said. 'Very unusual. But if it really is a scam that's being pulled by one or two people rather than a string of coincidences, then they must have cleared a lot of cash by now.'

'Over half a million after expenses, by my estimates,' I said calmly. 'They probably can't believe their luck. If I was them, I'd be planning to pull out before the shit hit the fan.'

'How do you know they haven't?' Della asked.

'I don't. I'm banking on the fact that they haven't. That way, the next time they pull one, I can get on their tail while the trail's still warm.' Much as I liked Della, I wasn't about to tell her that I thought I'd spotted the next target. I was perfectly happy for her to think I was playing a waiting game. It would keep the Regional Crime Squad off my back. Besides, I didn't want to get into a discussion on the subject of illegal phone taps. I hate the sound of people in glass houses throwing stones.

I scooped the last mouthful of scrambled egg on to a triangle of toast and managed to savour it, Della being between cigarettes. 'Let me know how you get on. I'm really fascinated by the sound of this one. I'm sure we could help.' She took a card out of the jacket of her charcoal grey suit. 'And if they do seem to have done a runner, get in touch anyway. You never know, we might be able to put something together with what you've got.'

'I appreciate that. Soon as I've something concrete, I'll call you. Josh, thanks for introducing us. It's the first time I've met someone you actually shut up for,' I said.

'You don't deserve me, Kate,' he said sadly.

'Thank God for that. Now, if you'll both excuse me, I've got to run,' I said. I stood up and shook Della Prentice's hand. 'I'll be in touch. Oh, and Josh? Thank Julia for that information she dug out for me.' I gave him a peck on the cheek.

My guilty conscience over talking to DCI Della Prentice about Ted's problem gave me a severe prick when I walked into the office to find the conservatory builder and the lovestruck secretary with their heads together. Ted Barlow was perched on the edge of Shelley's desk, while she ignored her computer screen and stared instead into his eyes. Before I'd even got my duffel coat off, Ted was apologizing for bothering me and Shelley was twittering about interim reports and mobile phones. I invited Ted into my office and brought him as up to date as I dared. I didn't trust him entirely with full knowledge of my current surveillance. He may have been footing the bill, but he was far too transparent for me to feel comfortable with him knowing my every move. Besides, he was so obviously one of life's honest guys that he might be uncomfortable at the thought of me bending the law on his behalf.

So I told him that I was making progress, and that I was close to working out how it all came together. He seemed satisfied with that. Maybe all he was looking for was some reassurance. When I emerged from my office a couple of minutes after he'd left me, he was still hanging round Shelley's desk looking nervous. I couldn't stand it, so I grabbed my coat and the mobile phone that had arrived that morning and headed for the door.

First stop was the hired Fiesta with the receiving equipment. At first, when I checked the cassettes, my heart sank. Nothing seemed to have been recorded at all since I'd left it the previous evening. When I reset it, I must have made a mistake, I decided. Then I noticed that the first tape wasn't quite empty.

I pulled it out of the machine and smacked it in the car cassette. There was the unmistakable sound of a door slamming, then a phone ringing, unanswered. I breathed a sigh of relief. Neither I nor the machine was faulty. It seemed the woman just hadn't come home. In case she or one of her neighbours was the noticing kind, I drove the Fiesta round the block and reparked it in an obviously different position. I didn't want to be in the embarrassing position of having the bomb squad called because some civic-minded nosy-parker thought the receiver on the parcel shelf was an IRA car bomb. It happened to Bill last year. Luckily for him, the receiver was switched off at the time. Luckily, because the offence is using the equipment, not possessing it, which is the kind of logic the law specializes in.

I reckoned it still wasn't safe to go back to the office, so I decided to poke a stick into the hornet's nest of Alexis's little problem and see what flew out. It was late morning when I reached Cheetham's office. His obliging secretary told me he was in a meeting, but if I cared to wait . . .

I took the computer magazine I usually carry out of my handbag and settled down with an article about ram expansion kits. If I decided we needed something similar, the technique is to leave the magazine lying around the office, open at the appropriate page, and wait for Mortensen the gadget king to fall upon it and embrace it as if it were his own idea. Never fails.

Before I could reach a firm decision, the door to the inner office opened and Cheetham ushered out the woman I'd seen with him in Buxton. He had his arm round her in that familiar, casual way that people use with the kind of partners you sleep with rather than work with. When he saw me, he twitched and dropped his arm as if he'd been jabbed with a cattle prod. 'Miss Brannigan,' he said nervously.

Hearing my name, the woman, who until then had been focused on Cheetham, switched her attention to me. She sized me up in an instant, from the top of my wavy auburn hair to the tips of my brown boots. She probably misjudged me, too. She wasn't to know that the reason I was wearing enough make-up to read the six o'clock news was that the bruises on my jaw and cheekbone had gone a fascinating shade of green.

She looked like serious business, groomed to within an inch of artificiality. I hated her. Our mutual scrutiny was interrupted by Cheetham stammering, 'If you'd like to come through, Miss Brannigan?'

I acknowledged them both with a nod and walked past them to his office. I didn't hear what the woman murmured in his ear after I passed, but I heard him say, 'It's all right, Nell. Look, I'll see you this afternoon, OK?'

'It had better be,' I thought I caught as she swept off without so much as a smile for the secretary. You can tell a lot about people by the way they treat other people's office staff.

I waited for Cheetham to return to his chair. I could see the effort it was taking for him to sit still. 'How can I help you?' he asked.

'I just thought I'd drop by and give you a progress report,' I said. 'Our builder friend, T.R. Harris, seems not to exist. And neither does the solicitor whom you appear to have corresponded with.' I knew this for certain, since I'd checked out the list of qualified briefs in the Solicitors' Diary.

Cheetham just sat and stared at me, those liquid dark eyes slightly narrowed. 'I don't understand,' he said, rather too late.

'Well, it seems as if Harris used a false name, and made up a non-existent solicitor for the purpose of conning your clients out of their money. It was lucky that Miss Appleby happened to discover the land had already been sold, otherwise they'd all have lost a lot more money,' I tried. If he was straight, he'd be at great pains to point out to me that they couldn't have lost another shilling, since he, their diligent solicitor, would have discovered from the Land Registry that the land in question had already been sold, or was at least the subject of other inquiries.

He said none of that. What he did say was how sorry he was that it had happened, but now I seemed to have cleared it all up, it was obvious that he had been taken for a ride as much as his clients.

'Except that, unlike you, they're all out of pocket to the tune of five thousand pounds each,' I observed mildly. He didn't even blush.

Cheetham got to his feet and said, 'I appreciate you letting me know all this,' he said.

'They might even have to take the matter to the Law Society. They have indemnity insurance to cover this sort of negligence and malpractice, don't they?'

'But I haven't been negligent,' he protested weakly. 'I told you before, the searches came back clear. And the letters from Harris's solicitor assured me that although he'd had other inquiries, no one else was in a position to pursue a possible purchase at that point in time. How was I to know the letters were fakes?'

'It's a pity you solicitors always have to put everything in writing,' I said. 'Just one phone call to the so-called Mr Graves' office would have stopped this business stone dead.'

'What do you mean?' he asked hesitantly.

'The number on the letterhead is the number of a pay phone in a pub in Ramsbottom. But I suppose you didn't know that either,' I said.

He sat down again in a hurry. 'Of course I didn't,' he said. He was as convincing as a cabinet minister.

'There was one other thing,' I said. I'd rattled his cage. Now it was time for a bluff. 'When I was here the other day, I saw a guy come into your office after me. I had some other business in the building, and when I left, I saw him getting into his van. Some company called Renovations, or something like that? Looked a bit like your friend from Buxton, which, of course, is why I thought *he* was a builder.'

Cheetham's eyes widened, though he kept the rest of his face under control. Clearly, he was one of those people whose eyes really are the windows of the soul. 'What about him?' he asked nervously.

'Well, my boyfriend and I have just bought an old house out in Heaton Chapel, and it needs a lot of work doing, and I noticed the van had a Stockport number on the side. I wondered if they specialized in that kind of job and, if they did, maybe you could give me their number? I tried Yellow Pages, but I couldn't find them,' I said.

Cheetham's mouth opened and closed. 'I ... er ... I don't think they'd be what you're looking for,' he gabbled. 'No, not for your problem at all. Old barns, that's what they do. Conversions, that sort of thing. Sorry, I ... er ... Sorry.'

Satisfied that I'd put the cat among the pigeons, as well as establishing Cheetham's guilt firmly in my own mind, I gave him a regretful smile and said, 'Oh well, when we do buy ourselves an old barn, I'll know where to come. Thanks for your time, Mr Cheetham.'

An hour later, I was lurking behind a fruit and veg stall in the indoor market at Stockport. The bright autumn sunlight poured in through the high windows of this recently restored cathedral to commerce. It illuminated a fascinating scene. Across the crowded aisles of the market, in a little café, Martin Cheetham was in earnest conversation with none other than Brian Lomax, alias T.R. Harris.

Now I knew all I needed to know. All that remained was some proof.

16

I bought a couple of Russet apples and half a pound of grapes from the fruit and veg stall to keep my mouth occupied while I watched Cheetham and Lomax talk. Cheetham appeared to be both worried and angry, while Lomax seemed not so much tense as impatient. Cheetham was doing most of the talking, with Lomax nodding or shaking his head in response as he munched his way through a couple of barm cakes and a bowl of chips. Eventually, Lomax wiped his mouth with the back of his hand, leaned across the table and spoke earnestly to Cheetham.

There are times when I wish I'd learned to lip read. Or to predict the future. That way, I'd have been able to plant a radio mike under the table in advance. As it was, I was stuck in my less than blissful ignorance. All I could do was keep on Martin Cheetham's tail as he left the café and pushed his way through the shopping crowds back to the supermarket car park where he'd left his black BMW. A black BMW which I'd last seen parked outside Brian Lomax's house on Saturday night.

It wasn't hard to keep tabs on him. He drove back to Manchester like a man who's preoccupied with something other than the road and traffic conditions. Expecting him to go straight back to his office, I hung back a little as we neared the city centre, and that's when I almost lost him. At the bottom of Fennel Street, instead of turning left towards the Blackfriars car park where he'd been parked that morning, he turned right. I was three cars behind him, and I barely made it to the junction in time to see him turn left by the railway arches, heading for the East Lancs road. 'Oh, shit,' I groaned, stamping on the accelerator and skidding across four lanes of traffic in his wake. The Little Rascal really wasn't my vehicle of choice for a car chase. I only hoped the cacophony of horns wouldn't penetrate Cheetham's apparent reverie.

He wasn't in sight when I got to the next set of lights. I had to gamble that he'd gone straight on, out past Salford Cathedral and the university, past the museum with its matchstick men Lowrys, as reproduced on a thousand middle-class walls. I stayed in the middle lane, on the alert for a glimpse of his gleaming black bodywork. I was beginning to sweat by the time I passed the grimy monolith of Salford Tech. It looked like I'd lost him. But I stuck with it, and two miles down the East Lancs I spotted him up ahead, turning left at the next lights.

By the time I hit the lights, they'd just turned red, something I chose to ignore, to the horror of the woman whose Volvo I cut across as I swept round the corner. I gave her a cheery wave, then put my foot down. I picked Cheetham up a quarter of a mile down the road. He turned right, then second left into Tamarind Grove, a quiet street of between-the-wars semis, not unlike Alexis and Chris's. The BMW swung into the drive of a trim example of the type about halfway down on the left.

I drew up sharply in the little red van, keeping my engine running in case he was merely dropping something off or picking someone up. Cheetham got out of the car, locking it carefully behind him and setting the alarm, then let himself in the front door with a key. I drove slowly past the house and parked. I stationed myself by the rear door, keeping watch through the one-way glass of the window. I wasn't even sure why I was doing it. This had started off as a search for hard evidence of what Cheetham and Lomax had done to my friends. But I couldn't help feeling there was a lot more going on. What was Renew-Vations up to that sent Cheetham running down the road like a scalded cat to front up his partner in crime? And what was happening now? I have the kind of natural curiosity that hates to give in till the last stone is turned over and the last creepy-crawly firmly ground into the dirt. I kept coming back to the thought that whatever was going down here, Cheetham was the key. He knew I was poking my nose into his business. And Cheetham's partner in crime drove a white Transit van. Admittedly, the van in his drive at the weekend had been unscathed, but I figured it was a strong possibility that his business ran to more than one van.

If there's a more boring job than staking-out someone who's enjoying the comforts of their own home, I've yet to discover it. To relieve the monotony, I used my new toy to call the Central Reference Library and asked them to check the electoral roll for this address. Cheetham was the only person listed. Then I rang Richard to tell him my new number. This week, his answering machine featured him rapping over a hectic backing track, 'Hi, it's Richard here, sorry, but I'm out, leave your name and number and I'll give you a shout.' At least it was an improvement on the throaty, sensuous one he'd had running the month before. I mean, you don't expect to find yourself in the middle of a dirty phone call when it's you who's done the dialling, do you?

Then I settled down to listen to the play on Radio 4. Inevitably, five minutes before the denouement, things started happening. A white convertible Golf GTi pulled up outside Cheetham's house. A brown court shoe appeared round the driver's door, followed by an elegant leg. The woman Cheetham had called Nell emerged, wearing a Burberry. Her choice of car came as no surprise, though I've never understood the fascination the Golf convertible holds for supposedly classy women. It looks like a pram to me, especially with the top down.

Nell followed Cheetham's path to the door, and also let herself in with a key. Then, about twenty minutes later, a white Transit van turned into the street and parked a couple of doors away from Cheetham's house. Lomax got out, wearing a set of overalls like a garage mechanic, a knitted cap covering his wavy brown hair. He didn't give my van a second glance as he marched straight up to Cheetham's front door and pressed the bell. He only had moments to wait before the door opened to admit him. From where I was parked, I couldn't actually see who opened the door, but I assumed it was Cheetham.

I thought about sneaking round the back of the house to see if there was any way of hearing or seeing what was going on, but it was way too risky to be anything other than one of those tantalizing fantasies. So I waited. The plot was thickening, and I was powerless to do anything about it.

I phoned the office, on the off-chance that Bill would have some emergency that required me to abandon my boring vigil. No such luck. So I baited Shelley about Ted Barlow. 'Has he asked you out, then?'

'I don't know what you mean,' she said huffily. 'He's just a client. Why should he ask me out?'

'You'll never make a detective if you're that unobservant,' I teased. 'So are you seeing him again? Apart from in reception?'

'He's coming round about a conservatory,' she admitted.

'Wow!' I exclaimed. 'Terrific! You be careful now, Shelley. This could be the most expensive date you've ever had. I mean, they don't come cheap, these conservatories. You could just ask him to Sunday dinner, you know, you don't actually have to let him sell you enough glass to double glaze the town hall.'

'Do you realize your feeble attempts to wind me up are costing the firm 25p a minute? Get off the phone, Kate, unless you've got something useful to say,' Shelley said firmly. 'Oh, and by the way, the garage rang to say your Nova is definitely a write-off. I've phoned the insurance company and the assessor's coming to look at it tomorrow.'

For some reason, the thought of a new car didn't excite me as much as it should have done. I thanked Shelley, pressed the 'end' button on the phone and settled down gloomily to watch Cheetham's house. About an hour after he arrived, Lomax appeared on the doorstep, struggling with a large cardboard box which appeared to be full of document wallets and loose papers. He loaded them into his van, then drove off. I decided it was more important, or at least more interesting, to follow Lomax and the papers than to continue watching the outside of a house.

I waited till he rounded the corner before I set off in pursuit. The height of his van made it easy for me to keep him in sight as he threaded his way through the afternoon traffic. We headed down through Swinton and cut across to Eccles. Lomax turned into a street of down-at-heel terraced houses and stopped in front of one whose ground floor windows were boarded up.

Lomax unlocked the door, then returned for the bulky box. He slammed the door behind him and left me sitting watching the outside of a different house.

I gave it half an hour then decided I wasn't getting anywhere. I decided to swing round via Cheetham's house to see if anything was happening, then head back to my other stake-out to see if the tapes were running with anything interesting. As I turned into the street that Cheetham's road led off, I nearly collided with a Peugeot in too much of a hurry. To my astonishment, I realized as I passed that it was Alexis. Unaccustomed to seeing me driving the van instead of my usual car, she obviously hadn't noticed the driver she'd nearly hit was me. I hoped she hadn't been round at Cheetham's house, giving him a piece of her mind. That was the last thing I needed right now.

More likely, she was hot on the trail of some tale to titillate her readers. There was nothing unusual in her driving as though she were the only person on the road. Like most journos, she operates on the principle that the hideous road accidents they've all reported only ever happen to other people.

The Golf had gone from outside the house in Tamarind Grove. Cheetham's BMW was still sitting outside the garage, but there were no lights on in the house, though it was dark enough outside for the street lights to be glowing orange. Chances were Cheetham had been driven off somewhere by the lovely Nell. Which meant there was probably no one home.

To make doubly sure, I got his number from Directory Enquiries. The phone rang four times, then the answering machine cut in. 'I'm sorry, I can't take your call right now ...' And all the rest. It wasn't proof positive that the house was unoccupied, but I figured Cheetham was too stressed out just now to ignore his phone.

I couldn't resist it. Within minutes, I'd changed from my business clothes into a jogging suit and Reeboks from the holdall I'd removed from my wrecked Nova. I added a thin pair of latex gloves, just in case. Out of my handbag, I took my Swiss Army knife, my powerful pocket torch, an out-of-date credit card, a set of jeweller's tools that double as lock-picks, and a miniature camera. All the things a girl should never be without. Checking the street was empty, I slipped out of the van and down the flagged path that ran by the side of Martin Cheetham's house. Fortunately, although the bell box on the front of the house indicated he had a burglar alarm, he hadn't invested in infra-red activated security lights, as recommended by Mortensen and Brannigan.

The back garden was enclosed by a seven foot fence, and the gloom was compounded by thick shrubs that cast strange shadows across a paved area which featured the inevitable brick-built barbecue. There was no sign of light through the pair of patio doors that led into the garden so I cautiously turned on my torch. I peered in at a dining room with a strangely old-fashioned air.

I switched the torch off and moved cautiously across the patio to the kitchen door. It was the solid, heavy door of someone who takes their security precautions seriously. So I was rather surprised to see the top section of the kitchen window ajar. I carried on past the door and glanced up at the window. It was open a couple of notches, and although it was too small to allow anyone to enter, it offered possibilities.

I shone my torch through the window, revealing an unadventurous pine kitchen, cluttered with appliances, a bowl of fruit, a rack of vegetables, a draining board full of dry dishes, a shelf of cookery books, a knife block and an assortment of jars and bottles. It looked more like a table at a car boot sale than a kitchen.

The door leading from the kitchen to the hall was ajar, and I shifted slightly to let the beam from my torch play across the room. Caught between the beam of my torch and the gleam of the street light out front, I could see the body of a woman twisting slowly round and round, round and round.

17

Next thing I knew, I was crouched down on the patio, my back pressed against the wall so hard I could feel the texture of the brickwork against my scalp. I didn't know how I'd got there. My torch was turned off, but the sight of the dangling corpse still filled my vision. I squeezed my eyes closed, but the image of the body hanging in mid-air was still vividly there. It sounds callous, but I felt outraged. I don't do bodies. I do industrial espionage, fraud and white-collar theft. The desire to curl up in a tight little ball was almost overwhelming. I knew I ought to get the hell out of there and call the police, but I couldn't get my limbs to move.

It looked like an open and shut case. The woman called Nell had arrived earlier in the afternoon; now there was a woman's corpse in the house, and her car was missing. What it meant to me was that Cheetham would be facing a murder charge rather than one of fraud. Either way, he wouldn't be practising as a solicitor again in a hurry. But Lomax, on the other hand, would almost certainly live to defraud another day. All he had to do was deny everything and blame it all on Cheetham.

I struggled to my feet. I wished Richard was with me. Not because he'd be any practical use, but because he'd be talking me out of what I was about to do. I knew it was crazy, knew I was taking the kind of stupid chance that Bill would seriously fall out with me over. But I'd come this far, and I couldn't stop now. If there was any proof of what had been going on, I wanted to have a good look at it before the police sequestrated it. As Richard has pointed out on several occasions, I subscribe to the irregular verb theory of language; I am a trained investigator, you have a healthy curiosity, she/he is a nosy-parker.

I took a deep breath and studied the kitchen window, carefully averting my eyes from the doorway leading into the hall. If I could get up to it, I thought I might be able to reach through the open window and slip open the catch on the side section, which would be big enough to let me climb in. Unfortunately, the sill wasn't wide enough to stand on, and there was no conveniently placed ladder. The only things that were remotely portable were the carefully arranged bricks of the circular barbecue. They weren't mortared together, merely assembled like a child's building bricks.

With a sigh, I started shifting the bricks to build a platform beneath the window. I was grateful for the latex gloves; without them, my hands would have been in shreds. It didn't take long to construct a makeshift set of steps that brought me high enough to slide my arm inside the unfastened window. My fingertips could barely brush the top of the window catch. I withdrew and opened the blade of my Swiss Army knife that looks as if its only purpose is to remove Boy Scouts from horses' hoofs. It has a sort of hooked bit on the end and almost certainly has some quaint name like 'cordwangler's grommet disengager'.

With the blade extended, I was able to flick the catch upwards. I pushed the window towards me, and it swung open. I stepped into the kitchen sink and closed both windows behind me. I searched the draining board for a cloth then carefully wiped the sill and the sink to remove any obvious traces of my entry. The last thing I wanted was to be lifted for murder. What I was really doing was putting off the moment when I'd have to confront Nell's dangling body. She must be suspended from the banister, I realized as I braced myself to go through the doorway.

I emerged into the hall, gritted my teeth and switched on my torch. The body was still twisting languorously in some faint draught. Steeling myself, I started at the floor and worked upwards. A brown court shoe like the one I'd seen emerging from the Golf a couple of hours ago lay on its side on the plain oatmeal Berber carpet, as if it had been idly kicked off. Its partner was on the left foot of the body. The ankles were lashed together with an incongruous Liberty silk scarf. The scarf was tied in a slip knot that had tightened to cut into the flesh above the ankle bones. She wore sheer dark-tan stockings. They looked like silk to me. I caught a glimpse of suspenders under the full, swirling skirt. I couldn't see the underwear. The smell made me glad of that. My eyes travelled upwards, over a silk tunic cinched in at the waist by a woven leather belt with gilt studs, like a stylized leather queen's. The shapely legs were bent at the knees, held in place by another scarf that was tied to the belt.

The wrists were tied together in front of the body with another scarf, clasped like an innocent Doris Day in a nineteen-fifties film. Again, a slip knot had been used. It looked like a bizarre sexual fantasy, the stuff of snuff movies. I tried not to look too closely at the ligature, but it was obvious that the woman had been hanged by a rope of silk scarves. I closed my eyes, swallowed hard and made myself look at the face.

It wasn't Nell.

Not by any stretch of the imagination was that swollen, engorged face the same one I'd seen in Buxton and later in Cheetham's office. From below, it was hard to say more than that, but the hair looked strangely asymmetrical. The one ear I could see was an ominous bluish purple, and the skin of the face was an odd colour. Horrified but oddly fascinated, I skirted the body to climb the stairs for a better vantage point. Five steps from the top of the flight, I was almost level with the staring eyes. Dots of blood peppered the whites of the eyes. I tried not to think of this as a human being, but simply as a piece of evidence. Close to, it was clear that the brown hair was a wig. What was also clear, in spite of the hideous distortion of the features and the heavy make-up, was the identity of the corpse. That was when I lost it.

I splashed cold water over my face, drawing my breath in sharply as it hit. I dried myself on toilet paper, then flushed it down the loo. Then I flushed the loo again, the sixth time since I'd lost my lunch. Just because you're paranoid doesn't mean the forensic scientists aren't out to get you. I gave the toilet bowl a last wipe down, then flushed again, praying the U-bend was now free from any traces of my reaction to discovering Martin Cheetham hanging from a banister dressed in women's clothing.

I closed the toilet lid and sat down on it. It was only my second corpse ever, and the discovery seemed to be taking a bit of getting used to. The voice of wisdom and self-preservation was telling me to get out of there as fast as possible and wait till I was in another county before calling the police. The bloody-minded voice from the other side of my brain reminded me that I'd never get another chance like this to get to the bottom of whatever had brought matters to this pass. I couldn't believe Cheetham had killed himself because he thought I'd uncovered his dishonesty in the land sale. There had to be more.

I forced myself out of the bathroom and back on to the landing. 'It's not a person,' I kept saying out loud to myself, as if that could convince me. I stood on the landing, above the banister where Cheetham's body was suspended by the rope of silk scarves. From here, it didn't look quite so terrible, though at this angle I could see what had been obscured from below, that he had an erection. I forced myself to reach down and touch the skin of the face. There was no perceptible difference in temperature between my hand and the corpse. I didn't know enough about forensic medicine to understand the significance of that.

I turned my back on the body and started my search. The first room I entered was obviously the spare room. It was lit dimly by the glow of the street lamps. The room was clean and neat, but again, curiously old fashioned, like a room in my parents' house. The wardrobe was empty except for a white tuxedo, dress trousers and a couple of frilly evening shirts. The chest of drawers was empty except for towels in the bottom drawer. On the off-chance, I lifted an insipid watercolour of the Lake District away from the wall. I couldn't think of any reason for keeping it except to obscure a safe. No such luck.

The next bedroom appeared more promising. It overlooked the garden, so I took the risk of drawing the heavy, floor-length chintz drapes and switching on the light. Mirrored wardrobes the length of the far wall doubled the apparent size of the room. A king-size bed dominated the other wall. The plain green duvet cover looked rumpled, as if someone had been lying on it. On the floor by the bed, a magazine lay open. I crouched down and studied it, gingerly turning the pages. It was sado-masochistic pornography of the kind that makes me feel like joining Mary Whitehouse and the Moral Majority. The key pages came just before the one that lay open on the floor. They featured an illustrated story about a man who got his satisfaction from pretending to hang himself.

As I crouched there, feeling soiled just looking at the porn, by a strange contrast I noticed the bed linen still smelled fresh and clean. I looked carefully at the pillows, then moved round the bed to the undisturbed side, where I lifted the duvet: no stray hairs, no wrinkles in the sheet, no depression in the pillows. I may not have had much experience of suicides, but I couldn't see someone changing the bedding before they topped themselves. On a hunch, I walked across the room to the wicker linen basket. It contained two shirts, two pairs of socks, two pairs of boxer shorts and a bath towel. But no sheets, pillow cases or duvet cover. Curiouser and curiouser.

I started on the wardrobes. The first revealed half a dozen business suits and a couple of dozen shirts, all from Marks & Spencer. A shoe rack along the bottom held a mixture of formal and casual footwear. A tie rack was fixed to the inside of the door, revealing a taste in ties as exotic as an undertaker's. The next section contained leisure wear – polo shirts, rugby shirts, jeans, all carefully pressed and hung. The next unit disguised a tower of drawers. T-shirts, underwear, socks, sweaters, jogging pants, all neatly folded in piles.

The last two sections appeared to be a double wardrobe, and it was locked. The lock was different from the flimsy ones on the other doors and their keys didn't fit. I wondered where Cheetham's key ring was, and doubled back to the drawer in the bedside table. It held a wallet and a bunch of keys, but not the key to the wardrobe. Oh joy, oh rapture. There was nothing else for it. I'd have to try picking the lock, and be careful not to leave it looking like someone had had a go at it.

I took out the slender tools and gently began to probe the inside of the lock with a narrow, flexible strip of metal. Just the thought of picking the lock had my hands sweating inside the thin gloves. I started to poke about in what I hoped was a reasonable approximation of what my friend Dennis had taught me. After a few minutes that felt like hours, my probe met the kind of resistance that shows a bit of give. Praying the strip I was using was strong enough, I twisted it. There was a click, and the doors slowly opened out towards me.

I could see why Martin Cheetham didn't want any casual snoopers to open them. It was the last thing you'd expect to find in a conveyancing specialist's wardrobe. There were a dozen chic outfits on hangers, each covered with a transparent plastic sheath. They ranged from a cocktail dress with a froth of multicoloured tulle and sequins to an elegant business suit with pencil skirt. There was also a mac and a camel wraparound coat. On a rack on the door was an exotic collection of silk scarves ranging from Hermès to hippie-style Indian. A chest of drawers occupied the lower section of half the wardrobe. The top drawer was filled with an astonishing and luxurious collection of ladies' underwear in both silk and leather. Believe me, I mean 'ladies'. The second drawer contained an assortment of foam and silica gel prostheses, which I managed to sort into three categories; breasts, hips and buttocks. It also held more make-up than I've ever possessed, even as an experimenting teenager, and a selection of false nails.

The lower drawers were filled with a bizarre assortment of straps, clamps and unidentifiable bits of leather with buckles and studs. I didn't even want to start imagining how they all fitted into the strange world of Martin Cheetham's sexual life. There were also a couple of vibrators, one so large it made my eyes water just to look at it. There were, however, no more magazines like the one by the bed. I slammed the drawers shut and concentrated on the less threatening contents of the wardrobe. Along the bottom was a shelf of shoes and matching handbags. They alone must have cost the best part of a couple of grand.

I picked up the first handbag, a soft black Italian leather satchel that Alexis would have killed for. The stray thought brought me up with a jolt. Alexis! I'd completely forgotten our close encounter at the end of the road! She couldn't have anything to do with all this. I knew she couldn't, yet the little traitor voice in my head kept saying, 'You don't know that. She might just have tipped him over the edge.' I shook my head vigorously, like a dog emerging from a river, and carried on with my search.

The third bedroom, little more than a boxroom, had been fitted out as an office, with a battered old filing cabinet, a tatty wooden desk and a very basic PC, compatible with the one in his office so he could presumably bring stuff home. A quick search revealed where Lomax had got his documents from. Three of the four drawers in the filing cabinet were empty. The fourth held only a couple of box files filled with what appeared to be personal receipts, credit card bills and the sort of miscellaneous garbage that every householder accumulates. I riffled quickly through the pair of boxes, finding nothing of interest.

The desk had even less to offer. The drawers contained only paper, envelopes and the bizarre mixture of odds and ends that always inhabits at least one drawer in every work space. The interesting thing was what wasn't there. There wasn't a single floppy disc in the place, a serious omission given that the computer in Cheetham's home office had no hard disc drive. In other words, the computer itself had no permanent memory. Every time it was switched on, it was like a blank sheet of paper. If Lomax had cleared the discs out, I suspected it had been done without Cheetham's permission or co-operation, for if he'd been trying to get rid of incriminating material, there was no reason on earth why he'd also feel the need to dump the software programs that were necessary to make the computer work.

Musing on this, I finished my search of the office and moved downstairs, trying to avoid looking at the body. As I entered the living room, I checked my watch. I'd been in the house just under an hour. I really couldn't afford to hang around much longer. All it needed was for Nell or Lomax to come back and find me here.

As it happened, it didn't take long for me to complete my search, ending up in the kitchen, where, incidentally, neither the washing machine nor the tumble drier contained bedding. The most useful thing I'd found was a spare set of keys in the cutlery drawer. As I let myself out of the back door, I felt an enormous sense of anti-climax. The tension that had been holding me together suddenly dissipated and I felt weak at the knees. Somehow, I found the strength to replace the bricks in something approximating the right barbecue arrangement, then I sneaked back round the house to the street, checking there was no one in sight before returning to the van. I could only hope that when the neighbours heard about Cheetham's death, none of them would remember any details about the strange van parked a few doors away from his house.

I drove home at a law-abiding speed for once. It was the traffic that was my downfall. I had to pass the Corn Exchange on my way home, and as I drove up Cateaton Street, everything ground to a complete halt. The lights at the bottom of Shude Hill had died, and the resulting rush-hour chaos brought the city centre to a standstill. It seemed like a sign from the gods, so I pulled off the main drag on to Hanging Ditch and parked the van.

Five minutes later, I was inside Martin Cheetham's office.

18

Kate Brannigan's Burglary Tip No. 3: Always burgle offices in daylight hours. People notice lights in offices at night. And people who notice lights in offices that shouldn't be lit up have a nasty habit of being security staff. However, rules are made to be broken, and besides, I wasn't the first unauthorized visitor to Martin Cheetham's office.

That much was obvious from the safe. The reproduction of Monet's *Water Lilies* that had covered it on my previous visit lay on the floor, while the door of the safe stood ajar. With a frustrated sigh, I took a look inside. I found exactly what I expected. Nothing.

I looked round the room in something approaching despair. There was enough paper in here to keep the least popular detective constable on the force busy for a month. Besides, I wasn't convinced that I would find anything enlightening. I was still pinning my hopes on Cheetham's computer files, particularly since he had the kind of scanner that would have allowed him to import a copy of any document straight into his computer. A quick check of the desk revealed the same absence of discs that I'd noted back at the house. But there was one difference here. The PC sitting on the desk had a hard disc. In other words, the chances were that the master copy of the material on the discs that had been stolen was permanently stored in the machine in front of me.

It was last resort time, so I did the obvious. I switched on the machine. It automatically loaded the system files. Then a prompt appeared, demanding input. I asked the machine to show me the headings under which it was storing stuff. In the following list, I spotted a couple of familiar software names – a word-processing package, a spreadsheet and an accounts program. The rest of the list were probably data files. First, I loaded the word processing package which would allow me to read the data files, then I tried a directory called WORK.C. It seemed to be all the correspondence plus details of deeds on the properties currently being handled. The files were subdivided according to whether Cheetham was acting for vendor or buyer, and what stage he was up to. It was incredibly boring.

The next directory I tried was called WORK.L. When I attempted to access it, nothing happened. I tried again and nothing happened. I tried one or two other ways of getting into the directory, but there was clearly some kind of access block on it. Desperately, I searched Cheetham's drawers again, looking for a single word scribbled somewhere that might be a password for the directory, but without success. I knew that, given time, Bill or I could hack our way into the hidden files of the locked directory, but time was the one thing I wasn't sure I had.

What the hell? I'd taken so many chances already, what was one more? Closing the door on the latch behind me, I left Cheetham's office and returned to the van. I unlocked the security box welded to the floor and took out our office laptop PC. It's a portable machine, more compatible with its desktop equivalents than any married couple I know. It can store the equivalent of sixty novels. I walked back into the Corn Exchange with the fat briefcase, trying hard to look nonchalant, and returned undetected to Cheetham's office by some miracle.

Amongst the resident software on our portable's hard disc was a program that could have been designed for situations like this. It's a special file transfer kit that is used to move data at high speed between portables and desktop machines. I uncoiled the lead that would form the physical link between the two machines and plugged it in at both ends. I switched on my machine and booted up the software.

The program sends over a highly sophisticated communications program, which is then used to 'steal' the files from the target machine. The big advantage of using these kits is that you leave no trace on the machine you've raided. The very process itself also often bypasses any security package that the target PC's operator has installed. The final advantage is that it's extremely fast. Ten minutes after returning to Cheetham's office, I was ready to walk out of the door with the contents of WORK.C and WORK.L firmly ensconced on my own hard disc.

There were just a couple of things I had to do first. I picked up the phone and dialled my favourite Chinese restaurant for a takeaway. Then I called Greater Manchester Police's switchboard. I calmly told the operator who answered that there was a dead body at 27 Tamarind Grove, and hung up.

The traffic had begun to clear, and I picked up my Chinese fifteen minutes later. I'd just parked the van on the drive of my bungalow when I remembered I hadn't checked the tapes from the surveillance. I had two choices. Either I could go indoors and eat my Chinese, preferably with Richard, then, once I'd got all comfy and relaxed, I could schlep all the way over to Stockport and do the business. Or I could go now, and hope that there was nothing that would require my presence there all night. Being what Richard would describe as a boring old fart, I decided to finish the day's work before I settled down. Besides, my bruises were aching, and I knew that if I sank into the comfort of my own sofa, I might never get up again unless it was to crawl into a hot bath.

The drive to Stockport was the Chinese aroma torture. There's nothing worse than the smell of hot and sour soup and salt and pepper ribs when nothing's stayed in your stomach since breakfast and you can't have them. What made it even more frustrating was that there was no one home in my nice little staked-out semi. And, according to my bug, no one had been home either. The phone had rung another couple of times, and that was the sum total of my illegal surveillance.

When I finally got home, the offer of a share in my Chinese distracted Richard from a pirate radio bhangra station he'd been listening to in the course of duty. Sometimes I think his job's even worse than mine. I brought him up to date with my adventures, which added a spice to dinner that even the Chinese had never thought of.

'So he topped himself, then? Or was it one of those sleazy

deaths by sexual misadventure?' he asked, doing his impersonation of a tabloid journo as he poked through the *char siu*
pork to get at the bean sprouts below.

'It looks like it. But I don't think he did,' I said.

'Why's that, Supersleuth?'

'A collection of little things that individually are insignificant, but taken together make me feel very uneasy,' I replied.

'Want to run it past me? See if it's just your imagination?'
Richard offered. I knew he really meant: because you're too
well brought up to talk with your mouth full, that means there
will be more for me. I gave in gracefully, because he was quite
right, I did want to check that my suspicions had some genuine
foundation.

'OK,' I said. 'Point one. I take Nell to be Martin Cheetham's
girlfriend, judging by the body language on the two occasions
I saw them together. She was in the house for about twenty
minutes, thirty max, before Lomax arrived. Now if she and
Cheetham were getting it on together, that might explain why
he was in his drag. But if they were busy having a little loving,
what was going down with Lomax and the files?'

'Maybe he just sneaked in and helped himself,' Richard suggested.

'No, he didn't have a key. Someone let him in, but I couldn't
see who. I'm convinced Lomax cleared the files out, without
Cheetham's co-operation.'

'Why?' Richard asked.

'Because if Cheetham had simply been trying to get incriminating evidence off the premises, he'd only have dumped
discs with data on. He wouldn't have ditched the discs with
the software programs, because he'd have known enough to
realize that a computer with no discs at all is a hell of a lot
more suspicious than one with only software and no data,' I
explained. Richard nodded in agreement.

'Also, the bedding was clean. It had been changed since the
last time the bed had been slept in or bonked on. And there
was no bedding in the linen basket or the washing machine or
the tumble drier either. So where are the dirty sheets? Now if
Cheetham and Nell had been having a cuddle, or whatever it

is that transvestite sado-masochists do in bed, there would
be forensic traces of her on the bedding. These days, every
television viewer knows about things like that. So if she and
Lomax had actually killed Cheetham and wanted to make it
look like an accidental death during some bizarre sexual
fantasy, they'd have to make it look like he'd been alone with
his dirty magazine. And that's the only explanation I can find.'

'Maybe he's got a cleaner who comes in and takes his
washing home with her,' Richard suggested, sharing his own
fantasy.

'Maybe, but I don't think so. The linen basket in the bedroom
had dirty clothes in it. Then there's another point about the
computers. Whoever cleared out the office safe and took the
discs from there, it wasn't Cheetham himself.'

'What makes you say that?' Richard asked. 'I mean, if he was
starting to get a bit unnerved by you poking around, wouldn't
he try to get rid of anything incriminating?'

'You'd think so. But it was his computer. Whoever did the
clearing up of evidence, it was someone who didn't understand
that the discs were just the back-up copies of whatever was on
the hard disc. They didn't understand about the hard disc,
because they left the data on it.'

Richard shook his head. 'I don't know, Brannigan. It's all a
bit thin. I mean, ever since you solved Moira's murder back in
the spring, you keep seeing suspicious deaths everywhere.
Look at the way you got all wound up about that client who
died after he changed his will, and it turned out he'd had a
heart condition for years, nothing iffy about it.'

'But this is suspicious, even you've got to admit that,' I
protested.

'I could give you an explanation that would cover the facts,'
Richard said, helping himself to the last of the prawn wontons.

'Go on then,' I challenged, convinced I could unravel any
theory his twisted mind could come up with.

Richard swallowed his mouthful, leaned back in his seat and
polished his glasses in a parody of the learned academics who
pontificate on TV. 'OK. He's had this showdown with you then
he's rushed off to meet Lomax. As a result of all this, he's really

wound up, but he thinks he's handled it beautifully and he deserves a treat. So he arranges that what's-her-name, the girl-friend, is going to come around for a bit of afternoon delight. Now, from what you've told me about his little treasure trove, who knows what that pair get up to when they're getting their rocks off? Just supposing he's staged this tableau to get her going – he's all done up in his drag and tied up and pretending to hang himself when she arrives. Only it gets out of hand and he snuffs it. OK so far?'

I nodded, reluctantly. Certainly, Cheetham had had enough time alone in the house for that scenario to be feasible. 'OK,' I sighed.

'So what would your reaction be if you arrived at your boyfriend's house to find him hanging dead from the bani-sters in a frock? Especially if you knew he was into some hooky business that was going to come on top now he's popped his clogs? Remember, for all you know, the lovely lady could be right up to her eyeballs in his little schemes. You'd want to cover your back, wouldn't you?' He gave me that smile of his, the one that got me in this mess in the first place.

'You would indeed,' I conceded.

'So Lomax turns up like a bat out of hell and the pair of them clear out everything that might be remotely connected to Cheetham's little rackets. Lomax takes off with all the incri-minating documents and what's-her-name . . .?' He gave me an inquiring look.

'Nell,' I prompted him.

'Yeah, Little Nell, how could I forget?'

'This is no time for obscene rugby songs,' I said.

'Wrong sport, Brannigan. *You'll Never Walk Alone* is more my speed than *The Ball of Kirriemuir.* Anyway, as you so correctly pointed out, any fool knows these days that forensic science could place Little Nell not just at the scene of the crime but in the bed if they'd bonked in it since the last time the sheets were changed. She does nothing more than take off the dirty linen so she can wash it in private. Meanwhile, Lomax goes down Cheetham's office and clears out the safe and has it away on his toes with the computer discs in the office. Pick the holes in that,' he ended triumphantly.

I thought about it for a moment, then I jumped to my feet. 'Hold everything,' I said on my way through to my spare room, which doubles as study and computer room. I pulled out a book on forensic medicine written for the popular market that Richard had bought me for my birthday as a kind of joke. I ran my finger down the index and turned to the section on body temperature. 'Got it!' I shouted. Richard appeared in the doorway, looking crestfallen. I pointed to the relevant sentence, '"The rule of thumb applied by pathologists is that a clothed body will cool in air at between two and five degrees Fahrenheit per hour", it says here,' I said. 'And, when I touched him, he was the same temperature as I was, near as dammit. No way was he between four and ten degrees colder than me, which he should have been if he'd died when you suggested.'

Richard took the book from me and read the relevant section. As usual, the journalist in him took over and he found all sorts of fascinating things he simply had to read about. Leaving him to it, I started to clear up the debris of dinner. I'd just dumped the tinfoil containers in the bin when he reappeared, brandishing the book with a look of of pure triumph.

'You should have kept reading,' he said sanctimoniously. 'That way, you wouldn't have given me half a tale. Look,' he added, pointing to a paragraph on the following page.

'"Typically, death by asphyxiation raises the body temperature. This must be taken into account in estimates of the time of death, and is known to have caused confusion in some historical cases,"' I read. 'Bollocks,' I said. 'OK, you win,' I sighed. 'I'm letting my imagination run away with me.'

'So you accept my theory?' Richard asked, a look of total disbelief on his face.

'I guess so,' I admitted.

'There's one good thing about it,' he said. 'I mean, I know I've just deprived you of all the excitement of chasing a murderer, but look on the bright side. It puts Alexis in the clear.'

'I never thought for a moment she wasn't in the clear,' I lied frostily.

'Course you didn't,' Richard said, with a broad wink. 'Anyway, now I've saved you all the work of a murder hunt, do I get a reward?'

I checked my body out for bruises and stiffness. I was beginning to heal, no doubt about it. I leaned into Richard's warmth and murmured, 'Your place or mine?'

19

The bulging eyes stared fixedly at me, the blue lips twitching some message I could neither hear nor read. I moved back, but the face kept following me. I shouted at it, and the sound of my voice woke me up with the kind of staring-eyed shock that sets the adrenalin racing through the veins. The clock said six, Richard was lying on his stomach, breathing not quite heavily enough to be called snoring, and I was wide awake with Martin Cheetham's face accusing me.

Even if he hadn't been murdered, Nell and Lomax had behaved unforgivably, always supposing there was anyone still around to forgive them. Nell's actions in particular sickened me. I know I couldn't behave like that if someone I'd been lovers with was hanging dead in the hall. There must have been a lot at stake for Nell and Lomax to have had the nerve to carry off their cover-up and, although the voice of reason said it was none of my business, I wanted to get to the bottom of it.

Since I was awake anyway, I decided to do something useful. I slipped out of Richard's bed and cut through the conservatory to my house. A steaming shower banished the morning stiffness that still lingered in my muscles, and a strong cup of coffee kick-started my brain. I chose a pair of bottle green trousers and a matching sweater to go under the russet padded silk blouson that I'd picked up for a song on Strangeways market.

It was a quarter to seven when I parked outside Alexis's house. As I'd expected, her car was still in the drive. I knew her routine of old. Up at six, in the bath with a pot of coffee, the phone and her notebook at five past. Morning calls to the cops, then out of the bath at half past. Then toast and the tabloids. I estimated she'd be finishing her second slice of toast about now. Unfortunately, she wouldn't be in the office at seven *this* morning.

I looked through the kitchen window as I knocked on the door. Alexis dropped her toast at the sound of the knock. I waved and grinned at her. With a look of resignation, she opened the door.

'I have a question for you,' I announced.

'Come in, why don't you?' Alexis said as I walked across the kitchen and switched the kettle on.

'When you left Tamarind Grove yesterday afternoon, did you already know that Martin Cheetham was dead?' I asked conversationally, spooning coffee into a mug.

Alexis's face froze momentarily. Always pale, she seemed to go sheet white. 'How the hell did you know about that?' she asked intensely. If she used that tone of voice professionally, she'd get all sorts of confessions she wasn't looking for.

'I don't suppose you remember a red Little Rascal van that you nearly drove into, but that was me. I remember it particularly because for a brief moment, I wondered what Bill would say if I wrote off a second company vehicle inside a week,' I said, trying to lighten the atmosphere a bit.

'I might have known,' Alexis sighed. 'If you're brewing up, I'll have another cup.'

I made the coffees and said, 'I'm listening.'

Alexis lit a cigarette and took a couple of deep drags before she spoke. I sometimes think it must be lovely to have an instant trank permanently to hand. Then I think about my lungs.

'I'd had a couple of drinks at lunchtime. I wasn't pissed, just a bit belligerent. So I bought a can of spray paint. I was going to spray some rude graffiti on Cheetham's house,' she said, looking as embarrassed as she must have felt. 'Anyway, I got there and there was his car in the drive. I thought about spraying "You dirty rat" on the bonnet, then I realized if he was home I might as well give him a piece of my mind. So I rang the doorbell. There was no reply, so I looked through the letter box. And I saw these feet, legs, just dangling there.'

'Tell me about it,' I said with feeling, remembering my own experience.

'So I took off like a bat out of hell,' Alexis said, dropping her head so that her haystack of unruly black hair hid her face.

'You didn't phone the cops?' I asked.

'How could I? I didn't have any legit reason for being there. I didn't even know who the body was. And I couldn't have done it anonymously, could I? Half the cops in Manchester know who it is on the phone the minute I open my gob.'

She was right. Anyone who'd ever spoken to Alexis would remember that smoky Liverpudlian voice.

'I'm sorry,' I said. 'I should have rung you about it last night. I was just too wiped out. So, when did you realize it was Cheetham?'

'When I did my calls this morning. They told me about it as a routine non-suspicious death. If he hadn't been a solicitor, I doubt they'd even have mentioned it. It made my stomach turn over, I can tell you.'

'Any details?' I asked.

'Not a lot. Unattributed, I got that he was wearing women's clothing and playing bondage games. According to the DI at the scene, he had a proper little torture chamber in his wardrobe. They reckon he died sometime yesterday afternoon. He didn't have any form for sexual offences. Not so much as a caution. He's not even on their list of people they know get up to naughties in their spare time. They don't think there was anyone else involved, and they're not treating it as a suspicious death. They don't even think it was suicide, just an accident. All I can say is thank God he didn't have nosy neighbours, or else the lads might be asking me what exactly I was doing kicking his door in yesterday afternoon.' Alexis managed a faint smile. 'Especially if they knew I had a private eye working on how to recover the five grand he helped to con me out of.'

'You weren't the only person who was there yesterday,' I said, and went on to fill her in on the events of the afternoon. 'I was convinced they'd killed him,' I added. 'But Richard persuaded me that I was just seeing dragons in the flames.'

'So what happens now?' Alexis asked.

'Well, theoretically, we could just ignore the whole thing, and

I could still follow Lomax like you asked me to and try to get some money back from him. The problem is that now Cheetham's dead, I'm afraid Lomax might try to deny any criminal involvement in the whole thing and blame it all on Cheetham.'

'You don't really think he'd get away with that, do you?' Alexis demanded, lighting up another cigarette.

'I don't honestly know,' I admitted. 'Personally, I think there's been a lot more going down between Lomax and Cheetham than we know about. And if there's any proof of a connection other than the fact that I know I've seen them together, it could be buried in the other stuff. So I want to keep digging.'

Alexis nodded. 'So how can I help?'

There are parts of Greater Manchester where it wouldn't be too big a shock to encounter a shop catering for the needs of transsexuals and transvestites. A back street in Oldham isn't one of them. I find it hard to imagine anyone in Oldham doing anything more sexually radical than the missionary position, which only goes to show what a limited imagination I have. The locals clearly didn't have a problem with Trances, since there was nothing discreet about the shopfront, sandwiched rather unfortunately as it was between a butcher's and a junk shop.

On the way over, Alexis had told me about the shop and its owner. Cassandra Cliff had endured a brief spell of notoriety in the gutter press a few years previously when some muck-raking journo had discovered that the actress who was one of the regulars in the country's favourite soap opera was in fact a male-to-female transsexual. In the flurry of 'Sex Swap Soap Star' stories that followed, it emerged that Cassandra, pre-viously Kevin, had been living as a woman for a dozen years, and that no one among cast or production team had a clue that she wasn't biologically of the same gender as the gossipy chip-shop owner she played. Of course, the production company of *Northerners* denied that the uncovering of Cassandra's secret would make any difference whatsoever to their attitude to her.

Two months later, Cassandra's character perished in a tragic accident when the extension her husband was building to their terraced house collapsed on her. The production company blandly denied they had dumped her because of her sex change, but that didn't much help Cassandra, on the scrap heap at thirty-seven. 'She didn't let them get away with it,' Alexis said. 'She sold her own inside story to one of the Sunday tabloids, dishing the dirt on all the nation's idols. Then with the money she set up Trances, and a monthly magazine for transvestites and transsexuals. She's got so much bottle, Kate. You can't help respecting Cassie.'

Alexis skirted the one-way system and cut round the back of the magistrates' court. Modern concrete boxes and grimy red brick terraced shops were mixed higgledy-piggledy along almost every street, a seemingly random and grotesque assortment that filled me with the desire to construct a cage in the middle of it and make the town planners live there for a week among the chip papers blowing in the wind and the empty soft-drink cans rattling along the gutters. I tried to ignore the depressing townscape and asked, 'So how come you know her so well? What's she got to do with the crime beat?'

'I interviewed her a couple of times for features when she was still playing Margie Grimshaw in *Northerners*. We got on really well. Then after the dust settled and she set up Trances, I gave her a call and asked if we could do a piece about the shop. She wasn't keen, but I let her have copy approval, and she liked what I wrote. Now, we do lunch about once a month. She's got such a different grapevine from any of my other contacts. It's amazing what she picks up,' Alexis said, parking in a quiet side street of terraced houses. It could have been the set for *Northerners*.

'And she passes stuff on to you, does she?' I asked.

'I suspect she's highly selective. I know that after what happened to her, she's desperately protective of other people in the same boat. But if she can help, she will.'

I followed Alexis round the corner into one of those streets that isn't quite part of the town centre, but would like to think it is. I glanced in the window as we entered. The only clue that Trances was any different from a hundred other boutiques was the prominent sign that said, 'We specialize in large sizes. Shoes up to size 12'. The door itself provided the warning for the uninitiated. 'Specialists in supplies for transvestites and transsexuals', was painted on the glass in neat red letters at the eye level of the average woman.

I followed Alexis in. The shop was large, and had an indefinable air of seediness. The décor was cream and pink, the pink tending slightly too far to the candy floss end of the spectrum. The dresses and suits that were suspended from racks that ran the full length of the shop had the cumulative effect of being over the top, both in style and colour. I suspect that the seediness came from the glass cases that lined the wall behind the counter. They contained the kind of prostheses and lingerie I remembered only too well from Martin Cheetham's secret collection. In one corner, there was a rack of magazines. Without examining them too closely, the ones that weren't copies of Cassandra's magazine *Trances* had that combination of garishness and coyness on the cover that marks soft porn.

The person behind the counter was also clearly a client. The size of the hands and the Adam's apple were the giveaways. Apart from that, it would have been hard to tell. The make-up was a little on the heavy side, but I could think of plenty of pubs in the area where that wouldn't even earn a second glance. 'Is Cassie in?' Alexis asked.

The assistant gave a slight frown, sizing us up and clearly wondering if we were tourists. 'Are you a friend of Miss Cliff, madam?' she asked.

'Would you tell her Alexis would like a word, if she's got a few minutes?' Alexis said, responding in the same slightly camp vein. I hoped the conversation with Cassie wasn't going to run along those lines. I can do pompous, I can do threatening, I can even do 'OK, yah', but the one style I can't keep up without exploding into giggles is high camp.

The assistant picked up a phone and pressed an intercom button. 'Cassandra? I have a lady with me called Alexis who would like a moment of your time, if it's convenient,' she said. Then she nodded. 'I'll tell her. Bye for now,' she added. She replaced the handset and said decorously, 'Miss Cliff will see you now. If you'd care to take the door at the back of the shop and follow the stairs ...'

'It's all right, I know the way,' Alexis said, heading past the clothes racks. 'Thanks for your help.'

Cassandra Cliff's office looked like something out of *Interiors*. It could have been a blueprint for the career woman who wants to remind people that as well as being successful she is still feminine. The office furniture – a row of filing cabinets, a low coffee table and two desks, one complete with Apple Mac – was limed ash, stained grey. A pair of grey leather two-seater sofas occupied one corner. The carpet was a dusty pink, a colour echoed in the Austrian blinds that softened the lines of the room. The walls were decorated with black and white stills of the set and stars of *Northerners*. A tall vase of burgundy carnations provided a vivid splash of colour. The overall effect was stylish and relaxed, the two adjectives that sprang into my mind when I first met Cassandra Cliff.

She wore a linen suit with a straight skirt and no lapels. It was the colour of an egg yolk. Her mandarin-collared blouse was a bright, clear sapphire blue. I know it sounds hideous, but on her it was glorious. Her ash blonde hair was cut short but full on top, shaped, gelled and lacquered till it resembled something out of the Museum of Modern Art. The make-up was the kind of discreet job that looks completely natural.

As Alexis introduced us, Cassie caught me studying her and the corners of her mouth twitched in a knowing smile. I could feel my ears going red, and I returned her smile sheepishly. 'I know,' she said. 'You can't help it. You have to ask yourself, "If I didn't know, would I have guessed?" Everyone does it, Kate, don't feel embarrassed about it.'

Completely disarmed, I allowed myself to be settled on one of the sofas with Alexis while Cassie ordered coffee then sat down opposite us, crossing a pair of elegant legs that certain women of my acquaintance would cheerfully have killed for. 'So,' Cassie said. 'A private investigator and a crime reporter. It can't be me you're after. The jackals that Alexis hangs out with left me not so much as a vertebra in my cupboard, never mind a skeleton. So, I ask myself, who?'

'Does the name Martin Cheetham mean anything to you?' Alexis asked.

Cassie uncrossed her legs then recrossed them in the opposite direction. 'In what context?' she said.

'In a business context. Your business, not his.'

Cassie shrugged elegantly. 'Not everyone who uses our services likes to be known by their real name. You could say that their real name is what they're trying to escape from.'

'He died yesterday,' Alexis said bluntly.

Before Cassie could respond, a teenage girl came in with coffee. At least, I'm pretty certain it was a girl. The process of pouring our coffee gave Cassie plenty of time to recover from the news. 'How did he die?' she asked. In spite of her conversational tone, for the first time since we'd arrived she looked wary.

'He was wearing women's clothing and hanging from the banisters in his home. The police think it was an accident,' Alexis said. I was content to sit back. Cassie was her contact, and she knew how to play her.

'Do I take it that you don't agree with them?' Cassie asked, moving her glance from one to the other of us.

'Oh, I think they're probably right. It's just that he ripped me off to the tune of five grand a few weeks ago, and I'm trying to get it back. Which means trying to untangle what he was up to, and who with,' Alexis said determinedly.

'Five thousand pounds? My God, Alexis, no wonder you're working with Kate.' Cassie smiled, then sighed. 'Yes, I knew Martin Cheetham. He bought a lot of stuff from Trances, and he was a regular at our monthly Readers' Socials. Martina, he called himself. Not terribly original. And before you ask, I don't think he had any particular friends among the group. Certainly, I don't know of anyone he saw socially between meetings. He wasn't someone who appeared to find it easy to open up. A lot of men really blossom when they're cross-dressing, as if they've suddenly become themselves. Martina wasn't like that. It was almost as if it was an obsession that he had to indulge rather than a release. Does that make any sense to you?'

I nodded. 'It fits the picture I have in my mind, certainly. Tell me, was he a particularly effective woman? I mean, without wishing to be offensive, some men are never going to look like anything other than a man in women's clothes. On the other hand, it's hard to imagine that you were ever anything other than a woman. Where on the spectrum did Cheetham fall?'

'Thank you,' Cassie said. 'Martina was actually superb. He had a lot of natural advantages – he wasn't particularly tall, he had small hands and feet, quite fine bones and good skin. But the real clincher was his clothes. He could get into a standard size sixteen, and he didn't seem to care how much he spent on clothes. In fact . . .' Cassie got up and went over to one of the filing cabinets. She returned a moment later with a photograph album.

She started flicking through the pages. 'I'm sure he's on a couple of these. I took a couple of rolls of film at the Christmas Social.' She stopped at a photograph of a couple of women leaning against a bar, laughing. 'There, on the left. That's Martina.'

I studied the picture and realized where I'd seen Martina Cheetham before.

20

I sat in the Ford Fiesta listening to *Coronation Street* on headphones. Mary Wright had returned to the house I was bugging, her appetite for soap opera unabated. The mysterious Brian was still nowhere to be seen or heard, however. Perhaps he didn't exist. At least his absence freed me from having to listen to domestic chitchat, which meant I could concentrate on trying to crack the password that would let me into Martin Cheetham's secret directory.

Alexis had been as puzzled as me when I revealed where I'd seen Martin Cheetham in his drag before. The photograph had jogged my memory as the distorted face of the corpse could never have done. But there was no mistaking it. The elegant woman who'd been looking at cheap terraced houses in DKL Estates was Martin Cheetham. No wonder he'd taken off like a bat out of hell at the sight of me. Whatever their little game was, he must have thought I was on to him, which also explained why he'd gone into panic mode when I paid my second visit to his office. If I'd needed proof that Cheetham and Lomax were up to something a lot more significant than the land fiddle, I had it now. The only question was, what?

As the familiar theme music from *Coronation Street* died away, a Vauxhall Cavalier drove slowly past me and pulled up outside my target. When I saw Ted's favourite salesman was driving it, I couldn't help myself. I punched the air and shouted 'Yo!' just like some zitty adolescent watching the American football on Channel 4. Luckily, Jack McCafferty wasn't interested in anything other than the house where he intended to sell a state-of-the-art Colonial Conservatory. I'd been right! The pattern was working out, just as I'd anticipated.

What I hadn't expected was Jack's passenger. Unfolding

himself from the passenger seat came a sight to quicken Shelley's pulse. Ted Barlow stretched himself to his full height, then held a quick conference with his ace salesman. Tonight, Jack McCafferty's designer suit looked almost black under the street lights, his flamboyant silk tie like a flag of success. His brown curls had the glossy sheen of a well-groomed setter. Beside him, Ted looked more like the assistant than the boss. He wore the only suit I'd ever seen him in, and the tight knot of his striped tie was askew. Shelley would never have let one of her kids out of the door looking like that. I didn't need to be Gipsy Rose Lee to predict big changes for Ted Barlow in the months to come.

The two men marched up the path. As Jack's hand reached out for the bell, I experienced the strange sensation of hearing it ring in my ears. The television was abruptly turned off, just as I was getting interested in the latest episode in the steamy series of instant coffee adverts. Unfortunately, because there was a wall between the bug and the door, all I could hear of the doorstep exchange was the murmur of voices, but it became clear as the three of them entered the living room.

'What a delightful room!' I heard Jack exclaim.

'Isn't it?' Ted echoed, with as much conviction as a famous actress endorsing the rejuvenating powers of a brand of soap.

'We like it,' the woman's voice said.

'Well, Mrs Wright, if I might introduce ourselves to you, my name is Jack McCafferty and I'm the chief sales executive of Colonial Conservatories, which is why your telephone inquiry about our range was passed on to me. And you are very privileged tonight to have with you my colleague Ted Barlow, who is the managing director of our company. Ted likes to take a personal interest in selected customers, so he can keep his finger on the pulse of what you, the public, actually want from a conservatory, so that Colonial Conservatories can maintain its position as a market leader in the field.' It flowed virtually without a pause. In spite of myself, I was impressed. I could picture Ted standing there, awkwardly shifting from foot to foot, failing dismally in his attempt to look like a Colossus of Commerce.

'I see,' said Mary Wright. 'Won't you sit down, gentlemen?'

As soon as his backside hit the chair, Jack was off and running, his pitch fluent and flawless as he sucked Mary Wright into the purchase of a conservatory she didn't need at a price she couldn't afford for a house that wasn't hers. Every now and again, he sought a response from her, and she chimed in as obediently as the triangle player in the orchestra counting the bars till the next tinkling note. They established that her husband was working abroad, what kind of conservatory she favoured, her monthly incomings and outgoings. Jack conducted the whole exposition as if it were a symphony.

Eventually, Ted was despatched out the back with a tape measure and notebook. That was when it really got interesting. 'Slight problem,' Jack said in a low voice. 'Ted's having aggravation with the bank.'

'You mean, because of us?' Mary Wright asked.

'Probably. Anyway, bottom line is, I can't get a finance deal through the usual channels. We're going to have to arrange the finance ourselves, but that shouldn't be too hard. I've got the names of a couple of brokerages where they don't ask too many questions. The only thing we'll lose out on is the finance company kick back to me, but we'll just have to live with that. I'm only warning you, because the close will be a bit different. OK?' he said, as laid back as if he was asking for a second cup of tea.

'Sure, I'll busk it. But listen, Jack, if the bank's being difficult, maybe we should pack it in before it starts getting dangerous,' the woman said.

'Look, Liz, there's no way they could trace it back to us. We've covered our tracks perfectly. I agree, we should quit while we're ahead. But we've already got the next two up and running. Let's see them through, then we'll take a break, OK? Go off to the sun and spend some of the loot?' Jack said reassuringly. If I'd have been her, I'd probably have fallen for it too. He had the real salesman's voice, all honey and reassurance. If he'd become a surgeon, he'd have had sacks of mail every Christmas from adoring patients.

'OK. Are you coming back here tonight?' she asked.

'How could I stay away?' he parried.

'Then we'll talk about it later.' Whatever else she was going to say was cut off by the return of Ted.

'If you'll just give me a minute with the old pocket calculator, I'll give you a price on the unit you'd decided on,' Ted said. The presumptive close.

The price Ted quoted made my eyes cross. Of course, Liz/Mary didn't turn a hair. 'I see,' she said.

'Normally, we could offer you our own financial package, sponsored by one of the major clearing banks,' Jack said. 'Unfortunately, we at Colonial Conservatories are the victims of our own success, and we have surpassed our target figures for this quarter. As a result, the finance company aren't in a position to supply any more cash to our customers, because of course they have limits themselves and, unlike us, they have people looking over their shoulders to make sure they don't exceed those limits. But what I would suggest is that you consult a mortgage broker and arrange to remortgage for an amount that will cover the installation of your conservatory,' he added persuasively. 'It's the most effective way of utilizing the equity you have tied up in your home.'

'What about a second mortgage? Wouldn't that do just as well?' Liz/Mary asked.

Ted cleared his throat. 'I think you'll find, Mrs Wright, that most lenders prefer a remortgage, especially bearing in mind that our house prices up here in the North West have started dropping a tad. You see, if there were to be any problems in the future and the house had to be sold, sometimes it happens that there isn't enough money left in the pot for the lender of the second mortgage after the first lender has been paid off, if you see what I mean. And then the holder of the second charge doesn't have any way of getting his money back, if you follow me. And lenders are very keen on knowing they could get their cash back if push comes to shove, so they mostly prefer you to get a remortgage that pays off the first mortgage and leaves you with a few bob left over.' I couldn't see Ted getting a job presenting *The Money Programme*, but he'd put it clearly enough. What a pity he'd wasted it on a pair of crooks who'd forgotten more than he ever knew about property loans and how to exploit them.

'So what happens now?' the woman asked.

'Well, you have to talk to a mortgage broker and arrange this remortgage. And of course, if you need any advice filling in the forms, don't hesitate to call me. I could fill these things in in my sleep. Then, as soon as you get confirmation of the remortgage, let us know and we'll have your conservatory installed within the week,' Jack said confidently.

'As quickly as that? Oh, that's wonderful! It'll be in when my husband comes home for Christmas,' she exclaimed. Shame, really. She could have been earning an honest living treading the boards.

'No problem,' Jack said.

Ten minutes later, Jack and Ted were walking back to the car, slapping each other on the back. Poor sod, I thought. I wasn't relishing the revelation that the person responsible for the wrecking of his business was his good buddy Jack. The whole thing had taken just over an hour. I reckoned that in a dozen of those hours spread over the last year, Liz and Jack must have cleared the best part of half a million quid. It was gobsmacking. The most gobsmacking thing about it was how simple it all was. I still had a few loose ends to tie up, but I had a pretty clear picture now of how they had scammed their way to a fortune.

Since Jack had promised he'd be back later, I decided to stay put. It was a freezing cold night, frost forming on the roofs of the parked cars, and my feet were like ice. I knew I couldn't endure a couple more hours of that, so I nipped back to the van swapped my thin-soled court shoes for a pair of thick sports socks and my Reeboks. The feeling returned to my feet almost as soon as I tied my laces. Wonderful invention, trainers. The only problem comes when you go striding into an important business meeting, done up to the nines in your best suit, then you look down and realize that instead of your chic Italian shoes, you're still wearing the Reeboks you drove there in. I know, I was that soldier.

Left to her own devices, Liz was clearly lost without the box. We caught the tail-end of the nine o'clock news, the weather (the usual tidings of comfort and joy; freezing fog in the Midlands, ground frost in the north, rain tomorrow), then a dire American mini-series started. I wished I could change channels. Instead, I turned the receiver volume down low enough to tune out anything other than phone calls or conversations and opened up the laptop.

I'd tried all the obvious ones. Martin, Martina, Cheetham, Tamarind, Lomax, Nell, Harris, scam, land, deeds, titles, secret, locked, private, drag, Dietrich, Bassey, Garland, Marilyn, password. No joy. I was running out of inspiration when my phone rang. 'Hello?' I said.

'Kate? Alexis.' As if she needed to tell me. 'Listen, I had a brainwave.'

My heart sank. 'What?' I asked.

'I remembered that the *Sunday Star*'s got a reporter called Gerry Carter who lives in Buxton. Now, I've never actually met the guy, on account of the Sundays don't usually hang out with the pack, but I dug his number out of a mate of his and gave him a call, hack to hack.'

I was interested now I realized her brainwave didn't involve me in anything illegal or life-threatening. 'And did he have anything useful to say?'

'He knows Brian Lomax. In fact, he lives about five houses down from Lomax.' Alexis paused to let that sink in.

'And?' I asked.

'I think I know who the mystery woman is.'

'Alexis, you already have one hundred per cent of my attention. Stop tantalizing me as if I was a bloody-minded news editor. Cough it!' I demanded, frustrated.

'Right. You remember we saw two names on the electoral roll? And we assumed the other one was his wife? Well, it's not. According to Gerry, Lomax's wife left him a couple of years ago. In his words, "Once she'd installed flounced Austrian blinds at every window and redecorated the place from top to bottom, there was nothing else for her to do. So she shagged Lomax's brickie and ran off to some Greek island with him."

Unquote.' Alexis chuckled. 'Where presumably she is complaining about the shortage of windows to clothe in frilly chintz, always assuming Laura Ashley's opened a branch on Lesbos. Anyway, once the pair of them had done their disappearing act, Lomax's sister moved in with him, on account of it's a bloody big house for one bloke on his own, and she'd just sold her own house to raise the capital to start her own business.' I could hear the sound of Alexis dragging smoke into her long-suffering respiratory tract.

'Carry on, I'm fascinated,' I said.

'D'you remember the second name on the electoral roll?'

'Not off the top of my head,' I confessed. Embarrassing, isn't it? The short-term memory's going already, and me only twenty-seven.

'Eleanor. And what's Nell short for?'

'Lomax's *sister*,' I breathed. 'Of course. Which would explain how they met in the first place. It would even explain why Martin Cheetham needed more money. She's an expensive looking woman; I can't see her settling for suburbia with a fortnight on the Costa Brava once a year. This business of hers – did your mate say what it was?'

'He did. She owns one of those small, select boutiques where the assistants sneer at you if you're more than a size eight and you've got less than five hundred pounds to spend. It's in the main shopping arcade, apparently. Called Enchantments, would you believe?'

'I would. Great work, Alexis. If they ever get round to firing you, I'm sure Mortensen and Brannigan could put the odd day's work your way,' I said.

'So what now?' she demanded.

I sighed. 'Can you leave it with me? I know that doesn't sound very helpful, but something I've been working on for a week now is about to come on top. With a bit of luck, I'll have it all wrapped up by tomorrow afternoon, and I promise that as soon as I'm clear I'll follow this up. How's that?'

'I suppose it'll have to do,' Alexis said. 'It's OK, Kate, I knew you were tight for time when I asked you to take this on. I can't start complaining now. You get to it when you can, and I'll try to be patient.'

That I really wanted to see. We chatted for a few minutes about the stories Alexis was currently working on, then she signed off for the night. I turned my attention back to the computer. At least Alexis had given me a couple of fresh ideas. I typed in ELEANOR, and the screen filled magically with a list of file names. Some days you eat the bear.

I'd only just started working through the files when the Cavalier returned. Jack drove straight into the garage, and closed the door behind him. I turned up the volume control, and a couple of minutes later he and Liz were doing the kind of kissing, fondling and greeting that brings a blush to the cheeks of even the most hard-nosed private eye. Unless, of course, you're the kind who gets off on aural sex.

However, it soon became clear that Jack and Liz had different things on their minds. While he seemed intent on making the earth move, she was more concerned about where the next fifty grand was coming from. 'Jack, cut it out, wait a minute, I want to talk to you,' she said. And all the rest. Eventually, it sounded like she broke free from the clinch, judging by the fact that her voice was noticeably fainter than his. 'Listen, we need to talk about this finance problem. What's gone wrong?'

'I don't know, exactly. All I know is that when I came into work tonight, Ted told me to stop writing finance proposals. He said the finance company were having problems processing applications, and that there was a temporary block on new business. But he was about as convincing as the Labour Party manifesto. I think what's really happened is that they've had enough of defaulting remortgages,' he said, his tone so casual I had to remind myself he was the man behind the problem. The man who faced at least a couple of years behind the picket fence of an open prison if he was ever nailed.

Liz wasn't anything like as cool. 'We're going to have to stop this, Jack. The bank won't just leave it at that. They'll call the Fraud Squad in, we'll go to prison!' she whined.

'No we won't. Look, when we started this, we knew it couldn't last forever. We always knew that one day, the finance company would notice that too many of Ted Barlow's conservatory customers were defaulting on their mortgages, and we'd have to pull out,' he said reasonably. 'I just didn't think they'd go straight to the bank before they warned Ted.'

'I always said we should spread the risk and go to outside lenders,' she whinged. 'I said it was crazy to use a finance company that's a subsidiary of Ted's bank.'

'We went through that at the time,' Jack said patiently. 'And the reasons for doing it my way haven't changed. For one, we're not involving anybody else. It's just you, me and a form that goes to a finance company who knew Colonial were a sound firm. For two, it's faster, because we never had to trail round mortgage brokers and building societies trying to find a lender, and run the risk of being spotted by somebody that knows me. And for three, I've been raking in commissions on the kick backs from the finance company, which has earned us a fair few quid on top of what the scam has made us. And doing it my way is why we're still safe, even though Ted's bank's put the shaft into him. There's no obvious pattern, that's the thing. Don't forget, we're in the middle of a recession. There'll be real mortgage defaulters in there as well as the ones we've pulled,' he said reassuringly. It was really frustrating not being able to see their faces and body language.

'Except that they'll still have conservatories attached to their houses. They won't have been up all night once a month dismantling a conservatory and loading it into a van so that Jack McCafferty can spirit it away and sell it on to some unsuspecting punter who thinks they're getting a real bargain! I'm telling you Jack, it's time to pull out!'

'Calm down,' he urged her. 'There's no hurry. It'll take them months to sort this mess out. Look, this one's in the home stretch. We can go and see a mortgage broker tomorrow and blag our way into a remortgage on this place, no bother. Where are we up to with the other two?'

'Just let me check. You know I don't trust myself to keep it all in my head,' she said accusingly. I heard the sound of briefcase locks snapping open and the rustle of paper. '10 Cherry Tree Way, Warrington. You've done the credit check,

I've got the new bank account set up, I've taken off the mail redirect, and I've got the mortgage account details. 31 Lark Rise, Davenport. All we've got on that is the credit check. I cancelled the mail redirect yesterday.' I really had got a result tonight. The two addresses Liz has just read out were identical with the ones Rachel Lieberman had already given me.

'So can we speed them up? Bring them in ahead of schedule?' Jack asked.

'We can try to speed things up at our end. But if we're going to have to find outside mortgagers to finance the remortgages, that's almost certainly going to slow the process down,' Liz said. I could hear the worry in her voice, in spite of the tinny quality of the bug's relay.

'Don't worry,' Jack soothed. 'It's all going to be OK.'

Not if I had anything to do with it, it wasn't.

21

Bank managers or traffic wardens. It's got to be a close run thing which we hate the most. I mean, if you got the chance to embarrass someone on prime time TV, would you choose the bank manager who refused your overdraft or the traffic warden who ticketed your car while you nipped into Marks & Spencer for a butty? I only had to talk to the guy in charge of Ted Barlow's finances to know that he deserved the worst that Jeremy Beadle could do.

To begin with, he wouldn't even talk to me, not even to arrange an appointment. 'Client confidentiality,' he explained superciliously. I told him through clenched teeth that I probably knew more about his client's current problems than he did, since I was employed by said client. I restrained myself from mentioning that Mortensen and Brannigan had standards of confidentiality and service that were a damn sight higher than his. We don't sell our customer list to junk mail financial services outfits; we don't indulge ourselves on the old boys' network to blackball people whose faces don't fit; and, strangely enough, we actually work the hours that suit our clients rather than ourselves.

But Mr Leonard Prudhoe wasn't having any. Finally, I had to give up. There was only one way I was going to get to see this guy. I rang Ted and asked him to set the meeting up. 'Have you sorted it all out?' he asked. 'Do you know what's been going on?'

'Pretty much,' I said. 'But whatever you do, don't so much as hint to anyone, and I mean anyone, that anything's changed.' I explained that he'd have to set up a meeting with Prudhoe so we could get the whole thing sorted out. 'Then, if you come to the office beforehand, I'll fill you in first.'

'Can't you tell me now? I'm on pins,' he said.

'I've got a couple of loose ends to tie up, Ted. But if you can fix up to see Prudhoe this afternoon, I should be able to give you chapter and verse then. OK?'

The relief in his voice was heartwarming. 'I can't tell you how pleased I am, Miss Brannigan. You've no idea what it's been like, wondering if I was going to lose everything I've worked for. You've just got no idea,' he burbled on.

I might not have, but I had a shrewd idea who did. When I managed to disentangle myself from his effusive thanks, I wandered through to the outer office. Shelley's fingers were flying over the keyboard as she worked her way through the proposals Bill had put together for our Channel Islands clients. 'Ted's little problem,' I said. 'I'm just nipping out for a couple of hours to tie up the last loose ends. He should be ringing back to let me know when we're seeing his bank manager. Give me a bell on the mobile when you know.'

She gave me one of her looks. The ones I suspect she reserves for her kids when she thinks they're trying to dodge out without finishing their homework. 'You mean it?' she asked.

'Brownie's honour,' I said. 'Would I lie to you about something so close to your heart? Are you familiar with the works of Rudyard Kipling?'

She looked at me as if I was out to lunch and not coming back for a long time. 'Wasn't he the one who went on about the white man's burden?' she said suspiciously.

'The same. Knew all about keeping the yellow and brown chappies in their places. However, he was not entirely a waste of oxygen. He also wrote the private eye's charter:

> I keep six honest serving men
> (They taught me all I knew)
> Their names are What and Why and When
> And How and Where and Who.

'Well, as far as Ted's case is concerned, I know the what, the why, the when, the where and the who. I know most of the how, and after I've paid a little visit to one of my contacts, I expect to know the lot.' I smiled sweetly as I shrugged into my coat and headed for the door. 'Bye, Shelley.'

'You worry me, Brannigan, you really do,' floated after me as I ran downstairs. The day had not been wasted.

Rachel Lieberman was doing front of house at DKL Estates when I walked through the door. The suit she was wearing looked as if it was worth about the same as the deposit on any one of her first-time-buyer properties. I pretended to study the houses for sale while she made appointments for a potential buyer to view a couple. Five minutes later, the grateful house-hunter went on his merry way with a handful of particulars, leaving Rachel and me facing each other across the desk. 'Lost your young man?' I asked.

'His mother says he's got a bug. I think it may have more to do with the fact that United won last night,' she said.

'You just can't get the help these days,' I commiserated.

'You can say that again. Anyway, what can I do for you? Still hunting for your mysterious con artists?'

I'd already decided that whoever was supplying Jack McCafferty and Liz with the information they needed, it wasn't Rachel Lieberman. I hadn't made that decision purely on women's intuition. I reckoned she'd have found a way politely to show me the door if she'd been involved. So I smiled and said, 'Nearly at the end of the road. I was hoping you could help me out with a couple of loose ends.'

'Fire away,' she said. 'You've got me quite intrigued. My son was enthralled when I told him I was helping a private eye with her inquiries. So I owe you some co-operation. It's not easy for a mother to impress a ten-year-old, you know.'

'Do you store all the details of your rented properties on your computer?'

'It all goes in there, whether it's for rental or for sale,' she said.

'So how does the Warrington office get your data, and vice versa?'

'I don't mean to be rude, but how well do you understand computers?' she asked.

I grinned. 'If you left me alone with yours for half an hour, I could probably figure it out for myself,' I said. I was almost certainly exaggerating, but she wasn't to know. Now, if I had Bill with me, he'd definitely be in there before I'd had time to brew a pot of coffee.

'I'll save you the bother,' she replied. 'Twice a day, at one and again at five, I access the Warrington office computer via a modem. The software identifies any new files, or files that have been modified since the machines last conversed. Then it exports those files from my machine and imports the ones from the Warrington computer. The system also warns me in the unusual event of the same file having been modified by both offices.'

'Sounds like a nifty bit of programming,' I said.

'Our software was written by my brother-in-law, so he had to make sure it does what it's supposed to, or I'd make his life hell,' Rachel said. I could imagine. One of the things I learned in law school was, never cross a Jewish princess.

'Now for the hard question,' I said.

'I can guess. Who has access to the computers?' she asked. I nodded. 'Is this really necessary?' I nodded again. 'And I suppose you won't be satisfied if I tell you that they're only accessible to members of my staff?' I began to feel like I was following the bouncing ball.

'You want names, do you?' she said.

'Photographs would be even better,' I said.

Her eyebrows arched, then she snorted with laughter. 'Have you ever considered a career in estate agency? With cheek like yours, you could stand in the middle of a decaying slum with rising damp, dry rot and subsidence and persuade the clients that the property has unique potential that only they are capable of exploiting.'

'Kind of you, but I prefer catching crooks to becoming one,' I said.

'It's flattery that's supposed to get results, not insults,' she retorted. 'All the same, would you mind terribly keeping an eye on the shop while I attempt to meet your demands?'

I even went so far as to sit behind the desk while Rachel disappeared into the back office. I suppose she could have been phoning the baddies to tip them off, but I didn't think so. Luckily, no one came in during the few minutes she was gone. Thursday morning obviously isn't the busy time for estate agents. Rachel returned with an envelope of photographs. 'Here we are,' she said. 'We had a staff Christmas dinner last year. The only person who's new since then is Jason, and you've already met him.'

Rachel handed me the bundle of snaps. They'd celebrated in one of the Greek tavernas, and the pictures had obviously been put back in reverse order, for the first few showed one of those organized riots that the Greeks, like the Scots, call dancing. There was no one that I recognized. I carried on. Then, on the seventh photograph, shot from the opposite end of the table, there she was. Small, neat features, sharp chin, face wider across the red eyes. Just like Diane Shipley's sketch, except that her natural hair was dark blonde, cut short in a feathered, elfin style. I pointed to the woman. 'Who's that?'

Rachel's face seemed to close down on me. 'Why? What makes you ask?'

'I don't think you want me to answer that,' I said gently. 'Who is she?'

'Her name is Liz Lawrence. She works two afternoons a week in our Warrington office. She has done for nearly three years. I think you must be making a mistake, Miss Brannigan. She's . . . she's a nice woman. She works hard,' Rachel insisted.

I sighed. Sometimes this job makes me feel like the bad fairy who tells children there's no Santa Claus. The worst of it was that I had another sackload of disillusion to dump on someone before the day was over.

Ted's suit was having yet another outing. When I got back to the office, he was perched on the edge of Shelley's desk, looking as cheerful as a bloodhound whose quarry has just disappeared into the river. 'And you know what garages are,' I heard him say as I came in. 'They don't know when they'll have either van back on the road.'

'More problems?' I asked.

'You're not kidding. Two of my three vans are off the road.

Which means my installations have slowed right down. It's a disaster,' Ted said mournfully.

'Are you sure it's just a coincidence?' Shelley demanded. 'On top of everything else, it's beginning to sound as if somebody's got it in for you!'

Ted managed to look both wounded and baffled. 'I don't think so, Shelley, love,' he said. 'It's just been bad luck. I mean, the first one was parked up when it happened. Somebody'd obviously smacked into it in the pub car park while Jack was busy inside.'

'Jack McCafferty? What was he doing with one of the vans? Surely he's got nothing to do with installations?' I asked, too sharply. They both gave me odd looks.

'He borrows it now and again. He runs a little disco business with his brother-in-law, and sometimes they're double booked so he borrows one of my vans overnight to run the disco gear around in,' Ted said. The final piece slotted into place.

Then I remembered what kind of vans Colonial Conservatories use. My stomach felt like I'd eaten too much icecream too fast. 'What night was it that he had the accident, Ted?' I asked.

Ted frowned and cast his eyes upwards. 'Let me see ... It must have been Monday night. Yes, Monday. Because we were running round like lunatics Tuesday trying to fit everything in, and that's why Pete was going too fast to stop at the roundabout. And now we're two vans down, and no sign of either of them back till next week at the very earliest.' Out of the corner of my eye, I noticed a flicker of movement as Shelley's hand sneaked out to pat Ted's.

Oh well, at least it hadn't been Ted's white Transit van that had tried to push me off Barton Bridge. 'I wish I had some good news for you, Ted,' I said, 'but I'm afraid it's a bit mixed. We're not due at the bank for another half-hour yet. D'you want to come into my office and I'll run it past you before we go and see Prudhoe?'

I thought I wasn't going to be able to get Ted to the bank. When I unfolded the tale of Jack's treachery, he went white round the mouth and headed for the door. Luckily, the sight of Shelley's astonished face slowed him down long enough for me to grab his arm and steer him into a seat. Shelley got a medicinal brandy into him and he recovered the power of speech. 'I'll kill the bastard,' he ground out between clenched jaws. 'I swear to God, I'll kill him.'

'Don't be silly,' Shelley said briskly. 'Kate will have him put in prison and that's much more satisfying,' she added. Taking me to one side while Ted stared into the bottom of his empty glass, she muttered, 'Which bastard are we talking about here?'

I gave her the last five seconds of the tale, which was enough to get her crouching beside Ted, murmuring the kind of comfort that it's embarrassing to witness. Of course, that was when Detective Chief Inspector Della Prentice chose to put in an appearance. I immediately steered her towards the door and said, 'Ted, I'll see you downstairs in five minutes.'

I'd rung Della as soon as Shelley gave me a time for the meeting with Prudhoe. I figured it would save me a bit of time if I outlined the case to her at the same time as I told the bank. I knew that the bank might be less than thrilled, but frankly, they were just going to have to lump it. I still had to find enough proof to nail Brian Lomax, and I simply didn't have the time to go into a ritual dance with Ted Barlow's bank manager about ethics.

Leonard Prudhoe was just as I'd expected. Smooth, supercilious, but above all, grey. From his silver hair to his shiny grey loafers, he was a symphony in the key of John Major. The only splash of colour was the angry purple zit on his neck. God knows how it had the temerity to sit there. Also, as I'd expected, he treated us like a pair of naughty children who've been reported to the head so they can learn how the grown-ups behave. 'Now, Miss Brannigan, I believe you think you might have some information pertinent to Mr Barlow's current problems. But what I really can't understand is why you feel it necessary to have Chief Inspector Prentice present, charming as it is to make her acquaintance. I'm sure she's not in the least concerned with our little difficulties . . .'

I cut across the patronizing bullshit. 'As far as I'm concerned, a crime has been committed and that's more important than your sensibilities, I'm afraid. How much do you know about fraud, Mr Prudhoe? Am I going to lose you three sentences in? Because if you're not well versed in major fraud inquiries, I suggest we get someone in here who is. I'm a very busy woman, and I haven't the time to go through this twice, which is why DCI Prentice is here,' I said briskly. He couldn't have looked more shocked if I'd jumped on the desk and gone into a kissagram routine.

'Young woman,' he stuttered, 'I'll have you know that I am an expert in financial defalcations of all sorts.'

'Fine. Pin your ears back and take notes, then,' I retorted. There's something about pomposity that brings out the toe-rag in me. It must be the Irish quarter of my ancestry.

Prudhoe looked affronted, but out of the corner of my eye, I noticed Ted looked a fraction less miserable. Della Prentice seemed to have developed a nasty cough.

'There's really no need to take this attitude,' Prudhoe said frostily.

'Listen, Mr Prudhoe,' Ted interrupted. 'You people tried to take my business away from me. Kate's been trying to sort it out and, as far as I'm concerned, that entitles her to take any attitude she damn well pleases.'

The turning worm shut Prudhoe up long enough for me to get started. 'On the surface, it looks as if what has happened to Ted is a sequence of unfortunate coincidences, culminating in you cutting off his line of credit. But the truth is, Ted is the victim of a very clever fraud. And if the perpetrators hadn't got so greedy that they decided to go for a second bite of the cherry no one would ever have cottoned on, because the frauds would have looked all of a piece with genuine mortgage defaulters.' In spite of himself, I could see Prudhoe's interest quicken. Perhaps, under his patronizing pomposity there was a brain after all.

I outlined the reasons why Ted had come to us in the first place. Della Prentice had her notebook out and was scribbling furiously. When I got to the missing conservatories, Prudhoe actually sat forward in his seat. 'This is how it works,' I said, thoroughly into my stride.

'You need a bent salesman and you need an insider in the office of an estate agency that specializes in decent-quality rental property. In this case, they used a firm called DKL Estates, who are as innocent of any criminal involvement as Ted is. The insider, let's call her Liz, picks houses that are to let where the owners have fairly common names and, preferably, where they are abroad, either working or in the services. Ideally, they want a couple who have been paying the mortgage for a fair few years, so that there's a substantial chunk of equity in the house. Liz then tells the office computer that she has found someone who wants to rent the place and whose references check out.

'The surname of the couple renting the house is identical with that of the real owners, but because they've chosen common names, if anyone in the office other than Liz notices the coincidence, they can all stand around going, "Well, stone me, isn't that incredible, what a small world, etc.". Of course, because Liz has access to all the original paperwork from the owners, they've got copies of the signatures, and possibly info on bank accounts, mortgage accounts, service contracts and everything else. With me so far?'

'Fascinating,' Prudhoe said. 'Do go on, Miss Brannigan.'

'The salesman, who has access to credit checking agencies via your financial services company, runs a check to see what other information about the owners it throws up. Then Liz opens a false bank account in the renter's name at that address, and stops any Post Office redirect on mail for the real owners. She spends a minimal amount of time in the house and pays rent for a while. Incidentally, they have three operations in the planning stage at any one time, so she never spends long enough in any of the houses for the neighbours to get close. They all think she works away, or works nights, or has a boyfriend she stays with a lot. She also changed her appearance with wigs, glasses and make-up to cover their tracks.

'Next, Jack McCafferty, Ted's top salesman, says he's had a call from her asking for an estimate for a conservatory. The following day, he comes in with an order, financed by a remortgage with this bank. And if it was one of those periodic nights where Ted goes out on the call with him, then Jack and Liz would just pretend they'd never met before and he'd pitch her just like any other punter. After all, remortgaging would be a perfectly legitimate way of doing it, and wouldn't ring any alarm bells with Ted or anyone else since everybody who can't sell their house right now is desperately trying to liberate some capital. I tracked all this down via the Land Registry's records, but I'm sure you can verify the remortgage details with your own records. I suspect they used your finance people all the time because they'd also earn the finance company's commission that way too,' I added.

'But wouldn't there be a problem with the original mortgage?' Della asked. 'Surely, once that had been paid off, either the building society would be alerted because payments were still continuing from the real owners, or else the real owners would notice that their mortgage was no longer being taken out of their bank account.'

I hadn't thought of that. But then I remembered an experience Alexis and Chris had had when they first sold their separate homes to move in together. Alexis, being a fiscal incompetent, had carried on blithely paying her old mortgage for six months before she'd noticed. I shook my head. 'It would have taken ages for the building society to spot what was happening. And then they'd send a letter, and the letter would drop into a black hole because of the mail redirect being cancelled. It could drift on for ages before anyone at the building society got seriously exercised enough to do anything about it.'

Della nodded, satisfied. 'Thanks. Sorry, do carry on. This is fascinating.'

'Right. So, when the bank checks the remortgage application, because the names are the same, all the information they get relates to the real owners, so there's never any problem. And the money is handed over. Think of the figures involved. Imagine a property bought ten years ago for twenty-five thousand pounds, which is now worth ninety thousand. The outstanding mortgage is only about seventeen thousand. They remortgage for the full ninety thousand, pay off the existing mortgage all above board to prevent any suspicion, then do a runner. Our friends Jack and Liz have netted approximately seventy thousand pounds after expenses.

'I reckon they've pulled the same scam at least a dozen times. And the only reason I was able to catch on is that they got so greedy they decided to dismantle the conservatories after they'd been installed and sell them on to another punter with an identical house at a rock-bottom price of a couple of grand.' I turned to Ted. 'That's what Jack was doing with the van when you thought he was playing at DJs.'

I didn't get the chance to enjoy their reactions. Now I remember why I resisted a mobile phone for so long. They always interrupt the best bits.

'He's got a passport application form,' Alexis announced triumphantly. 'I followed him to the Post Office. He's obviously planning to leave the country.'

It was a reasonable deduction. What it didn't tell us was whether he planned to take off to the Costa del Crime with his ill-gotten gains as soon as air traffic control would let him or whether he was simply planning ahead for his winter skiing holiday. 'Where are you?' I said.

'In the phone box just down the road from his yard. I can see the entrance from here. He hasn't moved since he came back from the Post Office.'

I gave in. 'I'll be there as soon as I can,' I said. After all, I'd given Ted and Prudhoe enough to keep them gossiping for hours. I ended the call and smiled sweetly at my fascinated audience. 'I'm very sorry about this, but something rather urgent has come up. No doubt the three of you have a lot to discuss, so if you'll forgive me, I'll leave you to it. Ted, I'll let you have a full written report as soon as possible, but certainly by Monday at the latest.' I got to my feet. 'I'd just like to say it's been a pleasure, Mr Prudhoe,' I added, reaching over his desk and seizing his hand in a firm grip. Poor sod, he still looked like he'd been hit by a half-brick. I seem to have this effect on men. Worrying, isn't it?

Della Prentice followed me into the corridor. 'Hell of a tale, Kate. You've done a great job. We'll need a formal statement, of course,' she said. 'When can we do the business?'

I glanced at my watch. It was getting on for three. 'I don't know, Della, I can't see me being able to sit down with you until the weekend, at the very earliest. Surely you've got enough to get a search warrant on the addresses they're using for the scam?' I opened my bag and took out my notebook, and copied down the addresses as I spoke. 'Look, talk to Rachel Lieberman at DKL Estates. The woman you're after is called Liz Lawrence and she works part-time in their Warrington office. And Ted can tell you all he knows about Jack McCafferty. I don't mean to be difficult, but I'm really up against it.'

'OK. I can see you've got problems. Let me know when you've got the time to sit down and put it all together. And

22

They say the Victorian era was the age of the gifted amateur. All I've got to say is that I'm glad I wasn't a private investigator then. I mean, if there's one thing worse than amateurs who insist on offering you the kind of help that completely screws up an investigation, it's the ones who are more on the ball than you. The way Alexis was operating in this case, I was soon going to have to start paying her, rather than the other way round.

What I'd heard when I went into a huddle with my telephone in Prudhoe's office wasn't the kind of news to gladden the heart. 'He's going to skip the country,' Alexis started the conversation.

'Mr Harris, you mean?' I said cautiously. I was trying to keep my end as short and uninformative as I could. After all, I'd suddenly become the rather embarrassing centre of attention. I wasn't bothered about Ted or Prudhoe, but the presence of police officers induces a paranoia in private eyes that makes Woody Allen look well-balanced by comparison.

'Of course, Harris, Lomax, whatever! Who else? He's going to do a runner.'

'How do we know this?'

There was a momentary pause while Alexis decided how to play it. 'After you'd explained how busy you were today, I managed to swap my days off. I thought if I kept an eye on him, at least we wouldn't have missed anything. And I was right,' she added defiantly.

I felt a guilt trip coming on. Somehow, I just knew that I wasn't going to be spending my evening as Emperor Brannigan of the Zulus, civilizing the known universe. 'What's happened?' I asked.

give me your mobile number so I can reach you if I need some background,' she said. I added my number to the sheet of paper and thrust it at her as I rushed off. I know that technically there was no desperate hurry for me to link up with Alexis, but if I hadn't got my adrenalin going, I might never have managed to drag myself back down the traffic-choked A6 and across that switchback road over the hills to Buxton. The locals must have amazing wrists.

I was back behind the wheel of the Fiesta. I'd got a taxi to drop me off there that morning, since there was no need to keep up my surveillance now. I swung round via the office to pick up the laptop with Cheetham's files, and a couple of my legal textbooks. I still hadn't had the chance to plough through the files, so I had no idea what twisted little schemes the dead lawyer had been up to. But I had a shrewd suspicion that they might need a bit more knowledge of the ins and outs of conveyancing than I had in my head. Better to have it at my fingertips instead.

It was nearly five by the time I overtook the last quarry wagon and dropped down the hill into Buxton. I cruised past Lomax's yard and clocked Alexis in her car. I had to admit I couldn't have picked a better spot myself. She was tucked in between two parked cars, with an uninterrupted view through the windows of the car in front to Lomax's yard. I parked round the corner and walked back.

I climbed into the Peugeot, shoving a pile of newspapers and sandwich wrappers on to the floor. 'Better be careful the bin men don't come round and claim you,' I said. 'Any action?'

Alexis shook her head. 'There are two vans. The one that Lomax drives and an identical one. The other one's been in and out a couple of times, but he hasn't shifted.'

'Unless of course he's lying in the back of the other van disguised as a bag of cement,' I pointed out. Alexis looked crestfallen. Oh great, now I felt even more guilty. 'Don't worry, it's not likely. He doesn't know anyone's watching him. Cheetham's death has been written off as an accident. As far as he knows, he's perfectly safe. Now, you can sod off home and let me earn a living instead of taking the bread out of my mouth,' I added.

'Don't you want me to hang on? In case he makes a run for it?' she asked, almost wistfully.

'Go home, have a cuddle with Chris. If he was planning to disappear over a distant horizon tonight, he wouldn't be sitting around in his yard. He'd be twitching in the queue at the passport office,' I said sensibly. Judging by the scowl on Alexis's face, she likes sensible about as much as I do.

She sighed, one of those straight-from-the-heart jobs. 'OK,' she said. 'But I don't want this guy to get away.'

I opened the car door. 'Don't forget, there's the small matter of proof,' I said. 'Now Cheetham's dead, Lomax can claim he did nothing dishonest. T.R. Harris is a business name, no more, no less. He just showed prospective buyers the land. He had no idea who bought it or when. Now, you and I know different, but I'd like to be in a position to prove it.'

Alexis groaned. 'All I want is a lever to get our money back, Kate. I don't care if he comes out of it all smelling of roses.'

'I hear and obey, oh lord,' I said, getting out of the car. 'Now shift this wheelie bin and let the dog see the rabbit.'

She waved as she drove away and I slipped the Fiesta into the space she'd left. I flipped open the laptop and accessed the WORK.L directory. The files were sorted into two directories. One was called DUPLICAT, the other RV. The files in RV each related to a house purchase. In some cases, the house had been sold about five months later, always at a substantial profit. I was about to check out the addresses in my *A-Z* when a white Transit van appeared in the gateway of Lomax's yard. My target was at the wheel. Fast as I could, I closed the laptop and dumped it on the passenger seat.

Don't let anyone tell you being a private eye is a glamorous way to earn a living. I followed Lomax from his yard to his house. Then I sat in the car for two hours, plodding wearily through Martin Cheetham's files. The houses in RV were all in the seedier areas south and east of Manchester city centre – Gorton, Longsight, Levenshulme. The kind of terraced streets where you can buy run-down property cheap, tart it up and make a modest killing. Or at least, you could do until the bottom started to drop out of the North West property market a few months ago. Looking at these files, it seemed that Lomax and Cheetham had been doing this on a pretty substantial scale. I did a quick mental calculation and reckoned they'd turned over getting on for two million quid in the previous year. Since my mental arithmetic is on a par with my quantum mechanics, I decided I'd got it wrong and scribbled the sums out in my notebook. I got the same answer.

Suddenly we were in a whole new ball game. I wasn't looking at a pair of small time operators chiselling a few grand on a dodgy land deal. I was looking at big money. They could have cleared as much as three-quarters of a million in the last year. But they must have had a substantial pot to buy the houses in the first place. Where the hell had the seed money come from to generate that kind of business?

While I'd been doing my sums, the last of the light had faded. I began to feel pretty exposed, which in turn made me feel deeply uncomfortable. I couldn't help remembering that less than a week ago someone had wanted to warn me off something so badly they'd taken the risk of killing me. If they were still around, I made a hell of a target, sitting all by myself in a car.

The answer to my fear was just behind me. I was parked on the opposite side of the street to Brian Lomax's house, about thirty yards further up the hill, outside a substantial Victorian pile with a Bed and Breakfast sign swinging slightly in the chilly wind. I collected a small overnight holdall from the boot, stuffed the law books into it and walked up the short drive.

I'd have taken the landlady on as an investigator any day. By the time I'd paid for a night in advance and she'd left me alone in my spotless little room, I felt like I'd had a bright light shining in my eyes for days. Never mind grace under pressure; there should be a private investigators' Oscar for lies under pressure. At least I was in a suit, which made it easier to be convincing about my imaginary role as a commercial solicitor acting for a local client who was interested in buying property in Manchester to expand his business. She'd gone for the lie, agog at my close-lipped refusal to breach client confidentiality. I was half-convinced that come the morning, she'd be tailing me just for the hell of picking up some juicy local gossip.

My room was, as requested, at the front of the house, and on the second floor, which gave me a better view of Brian Lomax's house than I'd had from the car. Glad to get out of tights and heels, I changed into the leggings, sweatshirt and Reeboks that had been relegated to the emergency overnight kit and settled down in the dark to keep watch. I passed the time dictating my client reports for PharmAce and Ted Barlow. That would take Shelley's mind off romance for a couple of hours.

Nell arrived home about half past six, parking her GTi in the garage. It was gone nine before I saw some more action. Lomax appeared round the side of the house, walking along his drive. He turned right and started towards town. I was out of the room and down the stairs a hell of a lot more quickly than I'd have been able to manage just a couple of days before. If Mortensen and Brannigan ever take on an assistant, I think we're going to have to stipulate 'must be quick healer' on the job description.

He was still in sight as I ran out of the guest house, trying to look like a jogger nipping out for her evening run. At the traffic lights, he turned left, walking up the hill towards the market place. I reached the corner in time to see him entering a pub. Wonderful. I didn't even have a jacket on, and I couldn't follow him into the pub because he knew only too well who I was. Furious, I walked right up to the pub and peered through the stained-glass door. Through a blue haze, I saw Lomax at the bar, talking and laughing with a group of other men, all around the same age. By the looks of it, he was having his regular Thursday night down his local with the lads, rather than meeting a business contact. That much was a relief. I stepped back and had a look round. Across the street, on the opposite corner, there was a fish and chip shop that advertised an upstairs dining room. I had nothing left to lose.

It's amazing how long I can take to work my way through steak pudding, chips, mushy peas, gravy, a pot of tea and a plate of bread and butter. Oddly enough, I actually enjoyed it, especially since I'd missed lunch. Best of all was the spotted dick and custard that tasted better than anything my mother used to make. I managed to make the whole lot string out until half past ten, then it was back out into the cold. Of course, it started to rain as soon as I emerged from the chippy. I crossed to the pub and had another look through the glass. The scene hadn't changed much, except that the pub had got busier. Lomax was still standing at the bar with his cronies, a pint pot in his fist. I couldn't see any point in getting soaked while he got pissed, so I jogged back to the guest house, my dinner sitting in my stomach like a concrete block.

He came back, alone, just on half past eleven. Five minutes later, a light went on in an upstairs room and he appeared at the window to close the curtains. Ten minutes after that, another light went on and Nell did the same thing in her room. I didn't bother waiting for their lights to go out. I bet I was asleep before they were.

I bet I was up before them too. I'd set my alarm for six, and I was out of the shower by quarter past. Lomax's curtains opened at a quarter to seven, and my heart sank. My landlady didn't start serving breakfast till eight, and it looked like he'd be out of the house by then. I consoled myself with the individually wrapped digestive biscuits supplied with the tea- and coffee-making facilities. (Fine if you like sterilized milk, tea bags filled with house dust and powdered instant coffee that tastes like I imagine strychnine does.)

Wearily, I packed my bag and returned to the car. I was beginning to wonder if there was any point to this surveillance. I sometimes think my boredom threshold's too low for this job. Twenty minutes later, the nose of a white E-type appeared in his gateway. I'd seen the Jag sitting next to Nell's GTi in the garage the night I'd spotted the T.R. Harris signboard. The classic car's long bonnet emerged cautiously, until I could see Lomax himself was at the wheel. He drove past me without so much as a glance. I watched him round the bend in my rearview mirror, then quickly reversed out of the guest house drive and sped after him.

I'd thought the road from Manchester had been bad enough.

The one we took out of Buxton was that nightmare you wake up from in a clammy sweat. The road corkscrewed up through a series of tight bends with sheer drops on the other side, just like in the Alps. Then it became a narrow bucking switchback that made me grateful for missing breakfast. The visibility was appalling. I couldn't decide if it was fog or cloud I was driving through, but either way I was glad there weren't too many side turnings for the E-type to disappear into. What left me gasping with disbelief was the amount of traffic on this track from hell. Lorries, vans, cars by the dozen, all bucketing along as if they were in the fast lane of the M6.

Eventually, we left the grey-green moors behind and dropped into the red brick of Macclesfield. I felt like an explorer emerging from the jungle after a close encounter with the cannibals. These were proper roads, with traffic lights, roundabouts, and white lines up the middle. Through Macclesfield, we emerged into the country again, but this was more my idea of what countryside should be. None of those dreadful moors, heather stretching to infinity, dilapidated dry-stone walls with holes in where someone failed to make the bend, grim pubs stranded in the middle of nowhere and trees that grow at an angle of forty-five degrees to the prevailing wind. No, this was much more like it. Neat fields, pretty farmhouses, Little Chefs and garden centres, notices nailed to trees announcing craft fairs and car boot sales. The kind of country you might just be tempted to take a little run out to in the car.

We roared down the slip road of the M6 at 8:14, according to my dashboard clock. I began to feel excited. Whatever Lomax was up to, it was more interesting than repairing guttering. As the speedo hit ninety, I really began to miss my Nova. It may not have looked much, but it was a car that only really ever seemed to get into its stride over eighty. Unlike the Fiesta, which had an interesting shake in the steering wheel between eighty-two and eighty-eight. As we changed lanes to head west down the M62, I remembered the phone call from Alexis that had started this latest phase of the operation. A passport application form.

To obtain a full British passport, you have to fill in a complicated form, have your photographic identity attested by a
supposedly reputable member of the community who's known
you for at least two years, and send it off to the passport office.
Then you sit back and wait for a few weeks while the wheels
of bureaucracy grind exceeding slow. If you're in a hurry, you
take yourself off to one of the five passport offices on the
UK mainland – London, Liverpool, Newport, Peterborough
or Glasgow. I remember the performance well. Richard and I
booked a fortnight's holiday in July driving round California
in a Winnebago. Two days before we were due to leave, he
materialized in my office mid-morning to announce his passport was out of date. Of course, he was too busy to sort it out
himself, could I possibly . . .?

If you get there on the stroke of nine, they deign to take your
paperwork off you and tell you to come back in four hours'
time. If you're late, you have to wait in the queue and pray
they get round to you before closing time. If that was where
Brian Lomax was headed, he was clearly determined to avoid
queuing all day.

He headed straight for the centre of Liverpool, and parked
his car in the multi-storey nearest the passport office at ten to
nine. I stayed in my car and watched him through the door of
India Buildings. He might well have been headed for any of
the offices on any floor except the fifth, but I doubted it. He
was out within twenty minutes but, instead of going straight
back to his car, he headed off towards the city centre. I swore
steadily under my breath as I tried to keep him in sight. As
long as he didn't turn into a pedestrian precinct, I might just
be OK.

I was and I wasn't. About a mile from the passport office,
Brian Lomax marched purposefully into a travel agency.

23

I burst through the door, fighting back the tears, rushed up to the assistant and wailed, 'Where's he taking her? Tell me! I've got a right to know where he's going with the bitch!' Then I burst into tears and collapsed into the chair that Brian Lomax had just vacated.

'I know it's stupid, but I still love him,' I sobbed. 'Whatever he might have done with that cow, he's still my husband.' Through the tears I could see the travel agent looking completely stricken. Her mouth was opening and closing.

'For God's sake, put me out of my misery! Let me know the worst. You're a woman, you should understand,' I added, accusingly.

Another woman pushed the younger assistant out of the way. 'What is it, queen?' she said soothingly.

'My h-husband,' I hiccuped. 'He's got a girlfriend, I just know it. So I've been following him. When he came in here, I thought, he's taking her away, never mind that me and the kids haven't had a holiday for two years. And something just snapped. You've got to tell me,' I added, on a rising note. Then I gulped noisily.

'Sharon,' the older woman said. 'The gentleman who was just in.'

'Lomax,' I said. 'That's his name. Brian Lomax.'

'Mr Lomax,' the woman echoed. 'What was he after, Sharon?'

'I thought we weren't supposed to discuss clients?' the younger girl muttered.

'Have you got no heart, girl? That could be you one day. Us girls have got to stick together,' the woman said. Then to me she said, 'Men. They're all the same, eh, girl?' Thank God for the legendary hearts of gold of Liverpudlians.

I nodded and made a great show of trying to get myself under control while Sharon nervously jabbed the keys of her computer with nails that would have had Cruella de Vil looking to her laurels. 'There, Dot,' she said, pointing at the screen.

The older woman nodded sagely and swung the screen round so I could see it for myself. 'Whatever he might be up to, he's not going off with her,' she said. 'Look. He's only booked for one person. Fly/drive to Florida. Flight, car hire and accommodation vouchers, including single person supplement.' As she spoke, I was taking it all in. Airline, flight number, price. Flying out of Manchester on Monday night. 'He paid in cash an' all,' Dot added. 'Now that's something we don't see a lot of in here these days.'

'What about his tickets?' I demanded. 'I bet he's not having them sent to the house.'

'No,' Dot said. 'With him going on Monday, he'll get them off the ticket agent at the airport.'

'Selfish bastard,' I spat.

'You're not kiddin', girl,' Dot said. 'Still, look on the bright side. At least he's not got the cow with him, has he?'

I got to my feet. 'By the time I've finished with him, he won't be fathering any more kids in a hurry,' I said.

'Attagirl!' Dot called after me as I stormed out of the travel agency.

By the time I rounded the corner and climbed into the Fiesta, which had miraculously escaped a parking ticket, the reaction to my performance had set in. My legs felt like jelly and my hands were shaking. Thank God for the solidarity of women whose men done them wrong.

So Alexis had been right, I thought as I drove back more sedately along the M62. Brian Lomax was about to do a runner. And the only thing that could stop him was me finding out what exactly he'd been up to. I decided to spend the rest of the day ignoring all distractions and getting to the bottom of Martin Cheetham's files. But before I did that, I reckoned I deserved the breakfast I'd missed out on earlier. On the horizon, I could see the Burtonwood motorway services building, a dead ringer for the Roman Catholic cathedral in Liverpool. If I tell you that the locals call the house of God 'the concrete wigwam', maybe you'll get the picture.

I pulled off the road and cruised into the car park. And there it was. Smack bang in the middle of the car park: Brian Lomax's E-type. I parked the car then cautiously explored the service area. He wasn't in the shop, or playing the video arcade machines. I finally spotted him in the cafeteria, alone except for a huge fry-up. Goodbye breakfast. With a sigh, I returned to my car and headed for the service road that led back to the motorway. When I reached the petrol pumps, I pulled off and parked. I nipped in to the shop and bought a bottle of mineral water and a bacon and egg sandwich, the nearest I was going to get to a proper breakfast that day. Back at the car, I let the engine idle while I ate my butty and waited for Lomax. I couldn't help myself; since the gods had handed him back to me on a plate, I just had to see what he was up to.

Quarter of an hour later, we were heading back towards Manchester. The traffic was heavy by now, but the E-type was so distinctive it was easy to tail. On the outskirts, he took the M63 towards Stockport. He turned off at the cheaper end of Cheadle, where you don't have to be able to play bridge or golf to be allowed to buy a house, and cut across to the terraced streets that huddle round Stockport County's football ground. Tailing him through the tight grid of narrow streets was a lot trickier, but luckily I didn't have to do it for long. And Lomax acted like the idea of being followed hadn't even crossed his mind.

He pulled up outside a house where a couple of workmen seemed to be removing the windows, and a youth up a ladder was clearing moss out of the guttering. A sign on the ladder had the familiar Renew-Vations logo, as did the scruffy van parked with two wheels on the kerb. Lomax had a few words with the workmen, then went inside. Ten minutes later, he re-emerged, gave them the thumbs-up sign then drove off.

We went through the same routine a couple more times, in Reddish then in Levenshulme. All the houses were elderly terraced properties in streets that looked as if they were struggling upwards rather than plunging further downhill. On the third house, it clicked. These were some of the most recent purchases in the RV directory. I was actually looking at the houses Cheetham and Lomax had bought cheap to do up and sell dear.

The last stop was on the fringes of Burnage, but this time it was a between-the-wars semi that looked completely dilapidated. There was grass growing through the gravel, the gate was hanging from one hinge. So much paint had peeled off the door and window frames it was a miracle they hadn't dropped to bits. Two men were working on the roof, replacing broken slates and pointing the chimney stack. Lomax got out of the Jag and shouted something to the men. Then he took a pair of overalls out of the boot, put them on over his jeans and sweatshirt and walked into the house. A few minutes later, I heard the high whine of a power drill. I decided I could use my time more fruitfully back in the office with the computer files.

Shelley was on the phone making 'new client' noises when I walked in, but judging by the speed with which the coffee appeared on my desk, she'd already had the run-down on my success with Ted's conservatories. 'Good news travels fast, huh?' I said.

'I don't know what you mean,' she said haughtily. 'Have you done the client reports for PharmAce and Ted Barlow yet?'

I took the cassettes out of my handbag. 'Voilà!' I said, handing them over with a flourish. 'God forbid we should keep Ted waiting. How is he, by the way? Happy as a sandboy?'

'As if it isn't bad enough spending my days with someone who thinks she's a genius, I now have to listen to Ted Barlow telling me you're a genius. The bank's agreed to restore his loan and his access to their financial services division, and he's got an advert in Monday's *Evening Chronicle* for a new sales person. The police raided the three houses last night and got enough evidence to arrest Jack McCafferty and Liz Lawrence. They should both be charged later today, and Ted's completely in the clear,' Shelley said, unable to keep the smile out of her eyes.

'Great news. Tell me, Shelley, how come you know all this?'

'Because it's my job to answer the phone, Kate,' she replied sweetly. 'Also, I've had calls from a DCI Prentice, a woman called Rachel Lieberman, Alexis Lee and four calls from

Richard who says he doesn't want to trouble you but have you charged the battery on your mobile because it's not responding.'

I knew there had to be a reason why I'd had peace all morning. I'd remembered to charge the phone up overnight. I'd just omitted to make sure it was switched on this morning. Feeling like a fool, I smiled sweetly at Shelley. 'I must have been in one of those black holes when he tried me,' I said.

Shelley gave me the look my mother used to when I swore blind I'd not eaten the last biscuit. 'If you're having that much of a problem, maybe we should just send it back,' she said.

I bared my teeth. 'I'll manage, thanks. So now he's got that load off his mind, how's Ted? Able to devote one hundred per cent of his attention to helping you achieve the full potential of your house?'

'Have I ever told you what a blessing it is for me to work with you, Kate? You're the only person I know who makes me realize just how mature my two kids really are.' She turned and headed for the door. I poked my tongue out at her retreating back. 'I saw that,' she said without turning her head. At the door, she looked back at me. 'Joking apart, it's OK.' Then she was gone, leaving me alone with the laptop and my phone messages, which I chose to ignore.

Now I'd worked out what the RV directory was all about and I'd actually seen some of the properties in question, I had to unravel the contents of DUPLICAT. At first sight, they seemed to be completely innocuous. They were files relating to the purchase of various properties by assorted individuals and the mortgages that had been arranged for them. The material seemed exactly the same sort of stuff that was in the unprotected WORK.C directory. The only difference was that in DUPLICAT, every single mortgage lender was different. In the few instances where the same building society had been used more than once, Cheetham's clients had chosen different branches.

It was only when I'd worked my way through to the most recent of the files that something finally caught my eye. Even then, I had to look twice and cross-check with another file to make sure it wasn't just boredom and tiredness that were tricking me. But my first reaction was right. The property in the file was a detached house on an exclusive development in Whitefield. But another couple had arranged a mortgage on the same property and their address was none other than the dilapidated semi I'd left Brian Lomax working on.

I could feel a dull ache starting at the base of my skull. The combination of staring into my laptop and trying to work out what was going on was getting to me. I stood up and stretched, then moved around the office doing some of the warm-up exercises I'd learned down the Thai boxing gym. I swear the routine sends my brain into an altered state. As my body found its rhythm, the tension flowed out of me, and my mind went into free fall.

Then all the assorted bits and pieces of information that had been swilling round in confusion inside my head came together in a pattern. Abruptly, I stopped leaping around the room like Winnie the Pooh's imitation of Mikhail Baryshnikov and dropped into my chair. I didn't have a split screen facility on the laptop, so I hastily scribbled down half a dozen of the addresses of the houses that had been mortgaged according to DUPLICAT, along with the names of their buyers. Then I called up the files from WORK.C, the directory of Cheetham's straight conveyancing business.

It didn't take me long to discover that for every file in DUPLICAT there was another file in WORK.C that corresponded to it. In each case, the house was the same but the buyers and the mortgage lenders were different. Now I understood exactly what Brian Lomax and Martin Cheetham had been up to. They'd exploited the system's weaknesses in a scam that would have given them a tidy profit almost indefinitely. The pair of them were committing the classic victimless crime. But someone had grown greedy, and that greed had led to Martin Cheetham's death.

I glanced at my watch. It was just on four. I still had no proof that Brian Lomax had been an active conspirator rather than a mug that Martin Cheetham and, possibly, Nell Lomax had exploited for their own ends. But I was convinced that whatever had gone wrong with Cheetham's carefully worked out scheme could be traced straight back to Lomax. There was something about his body language, a kind of swagger in the way he carried himself. Brian Lomax was no more one of life's victims than Warren Beatty. And I had to get him in the frame before a jumbo jet took off into the sunset on Monday night.

I closed the laptop and took it through to Bill's office. He was staring at an A4 pad, gnawing the end of a pencil. 'Bad time?' I asked.

'I'm trying to write a memory resident program that will automatically check for any date-activated programs hiding in the computer's memory,' he said. He dropped the pencil with a deep sigh and started chewing his beard instead. I'm often tempted to ring his mother and ask what experience he had in his infancy that's made him so oral.

'Virus protection?' I asked.

'Yup. I've been meaning to get to it since the débâcle on Yom Kippur, but this is the first chance I've had.' He pulled a face. Bill was still smarting from the computer virus that had attacked one of our clients at the beginning of October. The virus had been set to activate itself on the Jewish Day of Atonement. Our clients, a firm of accountants called Goldberg and Senior, had taken it very personally when all of their records had been turned into gobbledygook. They didn't find it a consolation when Bill told them it was a one-off that wouldn't recur in other years, unlike the really vicious Friday the Thirteenth and Michelangelo viruses that attack again and again till they're cleansed for good.

'I'm putting the laptop in the safe. It's got the data from Martin Cheetham's hard disc on it, and I think it's probably the only evidence left of what he and Brian Lomax were up to,' I said.

'You've cracked it, then?' Bill looked eager and stopped chewing.

'I think so. The only problem is that it's hard to prove Lomax was actively involved with the criminal aspect of it. So I've got a little experiment in mind to sort it out one way or the other.' I crossed the office and pushed the frame of the print of Escher's

Belvedere. The spring-loaded catch released itself and the picture swung back on its hinges to reveal the office safe.

'You want to enlighten me?' Bill asked as I keyed in the combination. The door clicked open and I cleared a space on the bottom shelf for the laptop.

'I'd love to, but I haven't got the time right now. I need to be in Buxton before six if this is going to work. Besides, this is not a tale you want to try and digest on a Friday teatime. The twists and turns in this make Yom Kippur look as simple as Space Invaders.' I closed the safe, then unlocked the cupboard that contains all our Elint equipment.

'I don't want you to think I'm being chauvinist about this, but you're not going to do anything dangerous, are you?' Bill asked anxiously.

'I wasn't planning to, no. Just a simple bit of bugging in the hope of picking up something incriminating.' I chose a directional bug with a magnetic base, and added the screen that indicates where the bug is relative to the receiver. I also helped myself to a couple of tiny radio mikes with integral batteries, each about the size of the top joint of my thumb, and the receiver that goes with them. The tape recorder was still in the Fiesta, so I'd be able to record anything I overheard. I screwed each mike into a plastic pen-housing that also contained a U-shaped length of wire which acted as an aerial.

Bill sighed. 'As long as you're careful. We don't want a repeat performance of last Friday night.' From anyone else, it would have sounded patronizing. But I recognized the genuine concern that lay behind Bill's words.

'I know, I know, the firm can't afford the insurance premiums to get any higher,' I said. 'Look, there's been no sign of anyone having another go. Maybe it was the real thing, a genuine accident. You know, someone a bit pissed or tired? Stranger things have happened.'

'Maybe,' Bill agreed reluctantly. 'Anyhow, take care. I haven't got the time to train a replacement.' He grinned.

'I promise. Like I said, just a simple bit of bugging, that's all.' I didn't want to upset him. That's why I chose not to tell him I was going out to find me a murderer.

24

Enchantments didn't. Enchant me, that is. There was something about their stock of expensive clothes that screamed 'girlie'. I'd only ever have shopped there if I'd been deliberately looking for something that made me look like a middle-class bimbo. It wasn't so much mutton dressed as lamb, as 'little baby lambikins'. It was obviously what the locals wanted, since it certainly wasn't a style that came naturally to the fiercely elegant Nell Lomax. Today, her wavy brown hair tumbled round the shoulders of what looked to me like a classic Jaeger suit and blouse. She looked like an advert for one of those richly spicy perfumes that we career girls are supposed to love.

I'd drifted past the shop to check she was there, then I'd slipped out the rear entrance of the modern glass and concrete shopping arcade where the boutique sat uneasily between a butcher's and a shoe shop. A quick prowl round the car park revealed there was only one white convertible Golf there. On the pretext of tying my lace, I slipped the directional bug inside the wheel arch. Now I could keep tabs on Nell without sitting tightly on her tail.

Nell was sitting on a high stool behind the counter reading *Elle*. She glanced up when I walked in, but clearly didn't think a woman who would be seen out of doors in jogging pants, sweatshirt and ski jacket was the sort of person worth lavishing her personal attention on. I'd pulled my hair back and tied it in a pony tail, and now my bruising had gone down, I was back to my usual light application of cosmetics, so it's not really surprising she didn't recognize me as the smartly dressed, over-made-up private eye she'd come face to face with a few days before. Besides, a lot had happened since then to take her mind off my face.

As she read on, I browsed among the racks of over-priced merchandise, trying to imagine anyone I respected wearing any of these clothes. I did find one skirt my mother would probably have liked, but she'd have wanted to pay about a third of the price for it, and I can't say I'd have blamed her. Keeping half an eye on Nell, I worked my way round the shop.

Eventually, I approached the counter from the side, so I was close to her coat, which was slung over a chair, and to her handbag, on the floor at her feet. 'We need to talk, Ms Lomax,' I said, dropping on to the chair with the coat and letting my bag slide on to the floor next to hers.

She looked startled, as she was meant to. 'I'm sorry, I don't think I . . .?' she said.

'We haven't been introduced,' I said, leaning forward to open my bag. I took out a business card and handed it to her. While she was frowning at it, under the pretext of closing my bag, I slipped one of the radio mikes into her handbag.

'I still have no idea who you are, Miss Brannigan,' she said uneasily. Not a good actress; I could see the nervous flicker of her eyes as she lied.

'We met in Martin Cheetham's office. The day he died,' I said. I leaned back and casually draped my arm over the back of the chair. I managed to slip the second mike into one of the deep pockets of her Burberry without taking my eyes off her face.

'I don't know what you're talking about,' she replied with a nervous shake of the head.

I sighed and ran my hand over my hair. 'Ms Lomax, we can do this the hard way or the easy way. Martin Cheetham was your boyfriend. He did business with your brother. Very dodgy business, some of it. You were both at his house on the afternoon he died, something which I don't believe you've seen fit to discuss with the police. Now, I know about the double dealing with the land, I know about the mortgage frauds and I know how the money's been laundered. And I know why Martin Cheetham had to die.'

Nell Lomax's chic façade crumbled, leaving a frightened woman whose eyes couldn't keep still. 'You're talking rubbish,' she gabbled. 'I don't know what you're on about. How dare you – coming in here and talking about Martin and my brother like that.' Her attempt at defiance didn't even convince her, never mind me.

'Oh, you know all about it, Nell,' I said. 'What you don't know is that your lovely brother is planning to skip the country and leave you holding the sticky end.'

'You're mad,' she said. 'I'm going to call the police.'

'Be my guest. I'd be happy to tell them what I know, and to show them the proof. It's in a very safe place, by the way, so there's no point in trying to get rid of me like you got rid of Martin Cheetham,' I added.

'I think you'd better leave,' she said, unconsciously backing away from me.

'I came to deliver a message. Your brother and your lover conned my client out of five thousand pounds. They did the same to another eleven people in the same scam. I want that sixty thousand back before he leaves the country on Monday, otherwise the police will be waiting at the airport for him.' I indicated my card, which she was still clutching tight. 'You've got my number. When he's got the money together, tell him to ring me and we'll arrange a hand over.'

I picked up my bag and stood up. 'I'm deadly serious about this, Nell. You're in the frame too, don't forget. That should be a hell of an incentive to convince your brother to refund my clients.' I walked briskly across the shop. At the door, I contemplated kicking over a rail of clothes, but I decided the air of low-key menace was probably more effective than going over the top. I marched out, not looking back.

I gambled on Nell shutting up shop and going off to find brother Brian. Since it was just after half past five, I thought there was a good chance that she'd head straight for home, so I checked back in to my cheap and cheerful guest house. The landlady nearly burst with curiosity at my return, especially when she spotted the electronic equipment. I closed the door firmly behind me and settled down at the window, the directional receiver on a low coffee table beside me. I plugged an earphone from the microphone receiver into my ear and waited. So far, nothing. Either Nell was too far away for me to pick anything up or she'd found the bugs and flushed them down the toilet. Given the state she'd been working up to when I left the shop, I frankly didn't think she'd have noticed if they'd jumped out of the bag and bitten her.

Then the screen started to flash. The bug itself has a radius of about five miles, and it transmits back to the receiver. The screen shows the direction of the bug relative to the receiver, and there's a display of figures along the bottom of the screen which gives the distance in metres between the bug and the receiver. At first, the numbers started climbing, which got me twitching. Had I guessed wrong? Was she heading for some building site where her brother would be working late? Just as I reached the point of panic, the direction changed and the numbers started to plummet. When it showed 157, I could actually see the white Golf racing up the hill towards the house. Then the earphone came alive and I could hear engine noise.

She was driving like a woman who'd lost control. It was a miracle she didn't leave her front bumper on the gatepost as she shot into the drive. As it was, I heard a harsh scraping as she pulled off the road. She didn't even bother garaging the car, simply abandoning it on the Tarmac in front of the house. I watched and listened as she jumped out of the car, slammed the door and let herself in.

'Brian,' she shouted. I could hear her footsteps, the rustle of her clothes and her quick breathing as she hurried through the house calling his name. But there was no reply. Then it sounded like she'd taken her coat off and thrown it down somewhere.

I heard the electronic chirruping of a phone as she keyed in a number. I could faintly hear the distinctive ringing tone of a mobile phone. Someone answered, but even I could hear the static on the line. 'Brian?' she said. 'Is that you? Brian, I've got to talk to you. Brian, it's that Brannigan woman. Hello? Hello? You're breaking up, Brian!' He wasn't the only one. Nell sounded like she was in pieces.

'Brian? Where are you?' she yelled. There was a pause, and I couldn't hear what was coming down the phone at all. 'You'd better get here soon, Brian. This is real trouble.'

It was working. I waited patiently while Nell poured herself a drink. Luckily she was one of those women who are attached to their handbags by an umbilical cord. More often than not, they're smokers, I've noticed. I heard the unmistakable click of a lighter. She was on her third cigarette by the time Lomax turned into the drive. Seemingly unperturbed by his sister's panicky phone call, he calmly garaged the E-type and strolled unhurriedly round to the back of the house.

A moment later, I heard Nell shout, 'Brian?'

'What the hell's the matter with you?' I heard, the voice muffled at first but growing clearer as he approached her.

A chair scraped on a hard floor, then Nell said, 'That Brannigan woman. The private eye, the one who was sniffing round Martin? She came into the shop this afternoon. Brian, she says she knows everything that's been going on!' She sounded as though she were on the verge of hysterics. It was like listening to a radio play, trying to conjure up the picture that matched what I was hearing. I checked that the tape was running, then concentrated on what I could hear.

'And you fell for that bullshit? Christ, Nell, I told you, no one can pin a thing on us. We're in the clear now. What did she say anyway? She could only have been bluffing.' He sounded angry rather than edgy, as if he wanted someone to blame and Nell was handy.

'She said she knew all about the land deals, and the mortgage scam, and about using the old houses to launder the money,' Nell reported, surprisingly faithfully.

'Jesus, that really is bullshit. She must have been guessing. And even if she did guess right, there's not a shred of proof.' Another chair scraped on the floor and a different lighter clicked.

'She said she had proof,' Nell said.

'She can't have. I got rid of everything after Martin. Every bit of paper, every computer disc. There isn't any proof. For Christ's sake, Nell, get a grip.'

'What if she does have evidence? What if there was something you don't know about? I'm telling you, Brian, she *knows*. And she knows Martin's death wasn't an accident.'

'Now you're really on Fantasy Island,' Lomax snapped. 'Look, the cops think it was an accident. The inquest is going to say it was an accident. You and me are the only ones who know any different. How the fuck could this private eye know anything? She wasn't there, was she? Or did I miss her? Was she there giving us a hand to drop your precious boyfriend over the banisters? Did that somehow escape my notice?' he demanded. 'Listen, there's no way she could know anything about that gutless little shit.'

'Don't talk about him like that,' Nell said.

'Well, he was. Saying he wasn't going to have anything to do with violence,' Lomax mimicked in a namby-pamby voice. 'Saying he was going to the police if I didn't lay off the nosy bitch. As if it wasn't his stupid fault in the first place that something had to be done about her. If I'd done the fucking job properly to begin with, we wouldn't be getting any fucking aggro off this Brannigan cow. She'd be on the bottom of the bloody Ship Canal where she fucking belongs.'

In spite of myself, I shivered. There's something very stomach-churning about listening to someone who's tried to kill you whingeing because they didn't succeed. A bit like reading your own obituary.

'Well you didn't do it properly, did you? And now she says she knows. And she wants sixty thousand from you or she'll go to the cops,' Nell said. Her voice sounded shaky, as if she was forcing herself to stand up to her brother.

'Sixty grand? She's trying to blackmail us?' Lomax's voice rose, incredulous.

'Not blackmail. She says you ripped off her client for five thou, and there's another eleven in the same boat. She wants their money back.'

'She wants their money back,' Lomax echoed, a snort of laughter in his voice.

'And she wants it back before you catch the plane on Monday night. What plane is that, Brian?' Nell's voice cracked. Even at my remove, I could sense the tension between these two.

'I told you, she's a bullshit merchant. She's just trying to drive a wedge between us, to make you crack and tell her all the stuff she doesn't know but wants you to think she does,' he said. He was as likely to win an Oscar as his sister.

'You're running out on me, aren't you?' Nell said. 'You're going off somewhere with all the money, leaving me to clear up the mess.'

'There isn't going to be any mess, I keep telling you. And I am not doing a runner,' Lomax shouted.

Confusion reigned in my right ear. It sounded like a chair scraping back, a scuffle then a slap. 'Oh no?' Nell almost screamed. 'So why have you got a bloody passport in your pocket?'

'Give me that,' he yelled.

'You thought you could just clear off and leave me? You bastard, Brian! You said we were in this together. I've put up with all the worry while you and Martin were playing your silly games. I was even stupid enough to listen to you when you said Martin was too much of a risk. And now you think you can just write me off and sod off with the money that's mine by rights?' She was ranting hysterically now.

'Fucking shut up,' Lomax exploded. I heard the sound of another slap. 'You silly bitch. All you ever wanted was the money. You didn't give a shit about Martin. You were willing to fuck your brains out to keep him quiet just so long as the money kept coming in. So don't give me all that stuff.'

There was sudden silence. Then Nell Lomax said softly, 'But nobody would ever believe that, would they? They'll believe me, though, when I break down and tell the police that I've discovered my brother killed my fiancé and now he's planning to skip the country with all the money they embezzled.'

'You wouldn't have the bottle,' Lomax said contemptuously.

'Wouldn't I,' Nell said bitterly. 'You're not leaving me without a shilling while you live it up on my money.'

There was a crash. 'You just went too far, little sister,' Lomax hissed.

The sounds of struggle intensified. Suddenly afraid, I whipped the earphone out and hit the floor running. I tore down the stairs, out of the front door and across the street, willing my stiff muscles to drive me forward. Up the drive, round the side of the house, the blood pounding in my ears, Lomax's voice echoing in my head.

As I rounded the corner of the house, I saw a long conservatory. Beyond it, I could see the kitchen. In an instant I took in the scene. Nell, bent forwards over the kitchen table, her hands scrabbling uselessly frantic behind her. Masking her body with his, Lomax leaned forward, bearing down on her with his superior weight, his hands round her throat.

I tried the door, but it was locked. Urgently, I scanned the UPVC door frame, estimating the weak point. Then I positioned myself and aimed a kick with my full weight behind it. The force of the blow cracked the frame, and had the added benefit of stopping Brian Lomax. I took a deep breath, trying to block out the pain that had jarred every bone in my body, and concentrated all of my body's energies into my leg and foot. The second kick jerked the door out of the frame, leaving it swinging inwards.

My momentum carried me forward into the conservatory. Lomax had abandoned Nell and was coming for me. He was bigger, heavier, stronger and fitter. I knew I'd only get one chance. I balanced myself and twisted round so I was side on to him. I feinted on one foot, then as he dived towards me, I brought the other foot round in a fast, short arc. The crack of bone as his femur snapped was sickeningly loud. He crashed to the floor like a felled tree. His scream of pain made the hairs on the back of my neck stand on end.

'Hanging in space over Barton Bridge wasn't a whole lot of fun either,' I said as I stepped over him towards Nell.

'Bitch,' he gasped.

I could hardly bring myself to talk to him, but, mindful that the tape was still running, I said, 'You brought it on yourself. You got greedy. You didn't have to kill Martin Cheetham.'

'What's it to you? He was a no-mark. I should have killed you when I had the chance,' I heard him say as I stooped over the slumped body of his sister.

I felt her neck for a pulse. There was a faint fluttering beneath my fingers. Gently, I raised her body and eased her to the floor. I loosened her blouse, then put my ear to her mouth. Her breathing was weak and ragged, but it was still coming. 'You'll be pleased to hear she's still alive,' I said.

'Bitch,' he repeated.

I stood up and moved to the phone. I was beginning to feel shaky, my muscles protesting at such a heavy work-out after no activity for a week. I picked up the phone and dialled 999. 'Emergency operator. Which service do you require?' The words were music to my ears. I looked round at the shambles I'd helped to create. This kitchen sure wasn't going to make this month's *Homes and Gardens*.

'You'd better make it the police,' I said. 'And throw in a couple of ambulances for good measure.'

25

I pulled up in a side street in Bolton. 'What are we doing here, Brannigan?' Richard asked.

I got out of the car, and he followed. 'After that Chinese in Buxton, I thought we deserved something a bit special,' I said, turning the corner and pulling one of the double doors open. Richard followed me down a flight of stairs and into a marble foyer with a fountain filled with koi carp. 'They do a ten-course Imperial Banquet,' I told him as we walked into the restaurant proper.

His face lit up. His eyes even twinkled. I doubt I'd have got that strong a response if I'd jumped on one of the tables and stripped off. I gave the waiter my name and we followed obediently to a table shut off from the main body of diners by tall lacquered screens. By the table, as ordered, was an ice bucket filled with Chinese beer and a bottle of Apollinaris mineral water for me.

'Times like this, I'm tempted to make you an offer you couldn't refuse,' Richard said as the waiter opened a beer.

'I don't do "married",' I reminded him. 'Married is for mugs, masochists and mothers. None of which I am.'

'Yet,' he said.

I scowled. 'Do you want to eat this meal or wear it?'

Richard held his hands up, palms towards me. 'Sorry!'

The dim sum arrived, and we both observed the requisite awed appreciation. Five seconds later, we attacked.

Through a mouthful of *char siu bau*, Richard said, 'So fill me in on the details. All I know is that these days, Friday nights the best place to find you is talking to a copper.'

The poor sod had finally reached me on my mobile some time after ten. I'd been sitting in an interview room at Buxton police station, going over the whole story with the local inspector plus Della Prentice, whom I'd asked them to ring because of the fraud stuff. Just for once, I fancied having someone on my side during a police interrogation. Neither of them had been particularly amused when I broke off to answer my phone.

I'd finally got home in the small hours, posted the 'Do Not Disturb on Pain of Castration' notice on my bedroom door and slept till mid-afternoon. By then, of course, Richard was at the match. Sometimes it's like being married anyway.

'Cutting a long and boring story short,' I said, 'when I put all the computer files together, the picture emerged. You have to remember that Martin Cheetham was an expert in arranging the sale and purchase of houses. What happened was that when he acted for the buyers of a property, he just omitted to forward all the paperwork to the Land Registry.'

'Sweetheart, you might as well be talking Mandarin,' Richard said. 'Let's have it from the top. Mortgage fraud for beginners.'

I sighed. 'This is how to get two mortgages on one property. Mr and Mrs X buy a house. They go to Martin Cheetham, solicitor. The mortgage is arranged and granted. Then Cheetham should send the paperwork to the Land Registry, who issue what's called a charge certificate, which shows that there is a mortgage outstanding on the property, and who carries the mortgage.

'But Cheetham used to delay a few weeks before he sent the documentation off to the Land Registry. He would then apply for a second repayment mortgage with another lender, as if it had never been bought by Mr and Mrs X. According to Nell, who couldn't stop talking once her throat started working again, she used to front up with Cheetham at the mortgage interviews and pretend to be his wife. As the first charge certificate hasn't been issued yet, there is therefore no official record of it when the lender checks it out with the Land Registry, so there's no problem and the mortgage is granted. You with me so far?'

Richard nodded. 'I think so.'

I scoffed a couple of prawn wontons and some tiny spring rolls before all the dim sum disappeared down Richard's throat.

A more suspicious soul than me might wonder why it is I always seem to end up explaining the intricacies of my cases when there's food on the table.

'That second lot of paperwork never goes anywhere,' I said. 'It sits in a safe in Cheetham's office. It would take the building society at least a year even to notice that they hadn't received the appropriate charge certificate, never mind do anything about it. Cheetham and Lomax have meanwhile got a (say) £100,000 cheque, because the building society paid the money to Cheetham on behalf of the second, fictitious buyers. As long as the mortgage instalments were made each month, there'd be no problem. No one would be any the wiser for at least a year. Multiply that by ten and a completely uncreditworthy person has a million.'

'Shit,' Richard breathed.

'Now, you can go for a short-term fraud and do a runner with the money, in which case you have the police looking for you. Or you can do what Cheetham and Lomax had been doing very successfully until a few months ago. What they did with the money was buy up derelict property. Lomax would send in his labourers and do it up, and then they'd sell at a huge profit, thus laundering the money as well. They could have carried on with this indefinitely if the bottom hadn't dropped out of the housing market, since they were paying off the bent mortgages within a year of taking them out.'

'You mean, before the lender noticed they hadn't got this charge certificate for the loan, Cheetham paid all the money back?' Richard asked.

'Correct. And in the meantime, he and Lomax had made about fifty per cent profit with the capital. It's a victimless crime. The lenders lose nothing; they don't even know anything dodgy's happened.'

Richard laughed. 'That's brilliant! And hey, they even did their own conveyancing, so they didn't have to fork out those exorbitant lawyer's fees. So why did it all come on top?'

'Like I said, the bottom dropped out of the market. Property stopped moving. They were lumbered with houses they couldn't sell. That's why they tried that hooky land scheme that caught Alexis and Chris. They were getting desperate for cash flow. So Lomax persuaded Cheetham to get a dozen new mortgages to keep them afloat. He'd no intention of ever paying a shilling on those mortgages. According to Nell, he reckoned that if they did that, they could have a million in capital. The three of them could flee the country to somewhere like Spain. Then when the market picked up, they could offload the rest of the houses and cash in on them too. We're talking twenty-seven houses, with an average value of thirty-seven thousand pounds, by the way. Which is another cool million.'

'Shit,' Richard said again. 'That is serious money, Brannigan. Why didn't you finish your law degree?'

I ignored him and concentrated on the aromatic crispy duck that had just arrived, piling shredded duck and spring onion on to a pancake covered in plum sauce. Some things are too important to be distracted from.

'So why did they kill Cheetham? I mean, everything seems to have been going OK. Why get rid of the only guy who knew how to work the scam?'

I fiddled with my food. 'According to Nell, that was my fault.'

'How'd she work that one out, then? Doesn't sound like she's got a degree in logic,' Richard said.

'Cheetham panicked when I started sniffing around,' I explained. 'Then when he was tarted up in his drag in DKL Estates and I turned up, he was convinced I was on to their major scam. So he told Lomax to warn me off. Apparently, he meant just that. Lomax or one of his labourers was supposed to threaten me in a dark alley. Instead, Lomax must have picked me up outside DKL, then followed me over to Ted's factory, and then, on the way home, he got a bit carried away, and tried to run me off Barton Bridge. He must have completely freaked out when I turned up the very next day on his home turf. Especially since he was actually with Cheetham.'

'So why kill Cheetham? Why not just finish the job they'd started on you?' he asked.

'Thank you, Richard. You don't have to sound quite so eager. The reason I'm still here is that they didn't know how much I knew, or how many people knew what I knew. But the Lomaxes figured Cheetham was the weak link in the chain, the one who'd crack under pressure. They also figured that with him out of the way they could destroy the evidence and leave themselves in the clear. So Nell arranged to meet Cheetham for one of their little games sessions. Then, when she'd got him all tied up, Brian arrived and smothered him. The pair of them tipped him over the balcony, so it looked like a nasty sex game that had gone horribly wrong.'

'And I thought my ex-wife was a bitch. Jesus. What kind of a woman does that to her lover?'

'One who's more in love with money than she is with him, I guess,' I said. 'They thought they'd got rid of all the evidence. But neither of them knew anything about computers. They thought all the data was on the floppies.'

'And will Alexis get her money back?'

'She'll probably have to take Brian Lomax to court. But at least she knows where he's going to be for the foreseeable future. She won't have any trouble filing the papers. Her money should be safe as houses.'